JIMMY COATES: TARGET

Also by Joe Craig

JIMMY
COATES:
ASSASSIN?

JOE CRAIG

JIMMY COATES: TARGET

HarperCollins*Publishers*

To Mary-Ann Ochota, *sine qua non*

Jimmy Coates: Target

Copyright © 2006 by Joe Craig

All rights reserved. Printed in the United States of America. No part of this book may be used or reproduced in any manner whatsoever without written permission except in the case of brief quotations embodied in critical articles and reviews. For information address HarperCollins Children's Books, a division of HarperCollins Publishers, 1350 Avenue of the Americas, New York, NY 10019.

www.harpercollinschildrens.com

Library of Congress Cataloging-in-Publication Data

Craig, Joe.

Jimmy Coates : target / Joe Craig.— 1st American ed.

p. cm.

Summary: Eleven-year-old Jimmy Coates is in France with friends and family, hiding from NJ7, the British secret intelligence agency that designed and programmed him, when he learns that there is another genetically programmed assassin—a new enemy whose mission is to return Jimmy to London.

ISBN-10: 0-06-077266-2 (trade bdg.) — ISBN-13: 978-0-06-077266-6 (trade bdg.)

ISBN-10: 0-06-077267-0 (lib. bdg.) — ISBN-13: 978-0-06-077267-3 (lib. bdg.)

[1. Genetic engineering—Fiction. 2. Assassins—Fiction. 3. Adventure and adventurers—Fiction. 4. France—Fiction. 5. Science fiction.] I. Title.

PZ7.C84419Jim 2007   2006020011

[Fic]—dc22   CIP

                                                                          AC

Typography by Christopher Stengel

1 2 3 4 5 6 7 8 9 10

❖

First American Edition, 2007

Originally published in Great Britain in 2006 by HarperCollins*Publishers* Ltd.

Thank you to the whole HarperCollins team, particularly Melanie Donovan. Thank you to Ann Tobias, Sarah Manson, Jack Martin, Dan Webber, and Oli Rockberger.

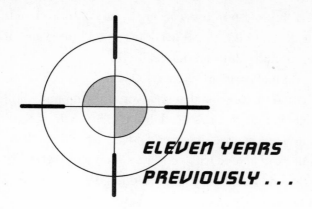

ELEVEN YEARS PREVIOUSLY . . .

The only thing that distinguished this man from everyone else on the bridge was his stillness. His collar was turned up against the wind of a typical Parisian autumn and his hat was pulled down to his eyes. Nobody noticed him. Then, with one deep sigh, he marched through the fog toward the Île St. Louis. I hope nobody will have to die today, he thought.

He reached a familiar wooden door. A sharp jab with his elbow snapped the old lock, and he slipped through unobserved. Around him was a small courtyard he didn't bother to inspect. Instead, he eyed the fourth floor of the adjacent building. Drizzle slicked the drainpipe when he clasped it, but he heaved himself up, strong and persistent. He hauled himself onto the balcony, careful to land silently, and drew his gun. It felt familiar yet horrible in his grip. It's just a precaution, he told himself.

After only a moment, he burst through the flimsy balcony doors. "*Levez les mains!*" he shouted.

An elderly man sat proudly at his desk among piles of papers. "There's no need to speak to me in French, Ian," he announced with just a hint of an accent as he raised his hands above his head. "And there's no need to point a gun at me. If you're going to shoot, shoot. If not, let's talk."

"You should have run farther away, Doctor."

"Where could I have gone that NJ7 wouldn't find me?" Still the gun pointed at the doctor's head, but neither man blinked. Dr. Memnon Sauvage rose slowly and edged around his desk.

"You know I can't come with you," he continued. "What I've done can't be undone, no matter what Hollingdale does to me."

"Turn around and put your hands behind your back," the other man replied flatly.

"How's Helen?" The doctor stayed facing the way he was. "Has the baby been born? It must be due any day now." Despite huge effort, Ian Coates's face flickered.

"Ah," exclaimed Dr. Sauvage with a dry smile. "Congratulations. A father for the second time!"

Ian Coates was scowling now, trying hard to detach his anger from his trigger finger. "Do as I say or I *will* shoot you."

"Go ahead. Shoot me," Dr. Sauvage snapped back. "Then NJ7 will never know what France is capable of."

"Then turn around and put your hands behind your back."

"So you can march me back to London? Back to NJ7? Back to your wife?"

At that, Coates slapped his hand viciously across the old man's face. The blow sent him straight to the floor.

"Hollingdale can do nothing without me," barked Dr. Sauvage, spitting blood. "Tell him that! And tell him this: the day he finds out what I've done will be the day it kills him."

Ian Coates approached slowly, leading with his gun. But Dr. Sauvage crawled backward, around his desk, and stopped at the foot of a huge bookcase. The two men stayed like that for what seemed like forever. Dr. Sauvage's blood dripped from Ian Coates's knuckles. Then the doctor's glance flicked for a moment toward the papers on his desk. Coates followed his gaze, but immediately regretted it. In that instant, Sauvage rose to his feet and heaved on the bookcase.

"No!" cried Ian Coates, dropping his gun and lunging forward. He was too late. The huge books hit Sauvage like a prizefighter's punches. Then the bookcase itself crushed his wiry frame.

Coates was stunned. Only the doctor's head was visible. Coates reached down to the man's neck and felt for a pulse— out of habit, not in hope. A cloud of dust settled on the body.

Coates didn't panic. He rifled through the stacks of papers on the desk. Everything was in code, of course, but he discarded the files at the top as obvious decoys. He paused when he came to a bright orange flash drive, the sort you could simply plug into a computer to make vast amounts of data portable. It was marked simply ZAF-1. The same initials recurred on documents, sometimes in bold. It meant nothing to him.

He snatched up his gun and stuffed as many of the files as he could under his arm, then slipped the flash drive into his pocket. He ran out of the room and followed the staircase to the roof. From there he bounded across to the next building, shoving the papers into his coat so that his hands were free.

ZAF-1, he thought, trying to shut out the image of the doctor's death. What could it mean?

He leaped to a balcony below, then down again, catching the arc of a lamppost. Finally, he let himself drop into the back alley and away he ran.

UNO STOVORSKY

"All rise!" Everybody in the courtroom obeyed the somber instruction except two bowed figures.

"This isn't fair!" shouted Olivia Muzbeke, her voice thin with fear and fatigue. Her husband tried to move a hand across to comfort her, but his wrists were chained to a metal bar in front of him. A guard dragged them both to their feet.

The stern-faced judge eased himself into his chair. "This is as fair as it gets for bad citizens," he mumbled.

Neil Muzbeke looked across the courtroom to where the jury used to sit, in the days when a jury was still part of the legal system. Inside, he felt as empty as those benches. He was past shouting. He had given everything. He had protested, he had pleaded, and now he was resigned to whatever fate the judge had been told to pass down to them. Any other thoughts were eclipsed by the image of the son he might never see again.

"You knew that the dangerous criminal Jimmy Coates was a fugitive from the authorities," the judge intoned, "yet you shielded him and then helped him to escape, putting the life of Prime Minister Ares Hollingdale at risk. Not only that, but your own son"—he scoured his notes for the name—"Felix Muzbeke, even at the age of eleven, has shown himself to be an enemy of the Neo-democratic State of Britain."

The judge wheezed and adjusted his glasses. Then, without even looking up, he passed sentence.

"Incarceration," he announced. "At the discretion of the Home Office." He slammed down his gavel to make the decision final. That noise killed any lingering faith Neil Muzbeke had had in his country's justice system.

At the back of the courtroom stood a woman who seemed too attractive for such miserable proceedings. But she looked satisfied with the result of the trial and the speed at which it had been conducted.

"Release the news," she whispered to a young man in a black suit, who trembled at the woman's complete authority. "Make sure it reaches France."

"Yes, Miss Bennett."

Jimmy was hardly conscious of the thud as the helicopter touched ground. The oleopneumatic shock absorbers of the EC975 were designed for the smoothest of landings. What woke him was the change in the noise of the rotors. The steady drone that had surrounded them since they left London was dying now.

Jimmy shook off his nightmare. As always, he had no recollection of what he had been dreaming, only shortness of breath and a thumping heart—the remnants of his terror. He pulled his blanket tighter around him. What did he have to be afraid of? In the past fortnight he'd crashed through brick walls, breathed underwater, and caught a bullet in his hand. Even stabbing a knife into his wrist had done no serious damage. The bloodless slit would heal abnormally fast. The bandage (which his mother had wound too tight) was unnecessary, but it was a comfort to him now. Nevertheless, he feared what might be out there waiting for him.

NJ7, Britain's most secret intelligence agency, could be anywhere. Their scientists had designed Jimmy to be an assassin when he reached eighteen, then sent him to kill seven years too soon. As soon as Jimmy had disobeyed that order, struggling against his physiological destiny, he had become an enemy. And there could be no less desirable opponent than NJ7.

Perhaps even more than that, Jimmy feared what was inside him. He felt so human, but now he knew that part of him was an inhuman power, created to kill.

Everyone else in the cabin was asleep. Christopher Viggo stepped out of the pilot's seat and stretched, his lithe physique outlined beneath the creases in his shirt. He turned to meet Jimmy's gaze, gave a tired nod, then stalked away. That was the man NJ7 had sent Jimmy to eliminate.

Viggo was fighting to make Britain a democracy again. Under the unlikely cover of running a Turkish restaurant, he had been building an organization that might one day be able to oppose the government. It had taken all of Jimmy's mental strength to reject his first mission and join Viggo's cause.

Now that they had landed, the others quickly woke up. The wind whipped around them as they alighted from the helicopter. Jimmy could almost taste the countryside air, so different from the city they had escaped. They were in the middle of a field, and the only building between them and the horizon was an ancient, half-timbered farmhouse, with its upper floor projecting out over the lower one.

So this is what France looks like, Jimmy thought to himself. He had never been out of Britain before. He had never even wondered what it was like anywhere else. Now he realized how strange that was. Perhaps he had always assumed everywhere else would be just like home. Anyway, he was too tired and scared to feel excited about finally being abroad. Besides, he wasn't on vacation. He was on the run.

Yannick Ertegun, the chef from Viggo's restaurant in London, led the way. Jimmy walked with his mother, Helen, followed by the dark and beautiful Saffron Walden, who was Viggo's girlfriend and a vital part of his outfit in her own right. Jimmy's older sister, Georgie, followed with her friend Eva, and Jimmy's best friend Felix Muzbeke stumbled after them, his face scrunched up against the elements.

Viggo hung back from the rest of the group. As they walked through an orchard at the back of the farmhouse, he stopped to fill his arms with fallen branches. Already the internal struggle in Jimmy began again: the agent in him realized he should help Viggo camouflage the helicopter, but the temptation of food and warmth kept him following the others toward the house. He held himself rigidly in line. Control meant everything.

At the farmhouse door was a tiny woman, who looked like the oldest person Jimmy had ever seen. Yannick bent down to kiss her on the cheek, and she clipped him around the back of the head.

"Everybody, this is my mother." The chef grinned.

Jimmy smiled cautiously at the woman, who scowled as they all shuffled awkwardly into the building. Clearly, she hadn't been expecting visitors. Despite being large, the interior of the farmhouse was dark and austere. The ceiling dipped at unusual angles as if the central beam were reaching for the fire that dominated the room. It didn't seem to be doing much to heat the house, thought Jimmy, shivering.

A staircase lurched upward out of the corner, and there was a door at each end of the room. Yannick's mother trudged through one of them, revealing a glimpse of a large, old-fashioned kitchen. Yannick followed her, pleading and explaining as best he could without being indiscreet.

Soon they were all sitting around the fire with giant mugs of hot chocolate.

"When will we start looking for my parents?" Felix whispered in Jimmy's ear. Jimmy stared deliberately into the flagstones and shrugged. He had almost forgotten that Neil and Olivia Muzbeke had been arrested for helping him escape NJ7. He had been completely caught up in his own thoughts. He silently scolded himself for being so self-obsessed. Even at that moment, he could feel the ever-growing presence of his powers, deepening the split between his heart and his instincts, his mind and his body. He could control his powers for now, but only by succumbing to them. It scared him beyond anything he had ever felt before to think that he might be relinquishing his humanity.

Whenever Jimmy did think back, he could only relive the last time he had seen his own father. Jimmy could picture in alarming detail Ian Coates's face as he refused to escape from the British government with Jimmy. The split inside him was forcing his family apart now too.

Felix started saying something else, but Jimmy hushed him and stood up. There was a tingle in his stomach. The assassin's instinct again. He'd heard something outside.

"Does anybody else live here?" he asked Yannick quietly.

"No, just my mother."

"You're being paranoid," said Georgie calmly. Jimmy wished that could be true, but his killer instinct had been infallible so far. Then Jimmy's mother stood up as well.

"I heard something too," she said.

"It must be Chris coming in," whispered Saffron.

Jimmy shook his head. His insides were swirling now. "Move to the center of the room."

Everyone did as he said except Eva. "This is ridiculous." She chuckled. "We're in the middle of the French countryside about a million miles from anywhere. How could they possibly find—"

Clunk!

The door slammed open. A masked figure in black crashed through with a battering ram. Another one stormed in behind him and dropped to his knees. Almost blending into the black of his gloves and sleeves was a Beretta 99G pistol. Then a dozen identical figures ran in, filling the room.

"Haut les mains!" came a shout from somewhere. Then, in a thick French accent, "Andz up!"

Jimmy could feel the overwhelming power of his killing instinct drumming through his body. But his mind was serene. He stayed as still as all his friends and raised his hands. One thought was utterly clear: This is not NJ7. If it had been, he would have been dead by now. Besides, NJ7 wouldn't have issued instructions in French.

The group backed toward each other. The shock on their faces changed instantly to puzzlement. Their gasps were drowned out by the protestation from Yannick's mother. She was screaming her head off in coarse French, while Jimmy was trying to concentrate.

"Ferme-la!" he shouted, then immediately clapped his hand to his mouth. Oh my God, he thought, I speak French.

The front door was flapping open, and in strode three more men. Two were dressed in black combat gear just like the others, but they carried FAMAT F9 assault rifles. Jimmy knew this for certain, in the same way he now knew French. It was all part of his conditioning—buried in his head, coming to the surface piece by lethal piece.

Between the two soldiers was a short man with a grim expression. His hair was thin and his shoulders hunched toward his ears. His skin seemed to blend in with his gray city overcoat, which was totally unsuitable for the rustic surroundings.

"By authority of the French military," he declared in perfect English, "you are all under arrest on suspicion of espionage. Keep your hands above your heads and—"

"You're making a mistake." It was Viggo. He was holding a gun to the back of the Frenchman's head. "Drop your weapons!" he shouted.

Even before Viggo had finished his sentence, the soldier to his left spun around. His rifle pointed at Viggo and his finger squeezed the trigger.

"Non!" snapped the man in the overcoat—just in time. The soldier held fire, but maintained his aim. Nobody moved.

"That sounds like Christopher Viggo," the man in gray continued, "but Christopher Viggo is not an enemy to France."

Then he calmly issued a stream of orders in French. As one, his team lowered their guns.

"Uno?" gasped Viggo, trying to peer around at the man's face. "Uno Stovorsky?"

"And only now do I see you've brought Saffron with you." The man shook his head in disbelief.

"Hello, Uno," Saffron called out, cool as ever. "How's the DGSE?"

"What's going on?" Felix whispered to Jimmy.

"The DGSE is the French secret service," he replied, but more than that he couldn't say. How come everyone seemed to know each other all of a sudden?

Viggo circled the man in the gray overcoat, his mouth hanging open in amazement. "Uno! I never thought—"

Then, without warning, Uno Stovorsky slammed his fist into Viggo's jaw.

"If I weren't on duty, I'd kill you right now," he growled.

Mitchell hoisted himself off the sofa, sweating. Another nightmare, but he had lost all memory of it now that his eyes were open. His alarm clock no longer worked, but he knew it was about 3:00 A.M. because he could hear the clubbers being thrown out of the bars below the apartment. He staggered to the bathroom and doused his face with the cold brown water that dribbled out of the hot tap.

His brother would be back soon. As usual, he'd come home, start a fight, then fall into bed, drunk. It made Mitchell angry just thinking about him. He had been forced to share this place since he and his brother had run away from their foster home. Sometimes, Mitchell wished he could go back there, but he knew what he really longed for wasn't possible—for his real parents to have come out alive from the crash.

Then he heard the click of the front door.

"Mitchell!" His brother sounded cheerful, but that wasn't necessarily a good sign. "Come here, mate, I have to do something."

Mitchell felt sick. He knew that greeting his brother face-to-face was the last thing he should do, but the apartment was so small there weren't exactly places to hide. He heard his brother stomp into the living room and pictured precisely what he was doing. First, he'd throw something at the sofa—probably his shoe. Then, when there was no reaction, he'd pull off the blankets and take on that mystified look, unable to comprehend why Mitchell wasn't lying there, waiting to be harassed.

"Mitchell?" This time his brother sounded confused. Mitchell's stomach turned over. He scrabbled through the bathroom cabinet for any medicine that wasn't out of date. "Listen, mate," his brother continued, still in the other room, "this guy said I could have ten grand, but, er . . ."

The bathroom door creaked open, and Mitchell caught sight of his brother's haggard face in the mirror.

"All right, bruv?"

"All right, Lenny." Mitchell turned to face his brother, but clutched his stomach. It felt like something in his belly was burning.

"Like I said," Lenny explained, blocking his brother in, "this bloke offered me ten grand. He had it there in a suitcase and everything."

It wasn't like him to talk so much, thought Mitchell. For some reason his brother had decided to make up some ridiculous story as a buildup to the violence. Then Lenny's face took on a leering grin. Mitchell knew what that meant.

"I have to knock you around a bit." Lenny chuckled. "Shall we do it in the living room?" He slapped Mitchell across the cheek, then turned to go. Mitchell wasn't following. The blood rushed to his face, and his breathing deepened.

"Come on," insisted Lenny, and slapped Mitchell again, harder this time. It really stung. As Lenny turned a second time, Mitchell's strange stomachache intensified into a ball of energy. It quivered inside him and leaped up his throat.

Mitchell wanted to shout, but the energy hit him in the head with five times the force of his brother's slap. Lenny's back was turned and, without even realizing he was going to do it, Mitchell pounced.

Lenny was a lot taller and three years older, but Mitchell yanked him backward by the throat, and they fell to the floor.

"Oi!" cried Lenny, elbowing Mitchell in the ribs.

"How stupid do you think I am?" shouted Mitchell through his teeth. He kicked his brother away and threw himself on top of him. He led with his knee and slammed it into Lenny's midriff.

"How do you like that?" Mitchell crowed.

Lenny rammed his fist toward Mitchell's face. Mitchell caught it. He had never had this strength before, but he was too angry to notice. Instead, he reveled in his new superiority.

"I'm sick of you!" he screamed as he pounded his fists into his brother's face. "This is how you make me feel!" Tears blurred his vision now, but fury kept his arms moving. He was numb inside. The pain that had built up all these years was pouring out. It felt like he wasn't even in the room, but watching from a distance.

Then something pricked his senses—a flash of blue reflected in the mirrors and tiles. It bounced around the bathroom and pulled Mitchell out of his frenzy. He sprang to his feet. His brother didn't move. His eyes were closed, and blood covered his face.

That wasn't me, thought Mitchell, but at the same time, What have I done? He ran to the living room and smeared his hand across the window. Through the streaks of blood on the glass, he saw an ambulance waiting in the street below. It was surrounded by three police cars.

Then the door of the apartment burst open, and Mitchell spun around to see two beefy men in black suits. They were pointing guns at him. His mind went blank. His brother's battered face appeared before his eyes and he couldn't think clearly. What was going on?

Before he could even raise his hands, his knees bent without him telling them to. Then his legs snapped straight and his entire body recoiled backward—through the window.

Glass peppered Mitchell as he fell, and in his head he heard himself scream. Then he landed—but not on the ground. Something cushioned his fall. He saw a dozen men staring at him with blank faces. Mitchell was lying on some kind of air cushion—it felt like a bouncy castle. Had all this been set up, waiting for him?

Then one man, tall and broad with a face like a wrinkled toad, pulled Mitchell to his feet.

"Looks like someone didn't play nicely," he said, cracking

his jaw. Mitchell could hardly hear for all the electricity running through his head. "You're under arrest for the murder of Leonard Glenthorne."

"Murder?" Mitchell gasped. His hands were shoved behind his back and roughly clasped in metal.

"Your brother's dead. Get in the car."

"But—" Mitchell's throat seized up. Nothing made sense. How had they come so quickly? How did they know Lenny was his brother? And worst of all, how could Lenny be dead?

Mitchell was grabbed on each side by two men. They rushed him to a long black car with leather seats and tinted windows. As his head was pushed down to guide him into the backseat, Mitchell saw a stretcher being wheeled out of the building. On it was a zipped-up black body bag. On the side of the bag was a thin green stripe.

2
BROTHERS

Uno Stovorsky signaled to his unit to move out. They obeyed almost silently, retreating to the ring of vehicles a safe distance from the building. Stovorsky remained, eyeball to eyeball with Christopher Viggo.

"Come on," Saffron said gently to the others, "we should leave them."

Yannick nodded and shepherded them through the door opposite the kitchen. But Felix and Jimmy were transfixed.

"Jimmy!" snapped his mother. "Come here now! You too, Felix."

The boys exchanged a glance. They knew they didn't have a choice, no matter how much they wanted to know what was going on between the two men at the front door. They trudged after the others, into what looked like an unoccupied dormitory. There were four beds in the room, but the sheets were dusty, as if they hadn't been slept in for years. Eva ran to one and curled up.

"It's cold in here," she squeaked, pulling her blanket around her.

"There are another couple of bedrooms upstairs," Yannick explained, though nobody was paying him much attention. As soon as the door closed behind them, the shouting started. The old wattle-and-daub walls were too thick for Jimmy to make out what was being said, but it was clearly a ferocious argument.

"When I was little we used to have loads of people coming to stay all the time," Yannick said with a nervous chuckle, as if trying to make sure nobody could hear what was going on in the next room. "For years nobody's been here but my mother, of course."

Nobody else in the bedroom said a word; they were all straining their ears to pick up any clues from next door.

"So let's have the girls down here and the boys upstairs. How about that?" Yannick was making a poor job of sounding cheerful. The only reactions he got were distracted grunts and nods.

Then Jimmy noticed Saffron sitting on the farthest bed, turned toward the window. She was the only person who wasn't trying to listen to the argument on the other side of the wall.

"What's going on?" Jimmy whispered. "Who is this guy, Uno Sto . . . whatever?"

Saffron glanced over to make sure nobody else was paying attention. "He's a French secret service operative," she explained. "They must have tracked us entering French airspace."

"I know that," Jimmy interrupted. "I mean, how come Chris knows him, and what are they arguing about?"

Saffron sighed and avoided looking into Jimmy's eyes.

18

"When Chris left NJ7, he needed to disappear. He hid in Kazakhstan for a while but wanted to use what he knew about NJ7 to put a stop to Ares Hollingdale. So he went to the DGSE." Her eyes scanned the room. Yannick and Jimmy's mother were doing their best to stop Felix, Georgie, and Eva from pressing their ears up against the wall.

"And that's when he met this Uno guy," Jimmy chipped in, to keep Saffron on track.

"Uno Stovorsky," Saffron whispered. "Remember his name. He could help us." Jimmy nodded. "But Chris fell out with the DGSE too."

"Why? What happened?" Jimmy implored. "What aren't you telling me?"

Saffron stood up and pulled in a deep breath. "Jimmy, they're arguing about me."

Moments later the door opened again, and Yannick's mother entered. "Jimmy," she grunted in a thick French accent.

He stepped forward, but so did his mother. "They can't keep me in the dark," she muttered.

Saffron glided out of the room after them, as elegant as ever, to join the discussion.

"Don't forget anything, Jimmy," Felix called out. Jimmy didn't have to respond. Normally, Felix wouldn't even have asked—Jimmy would always have filled him in. But the last few days had been far from normal, and the information Jimmy would be sharing was bound to be extraordinary.

"So this is your amazing automatic assassin?" Uno Stovorsky's eyes seemed to pierce Jimmy's skin. Jimmy opened his mouth to introduce himself, but before he could speak,

Stovorsky leaped from his chair. Jimmy's eyes snapped wide open, catching the glint of a knife in Stovorsky's fist.

Jimmy didn't have to think. With a minimum of movement, he swayed to one side and caught Stovorsky's wrist. With the knife point millimeters from his face, he chopped his other hand into the agent's stomach and threw him over his shoulder. Jimmy snatched the knife before it hit the floor, where Stovorsky lay gasping for air.

"Enough, Jimmy!" shouted Viggo. "He was just testing you."

"I know," Jimmy replied. "Why do you think he's still alive?" Jimmy started at his own words. He hadn't known what he was going to say. It seemed the urge to kill was still just below the surface. He pushed away the deep sickness in his gut and reminded himself to keep control at every moment.

"Uno," continued Viggo, "in return for your help, we are prepared to offer you a full display of Jimmy's abilities and an inventory of the technology Britain is developing for use against France."

Jimmy shuddered. What did Viggo mean by "a full display of Jimmy's abilities"? He wasn't a scientific sample! For a second he wanted to protest, but he quickly calmed down. He had learned to trust Christopher Viggo.

Stovorsky was still picking himself up off the floor. His expression was grim. "This information is as useless now as it was when you came to me all those years ago," he growled. Jimmy watched Viggo's face betray a hint of helplessness.

"Let me draw you a picture," Stovorsky went on. "Jimmy was designed in a test tube by scientists at NJ7. Dr. Higgins was one of them and he's still there. Ares Hollingdale was another, before he became prime minister. The new weapon was assigned to two agents, Ian and Helen Coates."

"Excuse me," interrupted Jimmy's mother. "I'm right here."

"I'm sorry, Mrs. Coates, I didn't realize it was you." He bowed his head slightly and took her hand up to his lips.

"How do you know this?" Viggo cut in.

Stovorsky's demeanor shifted again, back to the animal aggression he directed at his rival. "That's not all we know. We know Jimmy is not the first. There is another assassin, two years older, but he went missing shortly after his parents were killed. NJ7 thinks they died in a car accident."

Jimmy felt like each piece of new information was a brick being hurled at him. There was another genetically programmed assassin? Why had nobody told him? He was dumbfounded, though he made a point of trying not to show it. Fortunately, nobody noticed Jimmy's furrowed brow. Helen Coates and Saffron Walden were sharing a moment of concern. Viggo and Stovorsky were caught up in their own rivalry.

"Do you think I've been sitting on my hands since we last met?" Stovorsky jeered.

"But—," Viggo started.

"We have our own sources in England. You can't tell me anything I don't already know. All I can offer is that we let you live here in France. We can't protect you, and we certainly can't help you in your personal campaign against Ares Hollingdale." Viggo tried to interrupt again, but Stovorsky continued over him. "Hollingdale may be antidemocracy and he may be anti-France, but the DGSE can't meddle with anyone unless they pose a direct threat to France."

The reaction was silence. Jimmy's heart ached. He so

wanted to go back to Felix with some good news. But how could they get anywhere near Felix's parents without the resources of a major international agency? How else could they sneak back into England?

"Don't look so glum!" boomed Stovorsky suddenly. "I'm letting you stay in the country. I'll make sure you're not arrested and, if you stay on the move, the chances are NJ7 won't find you." He shook his head and sighed. "Honestly, you English. Don't you recognize a lucky break? Did you really think I was going to help you overthrow the British government?" He dusted off the shoulders of his overcoat and strode to the door, muttering under his breath in French.

"That's not why we need help." Helen's voice stopped him. "Jimmy, get Felix in here." Jimmy flung open the door to the next room. Eva, Georgie, and Felix all pretended they hadn't been trying to eavesdrop. Without a word Felix stepped forward.

"This is Felix Muzbeke," Jimmy's mother continued. "The government is holding his parents illegally. We just want to bring them here to safety." Felix put on his most winsome expression.

Only now did Stovorsky turn around. He glanced at Felix then quickly turned away.

"Do you have children, Mr. Stovorsky?" Jimmy's mother asked.

Stovorsky held his face in his hands then rubbed his eyes. "What do you need?" he huffed.

Viggo's response was immediate. "Safe passage back to London so we can find out where they are being held. We need money and equipment. We need all the help we can get."

Stovorsky groaned and raised his eyes to the ceiling. He waited a long time before speaking, then eventually he muttered, "I'll see what I can do." Wearily, he picked up a slat of a broken shutter from the floor. "Promise me this is just about the prisoners. Nothing else."

"Mr. Stovorsky," Helen Coates said calmly, "you have my word."

"You're a very smart lady." Stovorsky stared at Jimmy's mother. "You should have kept her, Viggo. And how I wish you had." His eyes darted to Saffron for just an instant, then away again. "I'll be in touch," he called out as he stomped from the farmhouse. "Until then, lie low."

Mitchell could hear the fizz of surveillance cameras tracking him through the corridors. He was keeping pace with the hands that dragged him roughly on either side. His blindfold itched but he was still cuffed, so there was nothing he could do about it. Inside, he was buzzing in a way he never had before. It was a mix of nausea and exhilaration. Every perception was pin sharp, but behind his stomach there was a swirling that threatened to throw him off-balance.

He still had nothing on his feet, so the cold of the floor crept up through his body. At last he came to a stop and his blindfold was yanked off. The first things he saw were the yellow teeth of an old man's smile. Mitchell's anger dulled instantly.

"Welcome to NJ7," the old man announced. "I am Dr. Higgins."

Before Mitchell could respond, the two men gripping his arms lifted him up and pinned him facedown on the desk in the center of the room. The smell of the leather worktop

23

swamped Mitchell's nose. He wriggled and kicked, but only for a second before he felt a sharp stab in his heel. He howled in pain. Then the two men lifted him off the desk and threw him down. Mitchell tried to stand, but his right foot was too weak and he fell to the floor.

"What's going on?" he shouted, his eyes darting around, taking in his surroundings. The walls were bare concrete. On the ceiling were strip lights and a girder loaded with two cameras that seemed to wink at him. All around were burly men in suits. Dr. Higgins stood out, with his aging physique and his white coat. A black cat curled around his ankles.

Then through a corridor at the back of the room came a wiry figure that Mitchell recognized immediately. "You're the prime minister!" he gasped.

Everyone stood to attention as Ares Hollingdale entered the room. His sallow skin almost glowed. "You're not running away this time, young man," he whispered, leering down at Mitchell. "Dr. Higgins has placed a satellite tracking device in your foot."

"What's going on?" Mitchell yelled again, but then into his head flew the idea that the answer was somehow obvious; it was like a distorted memory he couldn't bring out.

"Explain the situation to him," the prime minister snapped at Dr. Higgins. "Tell Miss Bennett as soon as you're finished. She's found the target." Then he turned back to Mitchell with a glare. "Cause any trouble, and we'll throw you in prison for the rest of your life."

Mitchell's mind was frantic. Pain throbbed up from his foot. They can't put me in prison, he thought, I'm only thirteen. But his ears replayed the sound of his fists landing on his brother's bloodied skull. With that came the most overwhelming emotion. Was it guilt? He told himself his brother had deserved it, but the next instant he knew that he had gone too far. He had never meant to kill. He had lost control of himself and now he was going to be punished for it.

"Do as we tell you," the PM continued, "and you could be a hero." The words meant nothing to Mitchell.

Then came Dr. Higgins's voice. "NJ7 is the most advanced military intelligence agency in existence. . . ."

Mitchell heard him through a daze. With the world twisting around him, he saw the shadow of the prime minister leave the room. Dr. Higgins's mouth was moving, but Mitchell picked up only fragments of his speech.

". . . you are thirty-eight percent human . . . an assassin . . . you will work for us. . . ." Whatever Dr. Higgins said, it barely registered.

Mitchell was crying for his brother.

SPECIAL DELIVERY

"It's been three days," Jimmy muttered almost to himself. "If I don't get outside soon, I'll go mad." The kitchen was thick with the smells of cooking, and Jimmy ripped into a bunch of parsley with bored vehemence. The bandage was gone from his wrist. The cut was hardly visible now—like a smudged line of ink.

"You know, that happens a lot," Felix chirped, struggling to hold on to a potato. "People don't go outside and then they lose their minds, and then they think the rest of the world has been destroyed by aliens or nuclear war or something, and—"

"You're holding the peeler upside down," Jimmy interrupted.

"Oh. Oh yeah. I *thought* it was a bit dodgy. So what was I saying?"

"The DGSE left three days ago," Jimmy went on, ignoring Felix's daydreams. "Don't you think we should have heard something by now?"

Felix shrugged and stared at his peeler, scrunching his face into a puzzled ball. "How come Yannick's mother gets to go into the village," he asked eventually, "but the rest of us have to stay indoors?"

"Well, somebody has to bring us food, and all the clothes and stuff."

"But won't she get spotted by imaginary intelligence?"

"It's 'imagery intelligence,'" Jimmy corrected. "From satellites. But she's always going into the village. It would look more suspicious if she didn't go."

"So I suppose bringing back nine times the amount of groceries, buying every item of clothing from some grimy charity shop, and being picked up in the truck by her son—that's not suspicious at all." Felix raised his eyebrows so high it looked like they might fly off his head at any moment.

"You've got a point," admitted Jimmy. "It's risky, but it's necessary, isn't it?"

Felix shrugged again. "S'pose," he mumbled. Then he tried juggling with three of the potatoes. He didn't have much success.

Jimmy turned his attention back to the cooking. His wrist flicked the knife through a carrot with the skill of a chef but the enthusiasm of an eleven-year-old boy. The heavy metal pans huffed and bubbled with delicious-smelling stews.

"And why have I done all the cooking?" Jimmy groaned.

"If you didn't want to cook," Felix replied, "you should never have helped out that first night we were here. Then we would never have found out that it's one of your, you know, skills."

Before Jimmy could respond, Georgie bounced in.

"When's dinner?" she asked, poking around the various

ingredients that lay on the work surfaces.

"When it's ready!" snapped Jimmy. He dropped the knife and flung the slices of carrot into a simmering pot. "Where's Yannick?"

"Outside. Let him have a break."

"Oh, 'let him have a break,'" Jimmy mocked. "Looks like I'm the one who'll spend my life cooking now."

"What's the matter with you?"

Jimmy tried to hold back his anger. "Sorry, Georgie," he said. "I shouldn't take it out on you. It's just that . . ." He paused midsentence to baste a chicken. "I hate this. How come I can cook?"

"It's your programming," Georgie answered as gently as she could.

"That's what I told him," Felix chipped in.

"But it's a stupid skill," Jimmy grumbled. "It's like whatever dumb idea Dr. Higgins had eleven years ago is inside me." He felt himself becoming more and more worked up, and he couldn't hold it back. "They don't know where I am," he yelled, "and they don't know what I'm doing, but NJ7 is still controlling me."

Helen slipped into the kitchen with concern on her face. "What's all the noise about?" she asked, picking up a potato from the floor.

"Jimmy doesn't want to cook," Felix announced.

"That's okay," Helen said immediately. "I'll help and —"

"No!" Jimmy screamed, "I don't want to be *able* to cook and I don't want to be *able* to kill."

Jimmy's mother looked across at Georgie, then back at her son. There was one thing they had to discuss, so she forced herself to bring it up. "Look," she began, "I know this must be confusing for you both. About me and your father, I mean."

Jimmy glanced at his sister, then dropped his eyes to the floor. Felix shifted uneasily from foot to foot.

"Er," he stuttered, "I have to, er, go finish my . . ." He edged toward the door. "You know, on that . . . string."

Once Felix had gone, Jimmy found the atmosphere even more stifling.

"Whatever happens," his mother continued, "none of this is your fault—either of you. Don't blame yourselves."

Jimmy let the words bounce off him. He knew what his answer was, but he refused to let himself say it. Then his sister said it for him.

"I don't blame myself," she mumbled. "I blame you and Dad."

Jimmy didn't know where to look. His sister's words had stoked the anger inside him. He noticed his hands were shaking slightly, then saw that his mother's were too.

"Okay," sighed Helen, "that's fine. But we both still love you just as much. And I know you still love your father."

"How can you still love someone," Jimmy shouted back, "when you know what they're doing is wrong?" He immediately regretted his words, but couldn't take them back now. His mother said nothing. She had no answer. For a few seconds she stared at Jimmy and Georgie, then she backed out of the kitchen. As she did, the seething liquid in one of the pots bubbled over.

Helen walked straight into Christopher Viggo, who caught her delicately by the shoulders and looked into her face.

"What's going on?" he whispered. Helen made sure the door was shut behind her so that her children couldn't see.

"It's nothing." She quivered. "Forget it."

"Listen," Viggo rasped, "the kids are just restless. They need to get out of the house — let off some steam."

"It's too dangerous."

Viggo looked deep into Helen's eyes and let out a sigh. "Yannick says the village up the road is pretty small. The risk of NJ7 picking it out is minimal. He says there's a lake nearby and stables. . . ." He softly lifted Helen's chin. "Let them have some fun. It could be days before we hear from Stovorsky."

"You think I'm being overprotective," Helen whispered, "but they're my children." She held his gaze for a moment, then pulled away and hurried upstairs.

Viggo was about to follow, but there was a pounding on the front door. Jimmy had heard it too and rushed out of the kitchen, followed by billows of steam. He looked to Viggo for guidance, and the ex-agent shook his head as if to say, "Don't worry." At that instant, Felix came tearing down the stairs.

"Who's at the d — ," he started. Viggo grabbed him and put a hand across his mouth. He was too late. Whoever was outside had heard them and hammered again.

"Coming!" Viggo called out, then stuttered the same thing in French: "On arrive!"

Jimmy pointed at the shadow in the crack under the door. There was clearly only one person there, but what if there were others farther from the door?

Jimmy ran upstairs and approached a window that over-looked the front of the building. Crouching low, he scanned the horizon. He could just discern the rooftops of the village up the road, but nothing out of the ordinary. His heart was pumping and he was almost relieved that at last he had something to occupy him.

He opened the window as quietly as he could and squeezed out, trampling the carnations in the window box. The wind tousled his hair; what a great feeling it was to be outside again. From here he could only just make out the person waiting at the front door—the overhang restricted his view. Jimmy quickly moved up the side of the building, clinging to the timber, each finger hard as rock.

It was a matter of habit now to call up his programming when he needed it. When the swirl from his belly engulfed his brain then saturated every muscle, it was a kind of comfort. Too much of a comfort in fact. He had to keep a part of his human self active. He knew how easy it would be for him to slip into the evil ways his body craved. He knew also that the programming would grow more powerful every day until he was eighteen. It was designed to completely swamp the human in him by then. That was a terrifying thought.

Jimmy reached the roof and stalked along until he was directly above the front door. Then he jumped. The wind rushed into his face. His eyes watered, his stomach lurched, then . . .

Bam!

Jimmy landed right on top of the figure, flattening him. Jimmy held him down but couldn't see anything. His face was full of flowers. The man under him was terrified, cursing in French. The front door swung open. Viggo was ready for action.

But there wasn't any—just a flower delivery man, quaking with fear. Jimmy brushed the man down while they were still on the ground, then rolled to one side, spat out a flurry of petals, and made a mental note to land with his mouth closed in future. Viggo seized the mangled bunch of flowers and flicked a tip into the dust. Jimmy muttered an apology and skulked back indoors, where Felix was laughing hysterically.

"That was so funny," he howled. "Did you see the look on his face?"

"What's going on?" It was Saffron, her eyes wide and expectant as if she too were ready for a fight. But then she saw the flowers in Viggo's arms and her expression melted.

"Oh, Chris," she gasped, "for me? They're so . . . squashed."

"They're not for you," he huffed. "I mean, they're not for anyone."

"If they're for Helen, just tell me now."

"No, they're—" Before he could finish, Felix jumped in and grabbed the card.

"The flowers are just a discreet way for Stovorsky to send us a message," explained Viggo. "Now what does he say?"

Felix's face was scrunched up in confusion. "It's gibberish," he said. "Just letters and numbers: 'P.p18N.2300.'"

"He's going to help." Viggo beamed. "We have to meet him in Paris."

St. James's Park, in the very heart of London, was as serene as ever. The thick bushes kept out most of the traffic noise, but there was the sound of two runners pounding along a path. Mitchell easily kept pace with the huge man at his side. His body was exhilarated by the crisp air, while Paduk breathed it in with heavy panting. This was the only part of Mitchell's training that took place outside the murky tunnels of NJ7 HQ: a daily run.

Mitchell asked no questions and made no objections. In fact, he had thrown himself into the training with more dedication than he had shown for anything in his life. It seemed to suit him. Yet still he could sense the unease of the people training him. He didn't know it, but the same team had trained Jimmy Coates. This was the same routine Jimmy had followed. This was the same run.

Paduk slowed to a walk and took a swig from his water bottle. Mitchell did likewise, though he didn't need to. Then they stopped completely. Paduk was staring through the foliage. At first Mitchell thought the man was simply catching his breath, but then he followed Paduk's eyes beyond the limits of the park. Buckingham Palace shone out, a majestic pearl.

Apparently unprovoked, Paduk spoke. "Mitchell," he began in an undertone, "you might be tempted to think that you're invincible." He wiped the sweat from his brow and cracked his jaw. "Don't. You're not. But neither are your enemies."

Without a glance at Mitchell, he ran on. Mitchell followed, keen to impress but confused by Paduk's words.

As soon as it was dark, Helen, Saffron, Viggo, and Jimmy crammed into the dilapidated truck. Felix banged on the window of the farmhouse and showed Jimmy a supportive fist. Jimmy smiled. It was great to see Felix in such good spirits, despite being so worried about his parents. Felix was the one who had the most to lose in this operation, but he hadn't complained once about being stuck in the farmhouse. While Eva,

Jimmy, and even Georgie had been going stir-crazy, Felix was nothing but supportive.

"What a bucket of tin," Viggo groaned as he started the engine.

Jimmy wondered whether Viggo would drive as wildly in this truck as he had at the wheel of his Bentley. That car had been abandoned in the garage of Viggo's restaurant, along with the rest of his London existence.

"It's only a couple of hours to Paris, but try to get some sleep." Viggo was addressing all of them, not just Jimmy. "After we've met Stovorsky, Saffron, you drive Jimmy straight back to the farm. Try to get back before the sun comes up. Helen, you and I will be heading for England."

"Hey," Saffron interjected, "I thought we were all going."

"It's too risky." Viggo bundled the truck over the rough tracks. "Helen and I are trained agents."

"And what am I?" Saffron snapped back. "A babysitter?"

"Who's a baby?" Jimmy remarked, indignant.

"She's right," Helen said calmly. "You should go with Saffron. I haven't been active for years and"—she drew a deep breath—"I don't want to leave the kids."

"Oh, Mum," Jimmy groaned, "you're being—"

"I know: overprotective. But whatever you say, I'm driving back to the farm with you, Jimmy."

They had reached a main road now, and Viggo picked up the pace.

"Why am I even coming then?" Jimmy mumbled. Saffron's response was firm.

"You're the only asset we have to offer. Without you, there's no reason for the French secret service to help us."

An "asset." Jimmy never thought he'd hear himself described like that. He realized it might be true, but it made him feel like an object. Saffron noticed his silence.

"Sorry, Jimmy," she added. "I didn't mean it like it sounded. An 'asset' can mean a person as well, you know."

Jimmy felt comforted by that. If he was ever to feel like a normal person again, the last thing he needed was for everybody around him to treat him as a machine. He smiled cautiously. Saffron smiled back.

There was a steel behind her grace that Jimmy admired. He'd seen Saffron in action and had no doubt that she should be the one to accompany Viggo back to London. He found it hard to imagine his mother being as effective if it came to a fight.

In Paris it was raining heavily and the traffic was as bad as the weather. Viggo spat and cursed as he maneuvered the truck through the back streets. All the time, Saffron kept her eyes on the side mirror, watching for any patterns in the vehicles behind them. It was imperative that they not be followed.

They drove along the line of the river into the center of the city. Viggo's fingers tapped impatiently on the steering wheel. "Clear?" he called out.

"Clear," responded Saffron.

Suddenly, the truck lurched to one side. Jimmy was thrown across his seat. They mounted the sidewalk and slipped through a narrow opening in the wall that ran alongside the road. It led to a cobbled ramp, and in seconds they were driving right beside the Seine. Viggo slowed down drastically until the truck was growling along, centimeter by centimeter.

They stopped under the arches of the next bridge, and Jimmy looked through the rain at the surface of the water. He shivered as they climbed out into the thick shadows. Water poured from the arches above his head, forming a curtain between him and the rest of the world. Here, the river exuded an eerie, sulfurous mist.

In silence, Viggo signaled the way. They ran through the rain, up a flight of thin stone steps onto the Pont de Sully. There, blending into the stonework, was Uno Stovorsky. In these conditions, his raincoat made perfect sense.

Still without a word, they followed Stovorsky along the bridge, onto the Île St. Louis. Jimmy gave up trying to keep the rain off. He wasn't even wearing the special shirt he'd been given by NJ7. He was shivering, but he would rather have drowned in the rain than wear the Green Stripe again.

Stovorsky unlocked an inconspicuous door and guided the others through a courtyard and into a building. When they reached the fourth floor, they stepped into a small office with a balcony overlooking the courtyard. Around the walls were bookcases stacked with leather-bound tomes. Stovorsky quickly pulled down the blinds. It was strange—Jimmy didn't feel any warmer in here than he had in the street.

Finally, Stovorsky spoke. "We don't have long. So I don't want any messing about."

"Messing about?" Viggo retorted. "You think it's messing about to make it into Paris undetected? Why couldn't we meet nearer the farmhouse? Somewhere in a wood maybe?"

"Chris, take it easy," Saffron cut in. "He's helping us out."

Stovorsky's response was icy. "Maybe in Britain you have secret meetings in the woods all the time," he mocked, "but this is France. We're still an old-fashioned democracy. This is a safe house, Viggo. Do you have a clue what that means?"

Jimmy thought he saw Viggo about to apologize, but Stovorsky rattled on. "It means we can jam listening devices, and it means we have routes to and from here that are sheltered from satellite surveillance. Now, you can go mess about in the woods if you want to, or we can get down to business."

Jimmy held his breath and watched Viggo out of the corner of his eye. The man nodded solemnly.

"Right then," Stovorsky continued. "We know where the boy's parents are being held." Jimmy's heart leaped.

"Well then," Viggo insisted, "where is it?"

"The French embassy in London."

Jimmy was buzzing—the natural buzz of excitement, not the sensation of his programming taking over. This was a huge step toward rescuing the Muzbekes.

"Wait a minute," Helen Coates cut in. "How did you find this out?"

Stovorsky nodded as if he had been expecting the question. "We have sources in England," he stated, then quickly added, "reliable sources."

Saffron turned to Helen and Viggo, concerned. "What if NJ7 planted that information? Do you think it could be a trap?" she asked.

Jimmy took in her somber mood, and his initial excitement faded. Don't ruin this, he thought. Just go and rescue them.

"There's only one way to find out," Viggo mumbled. "How

do we get to London?" Jimmy loved Viggo's determination.

"I shouldn't be doing this, you know." Stovorsky sighed.

Before Viggo could respond, Saffron took control. "We really appreciate it, Uno," she said with a voice coated in honey.

Stovorsky looked away for a second. Then, when he spoke again, Jimmy noticed that he looked anywhere except at Saffron. "Okay," Stovorsky began, "here's the situation. The French ambassador to London has been kicked out. Apparently, he provided transport to a group of dissidents."

Viggo looked sheepishly at the carpet. "Yeah," he muttered, "that was me."

"I realized that when we recovered the EC975 in the field behind your farmhouse." Stovorsky's tone was disapproving, but Jimmy detected a hint of respect in his half-smile. "The DGSE can provide cover for one of you to go in on a diplomatic visa. Officially, you'll be on the staff of the new ambassador."

Viggo stroked his chin, unsure how to ask for what he needed. Saffron did it for him.

"We need cover for two," she stated boldly.

"She's right, I won't be able to do it alone," Viggo added.

Stovorsky looked between the two of them, scratching his head. "Okay," he conceded with a sigh. "I think that can be arranged. So am I to assume that it will be you two?"

Again Viggo hesitated, and Helen broke the silence. "Yes, it's those two," she said.

Stovorsky nodded and pulled out a cell phone. He held it up and took one picture of Viggo, then one of Saffron. Then he buried himself in the keys, sending an encrypted text message.

"Who's going to examine Jimmy?" Viggo asked.

Stovorsky furrowed his brow without looking up from his phone. "What?" he muttered.

"In return for helping us," Viggo went on, "I assume one of your scientists will examine Jimmy?"

Jimmy prickled at the idea of being "examined." He realized it wouldn't be quite like going to the doctor. More than that, he felt indignation bristling in him again. Viggo was using him to negotiate, treating Jimmy as a commodity. The hurt quickly faded. All this was for Felix's parents—and Felix.

"I'm ready," Jimmy blurted out, aware that his voice betrayed his nerves. "I don't know everything about myself yet, but I'll show you what I've learned."

Stovorsky at last finished with his phone. He stared at Jimmy, incredulous. "No," he scoffed, "I told you. We don't need that information." Jimmy's tension eased.

"Then what do you want from us?" Viggo asked.

"Just this: you'll be working for the DGSE. We want any intelligence you can pick up while you're there. Particularly, what NJ7 knows about us."

"So you're asking us to spy on the British government?"

"Do you have a problem with that?"

The response was blank looks.

"That's fine," Viggo said at last.

Jimmy was surprised at the ease with which Viggo and Saffron accepted Stovorsky's price. Viggo had worked against the British government for years, but always for himself and his democratic ideals—never for France.

Stovorsky glanced again at his cell phone. "We have to move," he said, striding to the door. "You two come with me." Viggo and Saffron followed obediently. "You two"—Stovorsky indicated Jimmy and his mother—"get out of Paris. Now."

mission

Mitchell stood bolt upright in front of Dr. Higgins's desk. On the doctor's lap was a wiry black cat and in his hands was a photograph. Behind him were the other two people who had taken over Mitchell's life. First was the huge frame of the man who had brought Mitchell in. His military uniform was as crisp as the edges of his regulation haircut. This soldier's identity was a mystery; Mitchell knew him only as Paduk.

Dr. Higgins had the power of science at his disposal, and Paduk was as physically intimidating as any man Mitchell had ever seen. But the person he was most afraid of had a lipstick-red smile curling up one cheek and one eyebrow permanently cocked in an expression of disdain. Mitchell had no idea how a woman so beautiful could be so severe, but he couldn't imagine anyone disobeying Miss Bennett.

"You're ready," Miss Bennett announced, clearly relishing the moment. The sickness in Mitchell's stomach hadn't disappeared, it had just mutated into something else. An eerie power waiting to explode. He had to know when to push it down and when to let it take him over.

"Your target is dangerous," Miss Bennett continued. "We need him dead and you back here alive. You were very expensive." Mitchell nodded. It was almost an automatic response. "And if you attract the attention of the French police, you'll be useless on any future missions. So blend in and make it look like an accident."

She was about to walk away, but one more thought occurred to her. "There's no chance of you going off-mission, is there?" Her eyes narrowed. Mitchell shook his head hurriedly. "Remember: there's nowhere you can go that we can't track you. And working with us is the only chance you have to be forgiven for what you did to your brother."

Mitchell nodded again, this time trying to make it seem like the most natural thing in the world. He had no intention of going "off-mission," as Miss Bennett called it. The second he had seen his brother's battered face, he had begun to hate his human weakness. Learning that only 38 percent of him was human had come almost as a relief. Now he needed to build a new life. Killing an enemy of the state was the first step toward doing that.

He followed Paduk through the dark corridors of NJ7 headquarters. His mission had begun.

Dr. Higgins tutted wearily.

"Get over it, Kasimit," snapped Miss Bennett. "Soon only one of your babies will be left alive."

"Oh, they were never really my babies." Dr. Higgins sighed, gently stroking his cat. "The true genius behind them was chased out of NJ7 thirteen years ago."

He closed his eyes and let the photograph in his hand fall to his desk. It was remarkably detailed considering it had been taken from two hundred kilometers above the earth's surface. Every feature of Jimmy Coates's face was clearly visible as he ran across the roof of a French farmhouse.

Jimmy tried to sleep on the way back from Paris, but tension hunched his shoulders. The roads were quiet. It was easy to see no one was following, and his mother drove smoothly.

Jimmy leaned his head against the window. The vibrations of the truck drummed into his head. The road flashed past outside, but Jimmy wasn't watching that. From the corner of his eye he could make out his mother's face reflected in the glass.

Do I know her? Jimmy wondered. He knew he could trust her, but he no longer knew anything about her. She was just another ex-agent now, so different from the time before any of this business started. Jimmy wished he had happy memories of a normal family life, but he couldn't think about that time anymore without bitterness. His parents had been keeping secrets from him. Not just secrets about themselves and their jobs, but about him, Jimmy Coates, and who he was.

Helen glanced across at him as if she knew that he was thinking about her. Jimmy forced a smile, then turned away. What makes her right and Dad wrong? he wondered. His father supported Hollingdale's view that the public shouldn't be allowed to vote because they weren't qualified to know how to run the country. So what? That wasn't hurting anybody, was it? And if the prime minister held on to power through force, well, how was that different from his mother being prepared to use force to get rid of him?

"You okay, Jimmy?" his mother asked suddenly, interrupting the drone of the motorway.

"Yeah, I think so," he replied. He was going to leave it at that, but something was on his mind more than ever. "Mum," he started. His voice croaked, so he cleared his throat before going on. "If they'd examined me, what would they have found?"

Helen Coates didn't divert her eyes from the road, but Jimmy could see that his question had affected her. "I'm not a scientist, Jimmy," she said.

"But you are my mum."

There was a long silence. Helen's eyes flickered in the lights of the road. "I don't understand it completely," she said at last, "but I know that they programmed a special computer chip, and that chip controlled a laser—I think it was called a microlaser. The laser operated on a single strand of DNA, which eventually created you." She glanced across at her son. Jimmy was engrossed.

"But was I a baby like everyone else?" he asked.

"You were a beautiful baby," his mother said, smiling. "They put you in my womb, and they even implanted the computer chip into you when you were just an embryo so that nothing could go wrong while you were growing inside me."

Jimmy tensed up again. There was a chip inside him? His mother noticed and gave a short laugh.

"Don't worry," she said. "The chip was completely absorbed into your body by the time you were born. That's what guarantees you're unique."

They drove on in silence for a few more miles. Jimmy marveled at the years of research that must have gone into him. He tingled with excitement at the thought of the world's top scientists poring over his chemical makeup. But one thought still wouldn't let his mind relax.

"When Mr. Stovorsky was at the farm, he said there was another one of me."

His mother took her time answering, clearly choosing every word carefully. "There's only one you, but yes, there were two chips. There was another assassin. He would be two years older than you, but they don't know where he is. He ran away from his home. He's probably leading a normal life somewhere. I'm sorry you can't do that too, Jimmy."

"It's okay, I suppose," he replied, trying to work out how he felt.

"Jimmy," his mother said hesitantly, "if I'd known . . ." She trailed off. Jimmy watched her.

"If you'd known what, Mum?" Jimmy asked.

"Nothing" was the response. "It's just that . . . things were different back then."

"When?"

"When I agreed to be your mother."

Jimmy tried to imagine his mother as a younger woman. He shuddered at the thought of her standing with Dr. Higgins, Paduk, and Hollingdale, acting as one of them. Couldn't she have known then that the whole thing would lead to trouble?

"Why did you do it?" Jimmy asked.

His mother took in a deep breath. "A lot of reasons," she began, sounding distant, as if remembering was difficult—or painful. "It had to do with me and your father. It had to do with Georgie. She was a baby then. I suppose I thought that it would be a way for me to stay working for NJ7, but not *really* be working for them, do you see what I mean?"

Jimmy shook his head, but his mother wasn't watching him.

"It was a way out. I thought it would give me eighteen years of a relatively normal life."

"But what about me?" Jimmy whispered, unable to force out his proper voice.

"I knew that once you were eighteen you'd work for NJ7. But by then, with your programming fully developed, I thought you'd want that life."

Jimmy couldn't help himself. His brain vibrated with the words: I won't have a choice.

Helen reached across and ruffled Jimmy's hair. "I didn't realize you'd be . . . you," she added, trying a smile. Jimmy could see how sad she really was. He didn't smile back.

More than an hour later Jimmy shuffled into the farmhouse, ready to fall into bed. But as soon as they opened the front door, Jimmy heard whispers in the kitchen. He looked up at his mother, who gave a weary sigh.

"Well *I'm* going to bed," she whispered.

Jimmy smiled, totally exhausted, but desperate to share everything that had happened. In the kitchen, Felix, Eva, and Georgie were sitting around the table.

"Jimmy!" exclaimed Felix, jumping to his feet. "What happened?"

Jimmy didn't know where to start. "Ares Hollingdale is holding your parents at the French embassy," he blurted.

"And Chris and Saffron are going to bust them out?" Felix beamed, one big ball of energy.

"Something like that." Jimmy laughed.

Felix grinned one of his unmistakable grins. Eva and Georgie didn't look quite so happy. "At least *someone* will be getting out of prison," Eva grumbled.

"Yeah," Georgie added. "Who's going to rescue us?"

"What do you mean?" Jimmy asked.

"I mean that we've all been stuck in this house for days." Jimmy's sister toyed with a stale hunk of baguette. "It's no wonder we can't sleep—we don't do anything all day."

"At least we don't have to go to school," Felix chipped in with a bounce.

"So what?" Eva shrugged. "I'd rather go to school than be stuck in the middle of nowhere. I don't even have my phone with me."

Jimmy considered everything for a moment. He never liked it when Eva moaned, especially when Georgie started moaning with her, but she had a point. It did feel like being imprisoned.

"I'd rather be back with my parents," Eva went on, "and they're a pain. I bet they aren't even looking for me." Jimmy remembered Eva's parents with a shudder of disgust. They were supporters of the undemocratic British government.

Suddenly, Felix cut in. "Stop moaning," he said quickly. "This is the best night ever." Then his face suddenly changed, scrunched up in thought. "You're right, though. We've been stuck in the house long enough. If anybody's coming for us, they would have come by now. Tomorrow I'll persuade your mum to let us go out."

"Whatever you say." Jimmy shrugged and forced out a yawn. "Let's convince Mum in the morning. You do the talking. I'll watch."

❧   ❧   ❧

Miss Bennett followed the tunnels of NJ7 not to Downing Street, which was still being rebuilt, but to the deepest part of the complex. There, in a stark bunker, surrounded by three men in SAS uniforms and another two in NJ7 suits, Ares Hollingdale was huddled over his desk. Opposite him, leafing through a dog-eared orange folder, was Ian Coates.

"Who's there?" the prime minister panted when he heard his visitor enter. "An assassin! Security!"

The soldiers around him looked confused. They all recognized the director of NJ7.

"It's okay, Prime Minister!" shouted Ian Coates. "It's Miss Bennett."

"Ah yes, of course. Stand down, men; you're dismissed. I know this woman." Hollingdale's eyes darted around the room as if every second something tapped him on the shoulder unexpectedly.

"Mitchell Glenthorne has been deployed, sir," Miss Bennett announced once the room had emptied of security attendants.

"Don't let that thing near me," Hollingdale muttered. "I've seen what they're capable of."

"Prime Minister," Miss Bennett continued, "it's not too late to call him back."

Ian Coates jumped to his feet, startled. "Miss Bennett," he said, "if there's a way to safeguard our neo-democracy without hurting Jimmy, please don't keep it to yourself."

Miss Bennett flashed him a patronizing smile, then continued to address Hollingdale directly. "Now that we have found where Jimmy Coates is hiding, in less than an hour a single

UAV could flatten the entire area."

Ian Coates sank back into his chair, his face suddenly pale.

"Sending out another assassin is an unnecessary risk," Miss Bennett went on. "Haven't we learned anything from the last time we did it? Order the UAV strike."

"Are you mad, Miss Bennett?" the PM cried. "You're talking about sending an unmanned plane to bomb French soil!"

"The French would probably retaliate," Miss Bennett said, her voice devoid of emotion, "but it's nothing we couldn't handle."

Hollingdale's hands were shaking. He swung around in his chair to face the wall and waved over his shoulder. Ian Coates took that as his cue to stand again, and explain.

"The prime minister feels that provoking the French would be far too dangerous."

"What do you mean?" Miss Bennett asked flatly.

Hollingdale spun back around and pounded his fists on his desk.

"Sauvage!" he screamed, eyes flashing. "Until we know what the French are capable of, we must proceed with extreme caution."

Miss Bennett inspected the faces around her, each one rigid with anxiety. Ian Coates continued his explanation.

"We have reason to believe that when Dr. Sauvage fled, he passed classified technology to an agency called ZAF-1."

"ZAF-1?" queried Miss Bennett.

"Possibly the French equivalent of NJ7," Ian Coates replied. "We don't know. The details are encrypted in these files." He threw the folder onto the desk and pulled out a bloodstained orange flash drive in a clear plastic bag.

"And for eleven years nobody has told me about this?" She was furious.

"Nobody knows about this, Miss Bennett," the PM said. "Even within NJ7. If Dr. Higgins knew that we had this flash drive, the only explanation would be that we killed Dr. Sauvage. If he finds that out, he might be dangerous."

"You're completely paranoid!" Miss Bennett shouted. "Dr. Higgins isn't dangerous no matter how many of his friends we kill. He could decrypt those files in minutes."

Ares Hollingdale twitched almost imperceptibly. Miss Bennett sighed and ran her hands through her hair. "So," she stated in a matter-of-fact tone, "the French could possess weapons far more powerful than we thought."

"Exactly," Hollingdale snapped. "And they could use them."

Miss Bennett paced across the room. "But hold on," she said. "We have no intelligence suggesting they have these weapons."

"We have *this* intelligence," Coates insisted, pointing at the flash drive.

"Call that intelligence?" Miss Bennett mocked. "I've had enough of your sort of intelligence, Coates."

"I don't like your tone, Miss Bennett," Coates replied calmly, his eyes piercing Miss Bennett's.

"Why are you even in this office?" she sneered. "A month ago you were sitting at home with your feet up. Do you think your opinion matters? If you'd raised that boy properly, we wouldn't have this problem. You're no better than Christopher Viggo."

Ian Coates looked away. Christopher Viggo's name sent a pulse of anger across his face.

"Miss Bennett, that's enough," Hollingdale barked. "Ian's opinion is of the highest importance to me. His loyalty has been tested and he has proven himself." He rubbed his hands together, every vein clearly visible. His cuff rode up slightly, revealing a small tattoo of a green stripe on the inside of his left wrist. "We don't know for sure what the French are capable of," he continued. "Until we do, we must attack Jimmy Coates, not France."

IT'S RAINING UMBRELLAS

Mitchell's prey loomed large in his binoculars. It was Jimmy Coates. The circle of vision encompassed him like a tightening noose. At first, Mitchell had been surprised when he discovered who his target was. They had crossed paths before. It seemed so long ago that Mitchell had tried to mug him in London, and ended up showing him where the police station was. But that was a lifetime away. Nothing could surprise him now. Mitchell pushed back the memories of his old existence. Those miserable days were over. This was a fresh start.

His room at the Auberge de l'Aubergine overlooked the main square. From here he could keep an eye on anything that went on. The village held no secrets for him. It wasn't that Beuvron was so small—it was on the cusp of becoming a town—but Mitchell let no detail escape him.

He thought with pride of the hours he had spent in the grass outside Jimmy's farmhouse hideaway. His surveillance had even included close observation of the old woman that he now knew was Yannick's mother. He watched her buy food and clothes for her guests. He listened to her moan about it to the shopkeepers. All the information went toward building a rich picture of Jimmy's life in hiding.

Mitchell felt a surge of delight as Jimmy took a seat outside the *crêperie* across the square. It was perfect. Jimmy had done the same thing every day for the four days that he and his friends had been allowed out of the farmhouse by Jimmy's mother. Mitchell had spent the whole night in preparation, banking on Jimmy doing it again today.

Mitchell mouthed the words with him as Jimmy ordered a *citron pressé*. The blend of fresh lemon juice, water, and sugar that you mix yourself had become their favorite drink. Yes, Mitchell thought, your last drink. Such a shame you'll be dead before it arrives. Then he dropped his binoculars onto his bed and dipped his hand into a long slim pouch of black leather that hung on the bedpost. He drew out three separate sticks of bamboo, each about twenty-five centimeters long.

With the precision of a surgeon, he screwed them together, end to end. He went to the leather pouch once more and brought out a silver ring with a tiny clip attached to it. He clamped it onto the top of his bamboo rod. Finally, he reached up to his own head. With a deft tug, he plucked out two hairs. His hair was, as always, cropped short. It didn't matter. The strands were a perfect length for his purposes. He dabbed the ends on the tip of his tongue and secured them delicately across the ring.

What emerged in his hands was a specially adapted weapon

of his own design. It was probably the most sophisticated peashooter in the world, complete with a target sight and crosshairs.

Mitchell moved back to the window. He pulled up the glass just a crack and knelt on the floor. From his pocket he produced a handful of tiny pebbles. Afterward, there would be no bullet on the scene to arouse suspicion. The pebbles would disappear among the everyday debris of the street. It wouldn't even be a pebble that killed Jimmy Coates.

There was no question of sympathy as Mitchell loaded a stone into his shooter. Far from it. As far as Mitchell was concerned, Jimmy deserved his punishment. *So you're 38 percent human too*, Mitchell thought.

"Well, you've had it easy," he muttered, watching Jimmy leaning back in his chair, comfortable, smiling. "You're not like me."

Gently, he raised the bamboo and whispered, "Showtime."

"Deux citrons pressés, s'il vous plaît," announced Jimmy to the waiter, his French accent perfect.

"Oh, order one for me too," whispered Felix, licking his lips.

Jimmy raised his eyes to the sky. "Don't worry, you'll get one." He sighed.

"Oh, you think he knows what I want already?" Felix muttered, watching the waiter walk away.

Against his better judgment, Jimmy found himself laughing. "By the way," he added, "I think you should put sugar in it this time."

"No way," Felix replied. "I like the lemon flavor."

Jimmy had forgotten how much fun it was when Felix was

just being Felix. What's more, it felt fantastic to be outdoors. Jimmy's mother hadn't been able to justify keeping everyone in the house much longer. In any case, Yannick's mother was being driven mad by having kids around. If they hadn't been allowed out, she would probably have thrown them out.

In the four days since Viggo and Saffron left for London, there hadn't been any news from them. Jimmy realized it would take time to gather enough intelligence to raid the embassy without being discovered, but the waiting was still excruciating. Meanwhile, he and Felix had been taking advantage of being allowed out and not having to go to school.

Now they had a chance to enjoy spring in France. It wasn't all that hot, but there was enough sunshine for the *crêperie* to have umbrellas up over the outside tables. Except for the logo of some French beer company, they could have been giant blue lily pads. Jimmy and Felix made themselves comfortable in the shade. Jimmy was almost ready to forget his troubles.

But something wasn't quite right.

"What's the matter?" Felix asked, noting the concern on Jimmy's face.

"I don't know," he replied. "Maybe it's nothing."

"What's nothing?"

Jimmy shrugged, but still he couldn't relax. "It's my . . . you know"—he dropped his voice—"programming. It won't go away."

Felix leaned forward. "I thought it would always be there. You have to get used to it. Otherwise you could let it ruin a perfectly beautiful—"

Ping!

The noise cut off the end of Felix's sentence. At that

55

moment, the umbrella that sat in the center of their table wheeled off its pole.

Felix let out a laugh, half from amusement and half from shock. Jimmy found nothing to be amused about. The umbrella crashed down in front of him. It passed a centimeter from his face. He rocked back in his chair, startled. The spokes of the umbrella dug into the table like darts on a dartboard. The ends were unusually sharp. The umbrella came to rest on its side, the material sticking up from the table between Jimmy and Felix.

Jimmy leaned forward to regain his balance, but he couldn't. The back leg of his chair snapped clean off and he clattered onto his back. Then —

Ping!

The umbrella from the next table careered downward. Jimmy watched as its points glinted in the sun. They were heading straight for his face. At the last instant, he rolled out of the way. The spokes of the umbrella smashed on the sidewalk. Before Jimmy could get up —

Ping!

Another umbrella. Then: *Ping! Ping! Ping!* One after another, every umbrella rocked on its pole and wheeled toward him. Jimmy lunged between the spokes. They came like daggers. He snatched up a chair and used its legs to fend them off. At last, he made it under one of the tables.

The noise of crashing metal gave way to the shouts of the waitstaff. Jimmy looked around him at the forest of chair and table legs. Then Felix's face appeared, red but grinning.

"You okay?" he yelled over the hubbub.

"I suppose," panted Jimmy. "Except that a bunch of

street furniture just tried to kill me."

Felix roared with laughter. Jimmy didn't feel like joining in.

Mitchell knelt on his bed, forcing his disappointment down. So that plan had failed. Now he had to press on with a new plan straightaway. There was no time to dwell on his mistakes.

He looked around his room. There was barely enough space for a bed and a sink. It was filthy too, but Mitchell wasn't looking at that. He was examining the charts and maps that he had pasted up all over the walls. His mission surrounded him.

He tore down one of the maps and spread it out on the bed in front of him. He banged his fist on it, then scolded himself for letting his frustration show. Of course his first attempt hadn't worked. At the back of his mind he had always known that the plan with the umbrellas had been a long shot. Now he had to get serious.

Mitchell scratched at his heel. The itch was a constant reminder that Miss Bennett was watching him. There was nowhere he could go that she wouldn't find him. He felt toward her almost the way he would toward a very strict teacher. Facing her without having done his homework was out of the question. But there was a difference. Mitchell *wanted* to complete his assignment. For the first time in his life he felt like he had a real future. He couldn't wait until his eighteenth birthday. By then his conditioning would have taken over his entire being. And he'd never again be haunted by the face of his brother.

Mitchell drove those thoughts out of his head. They would destroy his concentration—and Miss Bennett's task demanded total concentration.

He traced his finger along a line on the map. It represented the road that joined the farmhouse and Beuvron. Jimmy and his friends walked along it every day. Here? Mitchell wondered. A traffic accident? He pictured the narrow roadway, the muddy ditch, and the poplars that bordered it. He shook his head. That would be enough to kill a normal human, but Jimmy Coates was faster, stronger, with reactions that would see him through almost anything.

Where then? Mitchell's finger wandered around the farmhouse in a spiral, searching the fields. It paused over a small collection of buildings. What's this? Mitchell asked himself. He peered closer. It was some kind of industrial site. The perfect place for an accident, he thought. But I have to get closer to the target. How?

He leaped off the bed and crouched low by the window, watching but invisible. He saw Jimmy in a heated discussion with the manager of the *crêperie* about the broken umbrellas. Felix was stumbling about trying to help clear up the mess. He wasn't doing terribly well.

Then two girls arrived. Mitchell knew they were Georgie and Eva. He knew too that they were about his age and that they spent most of their time in the Internet café around the corner. They had obviously heard that something had happened and come to check that Jimmy and Felix were OK.

Mitchell nodded gently, an idea trickling into his head. Yes, he thought. It's time to make my move.

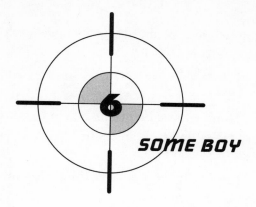

6
SOME BOY

Jimmy lay in the dark, staring up at the intricate cobwebs that decorated the ceiling. He was replaying over and over the accident at the *crêperie*. He tried to bring up exact images. That way he could search them for details he hadn't noticed before. He wanted to be able to zoom in as if his memories were photographs. Unfortunately, he wasn't doing very well, but something inside him wouldn't let him sleep until he'd examined every moment.

"You still awake?" came a whisper through the darkness. It was Felix.

"You can see I'm awake," Jimmy replied. The curtains at the window weren't doing a great job of keeping out the moonlight.

Jimmy and Felix were in neighboring beds in one of the two upstairs bedrooms of the farmhouse. The other room was just for Yannick's mother. On the other side of the room were another two beds. In one, Yannick's bulk heaved up and down to the rhythm of his snoring. The other was empty.

"Do you think Chris will be back soon?" Felix asked. "With my parents, I mean."

"Oh," Jimmy answered, distracted from his thoughts. "Oh, yeah. Sure. If anyone can do it, he can."

"Or you," Felix said quickly. "You could do it. You could do anything."

"Maybe. I dunno." Jimmy turned onto his side to face his friend. He smiled and closed his eyes but opened them again almost straightaway.

"Felix," he whispered hesitantly, "do you think that was really an accident in the village today?"

"That was so funny. The manager couldn't believe it when he saw that *all* of his umbrellas had broken!"

"The thing is, though, I don't think I believe it either."

"What do you mean?"

"I mean, don't you think it was a bit, kind of, funny that they all broke? And that the ends were all so sharp? That was really dangerous."

"Yeah," Felix replied, the moonlight catching the enthusiasm in his eye, "but you were so quick, you dodged out of the way like, like . . ." He wriggled about in his bed, acting out some of Jimmy's moves.

"And did you hear the noise just before each of them fell?"

"What noise?" asked Felix, completely tangled up in his bedsheets.

"That sort of pinging noise. As if something was knocking them over deliberately."

Felix stared at Jimmy, trying to make out whether his friend was serious.

"You mean," he started, "there was some invisible man, sent by Miss Bennett, who sharpened the ends of the umbrellas, then knocked them over, aiming for you?" He made a face that stretched one of his nostrils almost up to his eye. "You're crazy."

Jimmy let out a deep breath. Maybe Felix was right. There was no rational way to explain his suspicion. But there was a voice in his head that blared out like a trumpet. It told him over and over that when that many umbrellas, with sharpened points, all come within a centimeter of your head, it's more than a coincidence.

"What about my chair?" Jimmy insisted.

"What about it?"

"The leg snapped. How does the leg of a metal chair snap, unless somebody has weakened it?"

"Wait a minute," Felix said, sitting up. "How did this invisible man know you were going to sit in that particular chair?"

"He could have done it to all the chairs."

"Oh, *all* the chairs," Felix repeated sarcastically. "Then the invisible man *does* exist."

Jimmy huffed a little to disguise the fact that he was about to laugh. How could he take his worries seriously when Felix was there to make light of them?

"Thanks, Felix," he whispered. "I suppose I'm just paranoid."

"Yeah, and don't tell your mum any of your crazy theories, or she won't let us go out again."

They both turned over in a fresh attempt to get some sleep. Then Jimmy spoke again, quieter than ever, as if he was talking to himself.

"Felix," he muttered, "sometimes, just before I go to sleep,

I feel like my programming takes me over completely. I don't feel human at all because I don't feel anything."

Felix was silent for a second. Yannick's snores filled the room.

"Jimmy, don't worry," Felix replied eventually. "You'll always seem human to me. You *smell* human anyway."

With that, he burst out laughing—and so did Jimmy.

"That wasn't me!" Jimmy grinned. "It was Yannick!"

A few days later Jimmy and Felix were hanging out at the lake. In fact, Felix was literally hanging out. He was dangling from a tree trying not to fall into the water below him.

"Jimmy!" he shouted, the branch dipping drastically under his weight. "Get up here!"

Jimmy closed his eyes for a fraction of a second to feel inside himself for that powerful sensation. It washed over him so easily now, and for the time being he was still able to hold it in check. He ran three strides toward the tree and bounded upward. His hands scurried up the bark and his legs kept running as easily as if they were on the ground. It was only seconds before Jimmy was as high as Felix. But he didn't stop.

As he climbed higher, he glanced down to see Felix's amazed expression growing smaller. Looking up, Jimmy could see around the entire lake now. The branches grew thinner, but Jimmy didn't pause on them long enough for them to break. He kept dashing on to the next one until he could see all the way to the farmhouse and beyond that to Beuvron.

He stopped when he found a sturdy enough place to sit. His breathing was still steady, and the wind refreshed his cheeks. His smile had grown with every meter he'd climbed. Then something caught his eye. Between him and the farmhouse he could make out three figures walking toward them.

"Felix!" he called out. "Someone's coming!" He couldn't see his friend through the canopy of leaves, but there was something rustling below him. Then Felix's head popped up right next to him.

"Hey, looks like I have *special powers* to climb trees!" Felix said sarcastically. Jimmy blushed. It was so hard to separate what he was doing because of his programming and what he would have been able to do anyway.

"Oh, yeah," said Felix, looking out at the field below them. "Looks like Georgie and Eva."

"But who's that with them?" Jimmy squinted into the sun. The third figure definitely wasn't Yannick or Jimmy's mother.

"It's probably that boy," Felix grumbled.

"What boy?"

"Don't you listen to anything?" Felix asked, incredulous. "Georgie and Eva met some boy at the Internet café in the village. He's English. They've been trying to keep it secret from your mum. I think they fancy him."

Jimmy realized he hadn't really talked to his sister much lately, and he usually tried to avoid talking to Eva.

"They're always in the kitchen when I go down for a snack at night," Felix explained.

"They shouldn't be on the Internet and they shouldn't be talking to anyone they don't know," Jimmy whispered. The girls were close now and were obviously looking for them.

"Yeah, it might be Miss Bennett in disguise." Felix made a face, then began his climb to the ground. "Carrying a deadly umbrella."

Jimmy waited a moment. He shook off his concern and followed his friend down.

"Jimmy!" shouted Georgie just before she saw him jumping out of the tree. "Oh, hi, this is Mitchell. His family's on holiday nearby. He wanted to meet you two."

Standing between Georgie and Eva was a stocky boy with a short haircut. Jimmy did a double take. It couldn't be . . .

"Mitchell?" he said. The boy casually raised a hand.

"Hey, I know you," he said. "I took you to the police station, like, a few weeks ago."

Jimmy didn't answer. They had met before. The night NJ7 had first come for him, Jimmy had nearly been mugged by this boy. Jimmy tried to think back, but he had been so scared and confused at the time that he couldn't make out any distinct memories. He hesitantly shook the boy's hand.

"That's a coincidence, I suppose," Jimmy said steadily, looking him right in the eye.

"Yeah, I'm from North London too." Mitchell sounded confident and returned Jimmy's stare. "I overheard English voices, looked around, and saw two beautiful girls." He indicated Eva and Georgie. "I had to introduce myself."

The girls giggled and hid their faces behind their hands.

"Actually," said Eva, "I spoke to *him* first. You know, life here isn't so bad after all."

Felix shook his head and stuck out his tongue in disgust.

"We're going riding," Eva announced, her face flushed. "Wanna come?"

"What, on a horse?" Felix sounded nervous.

"Come on, it'll be fun," Mitchell said, turning to walk away with Eva and Georgie on either side of him.

Jimmy hesitated. Something was wrong. The boy Jimmy had met in the park when he was trying to find the police was surly and hated company. Now Mitchell was acting like everyone's new best friend.

"We should go with them," Jimmy whispered to Felix. "Make sure nothing happens."

"You want to sit on a French horse just because some boy fancies your sister?" Felix didn't look pleased about the prospect of riding.

"I have a bad feeling about him, that's all." Jimmy couldn't tell whether it was his assassin's instinct or the natural mistrust of a younger brother.

"Whatever." Felix shrugged, and they both set off after the others.

Jimmy's horse stank and clouds of flies surrounded him, but there was no backing out now. At the stables, Jimmy had settled a price with the man who owned the horses. He suspected it would have cost double if he hadn't negotiated in French. The mud-clad stable keeper wasn't too concerned about safety. There were no helmets, and he didn't care what anyone did with the horses as long as they were back before sunset.

The others trotted a little way ahead while Jimmy and Felix caught up, wobbling every step of the way.

"My bum!" Felix cried. "I don't deserve this kind of pain. My bum's going to die and fall off." Jimmy chuckled, despite suffering the same discomfort. But Felix wasn't finished. "I like my bum," he went on. "I need it for . . . sitting."

Eva was the only one of them who had ridden before, and she was keen to show off her expertise. Jimmy was glad he couldn't hear her simpering advice. Georgie's riding was shaky, but Jimmy's attention was fixed on Mitchell. He didn't want to take his eyes off him for a second.

At first, the group kept a measured pace and followed the paths, but Eva was quickly bored. "Let's go for a canter," she announced. Without waiting for a response, she leaned down to open the gate and kicked her heels in. Her horse moved steadily away into an orchard. Mitchell was quickest to follow, much to Jimmy's frustration.

Jimmy sighed and tried to block out the pain throbbing up from his backside. Why did they make saddles so uncomfortable? The leather creaked as he put every effort into persuading the horse to leave the road. At last he managed it.

Georgie and Felix weren't having such an easy time.

"This horse is such a donkey!" shouted Felix, flapping the reins to no effect. Jimmy wanted to laugh, but he was too concerned with watching the two riders ahead of him.

"Yours isn't a horse, Felix," Georgie corrected him. "You're on a pony." Then, desperate not to lose touch with Mitchell and Eva, she shouted, "Wait for us!" But her horse was going nowhere. She threw down the reins in frustration. "This is stupid."

"I agree," added Felix. "If humans were meant to ride horses, God wouldn't have invented motorbikes."

Jimmy was still waiting for them, growing more and more agitated.

"Jimmy!" shouted Georgie. "We've had enough. See you back at the farmhouse."

She and Felix waved frantically. Jimmy caught her words on the breeze and waved back. On any other day he would have gone with them, but he couldn't shake his suspicion of Mitchell. It was too much of a coincidence that they had both come to the same village. Was he right to feel so uneasy? Jimmy decided that if he was wrong, and just being paranoid, he wouldn't lose anything except the feeling in his butt. But if Mitchell had somehow found them deliberately, Jimmy had to find out why. This was his chance.

Mitchell could clearly handle a horse as well as Eva. The pair of them chatted and flirted while Jimmy kept close watch from behind. How come he can ride so well, Jimmy wondered, when he's a thief from London?

Jimmy bobbed beneath the branches, catching glimpses of Mitchell through the canopy of leaves. When the three of them rode out into the fields of low, green wheat, it was easier to keep an eye on him. They carried on for most of the afternoon, but Jimmy was never able to catch up completely.

He saw Mitchell pull up close to Eva. Their feet knocked against each other in the stirrups. What were they saying? Then Eva dug her heels in and sped away with a gleeful squeal. A moment later and Mitchell set off at a gallop in the other direction. They're trying to lose me, Jimmy thought. He would happily have let them go; he had nothing to base his suspicion on but an uneasy feeling, and knew he was no match for either of them on horseback. But they had come so far from the farm that Jimmy wasn't sure of the way back, and besides, something inside him didn't let him stop.

It was his programming. Of course, thought Jimmy—if he could cook, fence, and breathe underwater, why shouldn't he be able to ride a horse? Eva was nearly out of sight now in a clump of trees, but Mitchell was only a couple of hundred meters away. He glanced over his shoulder, almost teasing Jimmy, tempting him to follow. So that's what Jimmy did.

The muscles in his legs were taut. His posture in the saddle shifted. Now he was a rider. The horse responded to Jimmy's sudden transformation. It jerked into a gallop. Jimmy crouched low like a jockey, the horse's mane brushing his chin, dust flying into his face. The heavy thud of the hooves carried him flying toward the rider in the distance.

They rushed across the countryside, Jimmy gaining ground all the time. Ahead of him, Mitchell reached the edge of the field. His horse leaped effortlessly into the air, soaring over the hedgerow. Seconds later, Jimmy plunged toward the same obstacle. He gathered his horse, allowing the reins to fall slack in his hands. The horse lowered its head, then almost immediately Jimmy felt the huge force of its back legs surging forward and upward. He clung to the saddle with his thighs as the horse left the ground.

Squinting into the sun, Jimmy imagined he was in the air for minutes, but almost at once the horse's front legs hit earth. The impact jarred through Jimmy's body. The horse was racing away now and sped into the next field flat out.

Here the ground was uneven, and on the horizon was some kind of industrial complex, the only clutch of buildings for miles around. Jimmy watched Mitchell's head disappear over a dip in the landscape. Unable to see him for the moment, Jimmy charged on. He knew he could catch him.

He rounded the top of the hillock, looking for Mitchell up ahead. But the boy wasn't there. Then Jimmy felt a lash on his cheek. He turned to see Mitchell drawing up next to him, grinning. In one hand he held the reins to his horse and in the other he held a loop of strap. With one flick of his hand he sent it flying toward Jimmy, and it wrapped around his neck like a lasso.

Jimmy grabbed at it, but too late. Mitchell pulled him out of his saddle. The strap was tight around Jimmy's throat, and he flew off his horse. He smacked into the ground, face first, but still traveling. Mitchell had the strap wound tight around his wrist. The other end was choking Jimmy.

Mitchell dragged him through the dirt, never relenting in his speed. Jimmy's horse was still galloping behind, but it was no good to him now. He felt the ground cutting into him, scraping any bit of his skin that made contact. He twisted to try and free himself, but that only wound the strap tighter around his neck. He gasped for air, snatching for any breath he could force down. He gulped a mouthful of dust.

Jimmy's face was deep red. He scratched at his neck to loosen the strap, but it did no good. He could feel his brain crying out for oxygen and his vertebrae straining not to snap. Without realizing what he was doing or why, his fingers reached into his mouth. The taste of soil cut through him, but still no air.

He gripped one of his back teeth. Then came a burst of pain so intense he prayed to pass out, but his programming quickly swamped it and neutered the agony. Blood prickled on his tongue. He gripped his tooth tightly in his fist. It had come away whole; he felt for the spikes at its root.

He could hardly see now. Debris slammed into his face, and his eye sockets were swollen with bruising. It took all his effort to prevent himself from blacking out. Still not able to think, his life in the hands of his programming, he punched the tooth into his neck with a sharp jab, just above the strap. Trapped somewhere in his head was a human boy convinced he was about to die. His fingers twisted the tooth down and in, then ripped it straight out again. It tore his skin from the inside, but burst through the leather strap as well.

Felix and Georgie trudged into the farmhouse, covered in mud and bruises. Georgie's mother caught them in the hallway.

"What happened to you?" she asked.

"Horse riding," Georgie grumbled.

Helen Coates gave a little chuckle. "You were the ones who wanted to go out and have fun. Where are the others?"

"They were better at riding," Felix replied, as miserable with the afternoon as Georgie, "and Jimmy wanted to follow them."

Helen stood between them and the kitchen. "What do you mean, 'them'?" She stared into Felix's face. "Who else is there?"

Georgie glared at Felix. He looked sheepish, realizing he'd given her away.

"I suppose it's okay to tell you." Georgie sighed. "We met some boy in the village a few days ago. He wanted to come with."

Helen's shoulders tensed up instantly. Stay calm, she told herself. Don't be paranoid. "What boy?" she asked as casually as she could.

"He's just some boy, okay?" Georgie shrugged, turning to go upstairs. "His name's Mitchell."

Helen froze. "He's English, about your age," she gasped, "a little shorter than you, with light brown hair probably shaved very short."

"How do you know?" Georgie spun around to see the deadly serious look on her mother's face.

"I saw his projected imagery program thirteen years ago."

Georgie and Felix were stunned. Georgie tried to speak, but nothing came out of her mouth.

"Get in the truck, both of you," Helen said firmly. "You need to show me where they went."

7

ALWAYS RECYCLE

Jimmy heaved in a desperate lungful of air. He spat the grime from his mouth and wiped his eyes with the back of his sleeve. Instinctively, he patted the wound in his neck. It felt dry. But he couldn't rest yet. The ground was drumming under him. Looking up from the mud, he saw the silhouette of Mitchell turning his horse. He was charging back for Jimmy. He clearly wasn't going to stop until Jimmy was dead.

Jimmy pushed himself onto his feet, then ran toward his own horse. It was galloping past to meet its stablemate. Jimmy caught the pommel in his hand and threw himself up into the saddle. It took a commanding heave to wheel the horse around. He managed it with Mitchell still a few meters away.

"Come on," Jimmy whispered through his teeth, as if the horse could understand him. Somehow it must have sensed Jimmy's desperation because it kicked away with a burst of speed. Mitchell responded by digging his heels in, and they both dashed across the field.

In the open country Jimmy had nowhere to hide. The leak of blood in his mouth was already clotting, and the incision in his neck exposed only a smudge of gray beneath the surface. Still every gash cried out for him to stop. He fixed his eyes on the buildings up ahead. If he could make it there, he had a chance.

Mitchell was gaining ground. The two horses devoured the space in front of them, straining to race faster than they ever had. The shadows of the buildings grew as they approached. A rusty sign announced the entrance in French; it was an industrial recycling facility.

Jimmy didn't ease up. He couldn't; Mitchell was almost level now. In one more huge leap, Jimmy's horse soared over the fence and landed with a thud inside the complex. A second later, he heard Mitchell's horse do the same behind him.

Jimmy scoured the corrugated iron barns for some way of losing his attacker. The place was deserted. Mitchell was too close now. He reached forward and grasped the back of Jimmy's saddle. Locked together, they tore through the recycling plant, Mitchell pulling on Jimmy's horse to catch up. Soon he drew level and lashed out at Jimmy's neck. Jimmy was quick enough to stave off the blow. They traded one-armed hits while still surging forward.

Then they plunged through the entrance to one of the barns. Mitchell lunged out of his saddle to seize Jimmy's reins. Jimmy looked up and realized why. They were riding headlong toward the iron face of a machine. Jimmy tried to wrestle control away from Mitchell, but he couldn't turn the horse away. Mitchell clenched his jaw in a twisted grimace. Was he determined to clatter them both into a horrible crash?

Jimmy thought desperately for some way out, but Mitchell had control of both horses. Then, just in time, Mitchell pulled on the reins. The horses started to turn, but Mitchell had other plans for Jimmy. He gripped the back of Jimmy's shirt and, just as the horses came to a halt, hoisted him upward. The impetus sent Jimmy high into the air. He flew over the side of the machine ahead of them and crash-landed inside it.

He found himself sitting on a pile of metal panels, twists of wire, and torn sheets of plastic. Suddenly, the pile seemed to grumble. The grumble grew to an immense din, then Jimmy noticed that the rubbish beneath him was steadily shifting. Mitchell had turned on the machine.

Gradually, a hole emerged at Jimmy's feet. It opened up like a whirlpool. At the bottom he caught a glimpse of a block of wood dropping into a funnel, where rotating blades thrashed it to splinters. Jimmy was trapped in the loading receptacle of an industrial shredder.

He scrambled to the side, but it was sheer metal. Thinking fast, his injuries still burning for attention, he threw the biggest items he could find up against the wall. If he ever wanted his programming to take him over completely, this was the time. He willed it with all the power in his brain. Piece by piece his pile grew, but the ground was constantly sinking. At last he had done just enough. He clambered up until he could hook his fingers over the side of the container. Then he felt a huge force pushing down on his head.

It was Mitchell. He had climbed up the outside of the machine and he wasn't going to let Jimmy out. Jimmy's fingers were slipping. Smeared with blood, he had hardly any grip. He had to hold on. But Mitchell chopped his hand down hard into

Jimmy's shoulder, cutting off the nerves to his fingers. Staring into Mitchell's ice-cold eyes, Jimmy fell into the shredder.

He tried to swim up through the refuse, but it was churning with too much force. The hydraulic swivel system sucked him down toward the funnel. Could I survive that? Jimmy asked himself desperately. His mind was clogged with so many thoughts, but only one certainty—even he wasn't strong enough to withstand a shredding.

His arms reached out to grab on to something—anything— but one hand clasped only a length of wire and the other nothing more than a nail. Both sank with him. He heard himself scream as his leg came into contact with hardened alloy steel knives rotating at 1000 rpm. Pain erupted within him. I can't be in pain, he protested, I'm special. But the inferno inside him kept doubling.

Blood exploded upward, spattering Mitchell's face. He turned away. The scream faded. His job was done. He slid down the outside of the shredder and looked up to see he wasn't alone. Eva swung her body around and jumped off her horse, which immediately fled. She ran toward Mitchell, terror in her eyes.

Mitchell thought quickly. This wasn't in his plan. He had wanted to complete his mission without being seen, then tell the others there'd been a terrible accident. This could ruin everything. But then his head cleared—maybe he could use this to his advantage.

"The horse threw him off," he shouted over the noise of the machinery. "He landed in the shredder. I tried to help him, but the start mechanism is jammed." He glanced over to the control box he had smashed with a crowbar moments before.

"I know," Eva yelled back, tears running freely down her face. "I saw you reaching for him."

"Listen, you have to help me." Mitchell stared into Eva's eyes. "It was a terrible accident. But nobody will believe me."

"What do you mean?"

"I have a criminal record in England. I have to get away from here. Tell everyone I did my best and that I'm sorry." Mitchell waited for the lies to sink in. Eva was gazing at him strangely. Was that a look of admiration? He sprinted back to his horse, seized the reins, and hauled himself on. In the distance he could see a truck speeding up the farm track. He had to get away now. But Eva was running toward him.

"Go!" Mitchell shouted. "Get help."

Eva turned one last time to the huge mechanism that chundered on. Then she looked up at Mitchell. "Take me with you," she whimpered. Mitchell couldn't hear her, but he could make out the words from her lips.

Mitchell had seconds to make his decision. Should he kill this girl too? No—two deaths would look less like an accident. Before he could do anything, Eva ran over to Mitchell, clasped his arm, and heaved herself up behind him. The horse reared, adjusting to the extra weight. There was no time for Mitchell to argue. With one sharp kick, he sent them flying across the landscape and over the horizon.

The wire bit into Jimmy's palms as he clung on. The other end was slung over the side of the machine. On it was a nail, bent into a hook. Jimmy hoped Mitchell wouldn't notice it. That was the only thing holding him in this position: one foot flat against the side, leaning out almost horizontally over the hungry blades. His other leg hung down limp, spewing blood from half-shredded flesh. Only a layer of some inhuman gray substance held it together.

Jimmy closed his eyes, desperate to shut out the pain. He knew his programming wasn't fully developed, but he had never expected it to be tested beyond its limits by a situation so extreme. He listened. Until he knew Mitchell had gone, he was stuck there. But the noise of the machine was deafening. Then, against that thunderous backdrop, he made out two people shouting. As soon as he heard them, they stopped. Using every bit of strength he had left, Jimmy crept up the wire, hand over hand until he could peek out.

He was just in time to see Mitchell and Eva riding away.

He flopped over the side of the shredder and let go, not caring whether the fall was far or not. The ground was unforgiving, but it was nothing compared to what he had just been through. The noise oppressed his ears. His head was swimming. What if he blacked out? Would he bleed to death before anyone found him? A normal boy would, but would he? The mysteries of his own body tormented him. He could hardly move. He had to attract attention.

Come on! he ordered himself. Get moving or you'll die. He crawled on his belly across the floor of the barn until he was almost out in the open. At the entrance was a stack of oil canisters. Jimmy heaved one over. I have to attract attention, he thought. He looked back at the shredder. A thick trail of blood drew a line between him and the machine. Is that my blood? he wondered. Do I really bleed that much?

With all his might, he shoved the oil canister toward the pistons that drove the shredder. It rumbled across the floor. Just before it was crushed by the pumps in a flash of sparks, Jimmy sheltered on the other side of the barn wall. He slumped there in a heap. The last thing he remembered before he passed out was the heat of the explosion on his back.

The truck was traveling at top speed. Felix and Georgie bounced up and down as Helen charged along the country tracks.

"Are you sure they came this way?" Helen shouted.

"They were going in this direction but across the field," Georgie called back, her voice vibrating with the vehicle.

"We left them hours ago though," Felix cried. "It took us so long to get back."

Helen twisted her head from side to side, constantly scanning the horizon. Then a movement caught her eye.

"There!" Georgie shrieked. She'd seen it too. Two horses. One black, like Eva's, and the other chestnut, just like the one Jimmy had been on. But neither had a rider. They were both galloping toward the truck, away from a group of buildings that looked like a small industrial complex.

A split second later, thick orange flames roared into the sky. The ground shook. Helen reacted quickly. Even in the face of a giant explosion, she never lost control of the wheel. The view was obscured now by dense smoke, and they could only see snatches of where they were heading. That was enough.

The truck veered off the track, smashing through a fence. They were close now, and Helen slammed on the brakes.

"Stay here!" she shouted, but Georgie and Felix were already jumping out of the truck. The three of them ran toward the fire.

"Stay with me!" Helen cried, shielding her face from the dust and heat. As they approached the heart of the explosion, the smog cleared, blown high above them by the wind. It was Felix who saw Jimmy first: tattered and unconscious, slouched against the outside wall of one of the buildings. His leg was torn, leaving ribbons of flesh hanging over a layer of dull gray.

Felix waved to Helen and Georgie, and together they lifted Jimmy, carrying him step by step back to the truck. As they lay him along the seat, his eyes flickered half open.

"Mitchell . . . ," he murmured. "Eva . . ."

"Are they in there?" asked Helen desperately.

Jimmy managed a weak shake of his head before he passed out again. Blood oozed out of him, covering the seats. Georgie held his head steady as the truck rumbled back to the farmhouse.

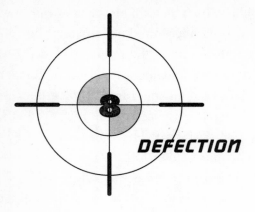

DEFECTION

Mitchell and Eva walked in silence through the clatter of the Gare du Nord. They'd left the horse at the next town on from Beuvron and reached Paris in a taxi. At every stage, Eva questioned her decision to come with Mitchell. For his part, Mitchell had hardly spoken. Perhaps it was just awkwardness now that he had a girl with him—and one who had clearly acted as if she had strong feelings for him. But Eva sensed it was more than that. He didn't act coldly toward her—but he seemed deep in thought.

They joined the line at passport control. Eva was about to ask what Mitchell meant to do about the rest of his family, who were supposed to be on vacation with him, when she suddenly froze.

"I don't have my passport," she gasped. She pictured it sitting in her father's desk at home. Collecting their passports certainly hadn't been on anybody's mind when they fled London in the helicopter. Mitchell sighed and looked around, distracted.

"Did you hear me?" Eva asked. "We can't go anywhere. I don't have my passport. Do you have yours?"

"We don't need them," Mitchell said quickly.

"What?"

"Look, I'm sorry, Eva." He lowered his voice and looked her straight in the eye. "I lied to you. I'm not here on holiday. I'm not with my family. And that stuff I told you about me having a criminal record?" He shook his head slowly.

Eva stared back at him. It felt like the station forecourt was melting beneath her feet. Mitchell took her by the shoulder and continued in an undertone. "I'm with the secret service," he confided. "I was sent to France to find you and bring you back."

Eva felt her knees wobbling. It was as if the station itself was dissolving around her. Could this possibly be true? Viggo had snatched Eva in the middle of the night by mistake; he and Jimmy had been trying to rescue Georgie from Eva's family, who were supporters of Ares Hollingdale. As far as NJ7 knew, Eva had been a hostage of theirs, rather than a willing helper.

But why had the secret service been looking for her, not the police? Why hadn't Mitchell just explained that when they first met? And why had he lied even after Jimmy had been killed?

Her questions tormented her, but she couldn't ask them. So much flashed through her mind: meeting Mitchell at the Internet café, flirting with him while they were riding, the roar of the shredder, Jimmy's blood on Mitchell's clothes. Should she run now? Would she get away? Beneath the confusion, another thought crept up on her. It was the same urge that had led her to come with Mitchell in the first place. Don't let him get away with this, it begged.

Before she could piece any of it together, Mitchell pulled

her forward, past the line. On the other side of the desk there was a booth with mirrored windows. From it emerged a tall, dark-haired man in the uniform of a customs officer. Mitchell gave a discreet nod, and the officer nodded back. He whisked them through passport control.

Everything was happening so fast, Eva couldn't take it in. They scurried through the terminal, the customs officer escorting them all the way into a first-class carriage. Only as she took her seat did Eva notice the enamel badge nestled against the man's lapel—a green stripe.

Semper Occultus—"Always Secret." Mitchell stared up at the secret service motto. It adorned the wall behind the desk, just beneath the crest of the royal family. It wasn't Miss Bennett's desk, because they weren't at NJ7. Mitchell and Eva had been met by a car at Waterloo station and brought to the headquarters of MI6, on the banks of the Thames. The building looked almost like a castle, but one that was peppered with security cameras. Mitchell was on the top floor now, and out of the window he could look from London's skyline to the people crawling across Vauxhall Bridge below.

He was here because it was out of the question to allow Eva, a civilian, into NJ7 HQ. Even the agent whose office they had borrowed had been shocked to learn that NJ7 really existed. He had always thought of it as some kind of ghost story. Now that he knew, he would be manning an observation tower in the Outer Hebrides by the end of the day.

Mitchell was keen to avoid eye contact with the woman who was technically his commanding officer.

"Well?" Miss Bennett stabbed Mitchell with a stare.

"Jimmy Coates is dead," he announced without emotion.

Miss Bennett made no response. Did her eyes flicker for a moment? Mitchell couldn't tell. He didn't want to look too closely.

"Anything else?" she said at last.

"There might be two hostile operatives gathering intelligence for a raid on the French embassy. One man, one woman."

"Might be?"

"It's possible the source was trying to impress me." Mitchell paused, then clarified. "She might have made it up."

Miss Bennett smiled, but still her eyes seemed dead. "And you've brought Eva Doren back with you," she mused.

"Yes," replied Mitchell. "I told her I was sent by the secret service—"

"Coming here would have looked a little odd if you hadn't," interrupted Miss Bennett.

"But she thinks I was sent to look for *her*, not Jimmy Coates."

Miss Bennett stroked her chin for a moment, then spoke softly. "That's quick thinking. Good." She flicked her eyes to the back of the room, where a man in a black suit guarded the door. "Send in the girl."

The man nodded discreetly and left. Mitchell's heart was thumping.

"What happens to me now?" he said, his voice betraying his trepidation.

"As long as you continue to work for us," Miss Bennett replied, unsurprised by his question, "you'll be in no trouble."

Mitchell had no time to say anything more before Eva

Doren came in. He stepped aside, taking up a position by the wall. Eva glanced at him, but again he avoided making eye contact.

He really is in the secret service, thought Eva.

"Good afternoon, Miss Doren," said Miss Bennett in a tone that was disgustingly friendly. "Your parents will be here shortly. In the meantime, if there is anything we can do to help you . . . counseling of any kind . . ."

Eva was only half listening. She knew the choice she was faced with. That's the easy way out, she thought. Her dilemma was clear. Go home, or stay near Mitchell to find out what's really going on. She'd made up her mind at the Gare du Nord.

Miss Bennett was still rattling on. Eva cut her off. "I don't want to go back with my parents," she blurted.

Miss Bennett was taken aback, but it took only a moment for her to adjust. "Eva, your parents have spent every minute since your abduction trying to find you," she explained.

"But I can help you," Eva said. "Let me work for you."

Miss Bennett let out an abrasive laugh. "I know the idea of being a 'spy' is all very glamorous, young lady, and maybe one day when you're older . . ."

"I mean now. You don't need to pay me. Think of it as work experience."

Miss Bennett stifled her laughter and waved to the man at the door to take Eva away.

"Christopher Viggo and Saffron Walden are planning to break into the French embassy!" Eva shouted as quickly as she could. Miss Bennett held up a hand to the man in the suit. "They're trying to rescue Felix Muzbeke's parents," Eva continued.

"Is this true?" inquired Miss Bennett slowly. "Or are you trying to impress me?" She shot Mitchell a wry smile.

"I know all about their operation." Eva waited, trying to work out what Miss Bennett was thinking. "And I know all about yours too," she added. "For example, if Mitchell is like Jimmy, I assume he's also only thirty-eight percent human."

Mitchell's head whipped around in her direction. "You know about . . . that?" he gasped. Eva nodded. "And you still"—Mitchell paused, searching for the right words—"*like* me?" Eva nodded again, and a sparkle lit up Mitchell's eyes that she hadn't seen before. Miss Bennett's expression still gave nothing away.

"I know about NJ7," Eva declared. At that Miss Bennett visibly tensed up.

"Your parents have been informed that we found you," she said calmly. "It would be a shame to have to tell them that what we found was your body."

Mitchell found himself short of breath, suddenly terrified for Eva. But she didn't need his help. "You're either going to have to kill me or employ me," she announced.

At that Miss Bennett really smiled. Something had clearly struck her. Then her cell phone rang and she flipped it open. Her eyes were still on Eva. Mitchell began to summon his programming. If they tried to kill Eva, he could intervene.

"Yes?" Miss Bennett barked into her phone. "Tell them it wasn't their daughter after all. . . . Tell them we're still looking." She snapped her phone shut and slipped it back into her pocket. "I like your attitude, Miss Doren," she said. "You're practical. Like me."

❀   ❀   ❀

"You were wise to call me, Stovorsky," said the doctor, still poring over Jimmy's ankle. "A civilian doctor would have gone straight to the authorities."

"Is he okay?" Stovorsky replied. They spoke in French, but even in his woozy state Jimmy had no problem understanding. Felix, however, was bewildered. He sat next to the bed with his mouth hanging open.

The doctor rubbed the back of his neck. "I don't know." He sighed. "Most of the bones in his leg were shattered, but they're not normal bones. They're as tough as girders and seemed to be replenishing even as I was examining them. The flesh around his calf is shredded to pieces, as you saw, but he's already clotting the wound from the inside. He stopped bleeding remarkably quickly, given the degree of trauma." The doctor was strapping up the injury as he spoke. Jimmy didn't squirm. His body appeared to have shut off all feeling below his left knee while that part of his leg healed. It was as if his brain had sent an anesthetic to be administered automatically.

The doctor wasn't finished with his report though. Now he turned to Jimmy's neck. "It looks like the skin here was split cleanly. There are no fragments of tooth or leather to infect the wound. And his body shut off the bleeding here before it even started, if such a thing is possible."

Jimmy had bandaging wrapped around his neck that meant he couldn't turn to either side, and gauze stuffed in his mouth that made it hard to speak. He felt like most of it was unnecessary, but he made tiny nods and grunts to show that he understood. The doctor looked into Jimmy's face, but there was no friendly smile to go with the medical attention.

"Any normal boy would never walk again," he said flatly.

"But as far as I can tell, you'll be fine. Just stay in bed for a few days with your leg up. And I've written out some exercises for you." He started to gather his instruments, but Jimmy wasn't satisfied.

"Og-oh," he tried, then spat out the lumps of gauze in frustration. "Doctor, I don't understand." His voice was raw and his throat hurt when he spoke—not that he cared.

The doctor rolled his eyes and gathered the bandages he had so carefully administered.

"Why wasn't my body tougher?" Jimmy implored.

The doctor stared at Stovorsky and was about to address him, but Stovorsky nodded as if to reassure him. "You might be specially built," the doctor began at last, his tone heavy with annoyance, "but you're not finished yet, are you?"

Jimmy didn't know how to answer. He felt so vulnerable—almost betrayed by his own deficiencies.

"Look"—the doctor sighed—"from what I've seen, even if you keep developing, you'll never be Superman. Sure, you'll be able to cope with some pretty serious knocks and cuts, and your body will heal itself far quicker than any normal body. But how can you expect not to bleed if you stick your leg in a shredder? And it's a fluke you didn't pierce a major artery with your tooth. Stupid boy. You're lucky to be alive."

Jimmy was shocked. No doctor had ever spoken to him like that. Medicine was obviously different in the military. He didn't want to provoke any more attacks, so he leaned his head back and opened his mouth, ready for the doctor to put the gauze back in. The doctor just laughed.

"You expect me to do all that again?" he scoffed. "So you can spit it out and ask stupid questions?" Jimmy sheepishly closed his mouth, anger welling up inside him.

"Listen, son," the doctor whispered, wagging a finger in Jimmy's face. "Arrogance is fatal. One day a bullet's going to bring you down. Believe me." For the first time his eyes really connected with Jimmy's and wouldn't let him look away. "Maybe the first bullet won't kill you—okay, you're special. But the second one certainly will. And it won't be a quick death like it might be for a human. Your body's as obstinate as your brain. You'll resist. You won't want to, but you will. You'll die slowly."

Jimmy's face was burning. He focused on the taste of blood to stop himself from crying. The doctor snatched his bag and strutted across the room, scowling at every person in it. He was met at the door by Jimmy's mother and sister.

"Thank you, Doctor," whispered Helen, shaking his hand before entering the room. Jimmy wanted to be sick. He let a fresh trickle of blood creep down his throat. Then he was pleased to be distracted by the sight of his sister. But something was wrong. Jimmy wasn't sure, but it looked like Georgie had been crying.

Helen cleared her throat. "Everyone, we have a problem."

The others waited expectantly to hear what it was; Jimmy felt a lump in his stomach like a bowling ball.

"If Mitchell is NJ7," his mother continued, "then NJ7 know about Chris and Saffron's plans at the French embassy."

"What?" Stovorsky exclaimed. "How did he find out?"

"I told him." It was Georgie, her voice clear but meek.

Jimmy was furious. "How could you do that?" he shouted, ignoring the sting in his gullet.

"Calm down," said his mother. But Jimmy was fuming.

"Did he torture you?" he rasped.

"I was trying to impress him." Georgie stared at the floor. "It was stupid. Eva overheard me telling him and she was furious. I thought it was because she was jealous of me talking to Mitchell privately. But she was right. And in the end he chose her over me anyway." The end of her sentence disintegrated as she burst into tears and ran out of the room.

Everyone else was left in silence. Even Felix had nothing to say for the moment. Jimmy could only imagine the kind of trouble Viggo and Saffron were in if their cover was blown. Stovorsky paced the room, his shoulders hunched.

"I can't believe it," he fumed. "How could Viggo be so stupid as to trust a bunch of children?"

"Georgie made a mistake, that's all," Helen said. "We can put this right."

"This could jeopardize all the DGSE field agents posted in the UK." As Stovorsky's anger grew, his English accent became more erratic. "NJ7 could trace their entry into the UK. Do you know what that could lead to?"

"Then you have a reason for helping us, don't you?"

Jimmy could see his mother was upset, but trying her best to stay calm for the sake of the situation. Stovorsky closed his eyes and let out a long, slow sigh.

"If NJ7 are on to us, then our lines of communication have been compromised," he muttered. "Someone has to go in and sort this out." He looked hard at Jimmy, then at Helen. "I'm the only one of us who can go in by traditional routes. You two will have your faces all over police lists."

Suddenly Felix piped up. He may have been silent, but his brain had been working away all this time. "What about me and Georgie?" he chirped. "We can go back—we're not targets, are we?"

Stovorsky grunted—it was a cross between amusement and horror. But apart from that, he didn't even bother to respond. Felix glanced at Jimmy, then down at the floor, crestfallen.

"I'll follow Viggo and Saffron to the embassy," Stovorsky said at last, pulling out a notebook and scribbling something down. "I'll find out what's going on, then you two follow in a couple of days." He pointed at Helen and Jimmy. "That should be enough time for me to arrange to smuggle you into the country, and it will have to be enough for you to recover, Jimmy." He tore a page from his notebook. Felix leaned over to read what was written on it. Stovorsky pulled the note away and thrust it into Helen's hands. "It's five P.M. You two will travel separately. Here are the details of a safe house. We'll all rendezvous there in exactly seventy-two hours. Memorize these instructions, then destroy them."

He glanced from Jimmy to Helen, checked his watch, and marched out.

Jimmy lay on his back on the kitchen table. His legs were in the air with his knees bent. His face strained with concentration and effort. This was because Felix was sitting on his feet.

"One more!" Georgie shouted from the side.

Jimmy straightened his knees, a millimeter at a time, lifting Felix toward the ceiling.

"One hundred!" Georgie cried. Felix jumped off and paraded around the kitchen as if he'd been doing the lifting himself.

Jimmy wiped his brow and took a few deep breaths. His injuries had healed well, helped by his determination to build up his strength again. His face was still slightly bruised and on his neck was a discreet bandage. He didn't pay too much attention to that, though, except for wearing his collar turned up to hide it.

"How do they feel?" Georgie asked.

"I dunno," Jimmy replied. "Stronger, I suppose."

"What are you talking about?" Felix cut in. "Those are the strongest legs in the known universe." Jimmy hopped off the table and gingerly took a turn around the room.

"I can't believe it," said Georgie. "Two days ago your leg was splattered all over the French countryside. Now you're hardly limping. It's amazing."

"Well, I don't feel amazing," Jimmy grumbled.

"Lean on me," Felix chirped, rushing to support Jimmy with his shoulder.

"I don't mean that." Jimmy slumped into a chair and took a swig from a plastic bottle of water. "I should never have let Mitchell put me in that shredder."

Georgie put a hand on his knee. "You're being too hard on yourself," she told him. "Mitchell's two years older than you, remember? So he's two years more developed."

"But that means his programming is two years less sophisticated," Jimmy countered straightaway. "What's the point of being the way I am if I still have to worry about getting hurt the whole time?"

"Jimmy—" Georgie tried to interrupt, but Jimmy wouldn't let her.

"You don't understand," he insisted, his eyes misting. "I have this thing inside me every minute of every day. All it means is that people chase me and stuff me in shredders and shoot at me. But you heard what the doctor said. Being subhuman won't help me. I'll just die slower when the bullet goes in."

"You're not subhuman," Felix reminded him.

"And so what if a bullet would kill you?" Georgie added. "You still have an advantage over the rest of us." She reached down inside her T-shirt and pulled out the chain that hung around her neck. Jimmy had never noticed her wearing a necklace like that before. Hanging from it was a small silver cylinder. She let it rest in her palm. Jimmy saw instantly what it was—a bullet.

"Where did you get that?" he asked.

"You gave it to me," Georgie replied. Then Jimmy realized: it was the bullet he had caught the last time an NJ7 agent had fired at him.

"So cheer up," Georgie said gently, peering into her brother's face. "I don't want my friends acting so miserable."

Jimmy couldn't help but smile when he heard that. He had never thought of himself as his sister's friend before. The happiness didn't last though. Georgie had reminded him of the last time he saw Eva.

Georgie read the change in his expression. "What's up now?" she asked, but then she worked it out. "Don't talk about her. She doesn't exist anymore."

"Unfortunately, she does," Jimmy replied quietly, "and she abandoned us."

"I don't understand it," Georgie muttered, shaking her head. "She was just getting used to being here. She said she was starting to like it. We even agreed that we could get along without our phones."

"She was certainly less annoying than she used to be," Felix added.

Georgie dropped her chin to her chest. "And then she . . . ruined it all."

Now it was Jimmy's turn to comfort Georgie. He put his arm around her as tenderly as he could.

"I'm proud of you" came a voice from behind them. They turned to see that their mother had slipped in without being heard.

"Hey, Mum," Jimmy chirped.

"Hey, Jimmy." Without another word, she strode over to them and crushed them in a hug. After only a second she took in Felix too.

"Mum!" cried Jimmy, hardly audible. "You're suffocating me!"

"Oh, sorry." She released them and stepped back. "I'm leaving now," she went on. "For London, I mean. Later, Yannick's going to drive you to meet your contact." She fixed Jimmy with a smile.

"Great," he said. "Jacob Estafette, right? From a Dutch meat company?" He had been repeating the details to himself over and over ever since Stovorsky explained the arrangements.

"Yeah," Felix said enthusiastically, "and you'll be Michael Vargas, secret agent." He said the name as if he was doing the voice-over for a movie trailer, then burst out laughing.

"Shut up!" said Jimmy playfully. "You're not supposed to know any of that." Jimmy was embarrassed at having shared his alias with Felix.

Jimmy's mother didn't seem to mind. "Don't worry." She laughed. "You don't have to remember anything. He'll know you."

"Of course," Jimmy replied, gathering his thoughts together. "Cool."

"But listen," his mother went on, addressing all three of them. "It isn't easy to smuggle people through border controls. Especially into Britain. In a way, you've got a better chance of making it than I have, simply because you're smaller."

"Mum, you'll be fine," implored Georgie.

"I know. Thanks, Georgie. But if for some reason I don't make it to the rendezvous, don't worry. I can find my way back here and make contact with you later." She looked deep into Jimmy's eyes. He looked away, not wanting to deal with the nerves in his stomach.

There was a strange familiarity to this feeling. It brought back all the terrible memories of the first night NJ7 had come for him. Miss Bennett had taken his mother away from him then, though he hadn't known it was Miss Bennett at the time. Jimmy couldn't help thinking that she was doing the same thing again.

"Good luck, Mum," he whispered.

"Yeah, good luck," Georgie agreed. "I know you won't need it."

"Good luck," chimed in Felix.

She hugged them each individually one more time and kissed them hard on the cheek.

"See you in London," Jimmy announced as proudly as he could.

Helen nodded. "See you in London," she replied, with a

hint of a smile. Then she was gone.

As soon as he heard those words, Jimmy felt something jolt inside him. It wasn't fear and it wasn't his programming. It was nothing to do with Viggo and Saffron being in danger. It wasn't even because they might soon find Felix's parents. Jimmy knew in his mind that he should be pleased about that, but his heart's response was blank.

He was going back to London. What was it that confused him so much about that? Then he realized.

He rolled the lid of his water bottle in his fingers. In his other hand he felt the weight of the bottle, half full. Then, in a deluge of fury, he hurled the bottle top against the wall. The bottle itself followed, smashing against the plaster in an explosion of water and plastic.

In London he would see his father.

VARGAS MEETS ESTAFETTE

Jimmy was delighted when Felix insisted on coming with them. Jimmy felt so much calmer when they were together. No matter what happened, Felix treated Jimmy the same way he always had.

"You'd think that they would have designed a way to stop this from happening," groaned Jimmy. He took a deep breath and closed his eyes.

"Stop moaning, will you?" said Felix. "So you feel travel-sick if you read in a truck. So what?"

"I'm not moaning," Jimmy replied. "I'm just saying that if it was up to me to design a person, I'd make sure they didn't get travel-sick."

"Well, one of you has to follow the map," Yannick grunted, "or you're never going to get anywhere, let alone London." He accelerated hard.

Jimmy passed the map over to Felix, who curled up his nose. "It's all in French," he protested.

"What do you mean, it's all in French?" asked Yannick, taking his eyes off the road for a split second. "A map's a map. The lines can't be in French, can they?"

"Okay," sighed Felix, twisting the map from side to side. "Let's see. We're here, yeah?" His finger almost poked through the paper.

Jimmy opened one eye. "Yes." He groaned. "We're there."

"Great," announced Felix. "Then we need to take this blue one."

"Blue one?" said Yannick. "It's not blue in real life, you know."

"Obviously," Felix replied. "It's road-colored. But this is the one we need. Now how do we get onto it?" He studied the map up close, every now and again lifting his head to peer out of the window for any landmarks.

Jimmy opened his eyes again. He couldn't help watching what Felix was doing. "Do you mean *that* blue one?" he asked.

Felix nodded frantically and flapped him away. "Shhh, I'm working it out."

"Er, Felix," Jimmy said carefully, "that's a river."

It took another hour before they finally found the meeting point. It was a rest stop, or an *aire*, off one of the *autoroutes* that ran like veins through northern France. This one was as basic as they came—just a telephone, a toilet, and a couple of rotting picnic tables.

"This is it, Jimmy," muttered Yannick. "We're not supposed to wait with you, you know."

"I know," Jimmy replied.

Yannick didn't even shut off the engine as Jimmy jumped out of the truck, following strict instructions from Stovorsky.

Jimmy turned back to his friends and made himself smile. He quickly regretted it. It would probably make him look even more nervous than he actually was, he thought.

"Say 'hi' from me," Felix blurted.

"What?"

"When you see my parents. Tell them 'hi.'"

Jimmy looked into his friend's face. "Pretty soon you can tell them yourself," he said, then he slammed the truck door.

Yannick gave a cautious wave and drove off. Felix pressed his face hard to the glass and inflated his cheeks. He looked hideous. Jimmy coughed up a chuckle. Then he turned away and strolled to a picnic table, raising his arm to wave. He wanted to look as casual as he could. He certainly didn't want to watch the others driving away. It was time to adjust to being on his own again.

The place was desolate. Even the roar of the roads was dulled by thick and wild hedges, making it sound like a ghostly whine. There was a chill in the air and Jimmy breathed it in, keeping himself calm. He wasn't really on his own, he thought. He had a whole underground operation working with him. Uno Stovorsky, a top agent of the French secret service, had sewn together a chain of contacts. In no time he would be in London, working with a team again. Despite his efforts to convince himself otherwise, it still felt as if Jimmy was sitting alone, in the middle of nowhere, as the sun went down.

While he waited, Jimmy went over his backstory. His contact was not to know his real name, nor his reasons for smuggling himself into the UK. But Jimmy didn't have to wait long before a van pulled off the road.

It wasn't one of the biggest vans—only about six meters long—and it certainly didn't look very new. The cabin was smeared with mud and the trailer wobbled as the truck slowed down. It bore a picture of a ridiculously cheerful cartoon pig above bold bubble writing that said "Thoosavlees."

The vehicle hissed and spluttered to a halt. Then out of the cabin lumbered a stocky man bundled from head to toe in densely padded rain gear. His face was mostly hidden by a wild black beard, but when he drew closer Jimmy could see enough to know that this man had been in a few fights over the years. His nose looked as if someone had flattened it, then twisted it askew for good measure, and his gnarled left eye was lower than the right. The smell of stale sweat drifted from the man's clothes.

He stopped right in front of Jimmy but didn't look at him. "Michael Vargas?" he huffed in a voice as gruff as his beard. Jimmy turned away from the reek of the man's breath. "Eleven years old, traveling alone, collar turned up," the man continued. "That's you, isn't it?"

"You must be Jacob Estafette," said Jimmy at last, mustering his confidence.

The man's fists were buried in his pockets, but now he twisted his right hand. Out of the top of the pocket peeked the tip of a knife. "Say my name again, and I slit your throat."

Jimmy didn't need to look at the knife. He had noticed it already in the way the man's coat bulged. He stared intently into Estafette's eye—the one that wasn't almost obscured by the flesh hanging down over it. He recognized the nervous energy behind this man's bravado. Estafette was obviously wary of anyone who wanted to sneak *into* the UK. Usually it was goods in, people out. He was a small cog in a tidy operation, making money by smuggling any of the foreign products that Hollingdale had banned from Britain: Coke, Nike sneakers, even music by foreign artists.

Jimmy nodded slowly, calming himself. There was no need to reveal that he was far more dangerous than this small-time criminal. Estafette obviously had no idea who Jimmy was and probably didn't even suspect that the secret service was involved. They walked together to the back of the van, and Estafette hauled it open.

Jimmy felt like he'd been slapped on the forehead. He reeled backward and had to steady himself. It was only then that he realized what had hit him wasn't actually solid. It was the smell. In the back of the trailer, hanging from the ceiling in three rows, side by side, were dozens of huge smoked hams. The beasts they came from must have been some of the biggest pigs in Europe.

Jimmy raised the back of his hand to his nose. Am I supposed to get in there? he thought, looking up at Estafette with the question in his eyes. The man smiled, and beneath the mustache Jimmy glimpsed a gaping hole where there should have been teeth.

Jimmy climbed up into the back of the trailer, swallowing up gulps of the smell. It could have been worse, he realized. It was then that the cold wrenched his breath away—the trailer was refrigerated.

"This . . . is . . . ridiculous!" Jimmy gasped, snatching air

100

into his lungs between each word.

Estafette held out a finger. Jimmy followed its stubby point to the floor of the van. At first he saw nothing except the pattern in the metal, but when he looked again there was a hole. Checking each action with Estafette, who nodded his assurance, Jimmy bent down and pushed his way through the meat, with the hams thudding into his back. When he reached the middle of the trailer, Jimmy stuck his finger into the hole and pulled. A thick section of insulated flooring came up—the lid of a hatch. It revealed a small hidden compartment beneath the truck.

Jimmy didn't need confirmation from Estafette to know what to do next. He lowered himself through the floor, teeth chattering, and curled up in the hole on his side. There wasn't enough room for him to stretch out.

Estafette climbed into the back of the truck, too, and leered down into the hole. Just a fat ham with a coat and beard, Jimmy thought to himself.

"You a fan of sardines?" Jimmy quipped, settling into his tin can.

"I like anything that doesn't talk" came the reply.

Then Jimmy asked, "That meat—can I have some?"

Estafette peered at the ham as if he'd only just noticed it was there. Then, with a note of amusement in his face, he tore off a strip and dropped it into Jimmy's hand. "Sorry. No blanket." He smirked.

"Just get me to England," Jimmy hissed back. Estafette clanged shut the cover of Jimmy's hiding place. The darkness brought with it the relief of relative warmth—it was only the main section that was refrigerated. Then there was the second crash of the van door closing. Jimmy was entombed.

Jimmy wasn't sure how much more of this he would be able to take. He twisted as much as he could, but he'd been stuck in the same position for almost four hours. At first he'd thought that the journey was going to be fine, but he hadn't accounted for the added discomfort of crossing the Channel. The ferry rolled unsteadily from side to side, never relenting. It seemed that Jimmy's programming had no mechanism to combat sea-sickness.

Don't puke, he told himself over and over. Don't puke. He closed his eyes, trying to imagine himself lying in the park on a glorious sunny day. It didn't do much good. There was no light, but nothing to see even if he had used his night vision. All he was aware of was the listing of his stomach. His ears seemed to magnify the creaking of the boat and background groan of the sea.

Nearly there, Jimmy told himself, though he knew that he had completely lost track of the time. He had long since finished his strip of ham, which meant that now he was the worst possible combination: hungry and queasy.

At last, he made out the snorting of car engines. Soon they'd be on the move again. "Thank you," he sighed, feeling a burst of joy when the truck drove off the boat. England, he thought. He couldn't see it, but he was there. It was only a couple of minutes before the truck stopped again. This was the real test — passport control. There had been a time when people could come and go freely across British borders, but Hollingdale had changed all that. Now there were rigorous checks on every-body.

The truck engine fell silent. Jimmy strained his ears, trying to make out what was going on. There were murmuring voices. Jimmy's heartbeat drowned out the words. The injury in his neck throbbed. Why are we waiting so long? Jimmy shouted inside his head.

He was sure that at any moment the lid of his hiding place would be ripped off. He pictured the face of Miss Bennett leering in at him. Instinctively, he held his breath.

He needn't have worried. After three tantalizing minutes, the truck rumbled on. Jimmy breathed heavily and felt a little silly for being so scared. He wondered whether his mother was going through the same ordeal. He knew it would be harder for her. It wasn't just that Jimmy was smaller. One of the first things he had discovered about his design as an assassin was that dogs couldn't pick up a scent from him. His mother didn't have that advantage.

A couple of hours later the truck stopped again. A gurgling noise gave away that they were at a filling station. Once Estafette had filled the tank, Jimmy heard the clang of the doors opening. Suddenly, the hatch cover flew off, and Estafette's craggy face appeared. As always, Jimmy's eyes adjusted quickly to the new light.

"Come on," grunted Estafette. "You can sit up front the rest of the way. We're nearly there."

"It's about time," Jimmy replied. He hauled himself out of his hole while Estafette trudged off to pay for the fuel. Jimmy shivered and tore himself another strip of meat. His knees wobbled. He had spent so long cramped up in that compartment that he had to lean on the meats as he stumbled out of the van. The service station glowed in the night, a neon oasis.

Every bit of Jimmy tingled; the blood was returning to all corners of his body. He stretched and moved to the front of the van, casting his eyes around the service station forecourt. About a dozen people were filling their cars, staring into the middle distance. Were any of them watching Jimmy? Don't be paranoid, he told himself.

He pulled himself up into the passenger seat, chewing on some ham. The cabin of the truck was decorated with all sorts of paraphernalia. There were photos stuffed around every edge of the windshield, some faded and crumpled. Smiling kids, people playing on the beach—Jimmy could almost have pieced together Estafette's entire life from these scenes. Then something caught his eye that completely took his mind off Estafette's decorations. A police car pulled in to the service station. The driver got out and grabbed a pump.

Jimmy froze. If he looks my way, he told himself, don't flinch. He didn't want to arouse the policeman's suspicions. Jimmy's programming rumbled inside him, holding him still. There was no reason to believe the patrol car had been sent to look for him. NJ7 thought Jimmy was dead. If Mitchell had believed otherwise, he would have stayed to complete his mission. This was just bad luck.

The policeman was a young man whose lean frame seemed to bend under the weight of his body armor. He surveyed the scene while the gas dribbled into his tank. Come on, Jimmy urged silently, both to the policeman and to Estafette. Jimmy kept his eyes straight ahead, deliberately not watching the policeman. But the policeman's head had stopped turning from side to side. His face was toward the truck.

Jimmy chewed on another hunk of meat. He held himself low in his seat, trying to look small, insignificant, like every regular child in the country. His fingers picked at the black duct tape that covered a tear in the fabric of the seat.

At last Estafette was on his way back. He headed straight for the truck, paying no attention to the policeman. This is good, thought Jimmy. Keep coming.

Estafette was within two meters of the truck when he stopped. The policeman was calling him over. Jimmy looked into Estafette's face. He read the doubt in the man's eyes. Should he turn around? Should he pretend he hadn't heard? Do something, Jimmy implored, unable to move a muscle. The policeman had a clear view of him.

At last, Estafette turned. He pulled an apple from his pocket and began peeling it with his knife casually—too casually. Jimmy couldn't watch. The policeman was pointing at him. Estafette threw his head back, laughing. The long curl of his apple peel bounced around, like a spring waiting to uncoil.

From the corner of his eye, Jimmy could make out a second policeman inside the patrol car. He was reaching for something. What if he was checking the computer or radioing for more information? Or was that the silhouette of a police rifle?

Jimmy felt the blood pumping through his body. He was aware of something revolving around his head. His programming was preparing. But for what? Then he realized that he was calculating how best to kill every last person on the forecourt. Keep control, he told himself, closing his eyes to regain his composure. The other half of his brain kept turning: take out one with the knife, two with a wheel kick to the head, three and four with the rifle—Stop! he shouted inside his head.

Jimmy desperately held his legs in check. If he moved, it would mean a dozen men would end up dead. He pleaded with his programming: Don't risk it.

At last, Estafette turned and made his way back to the truck. The policeman was still watching. "They asked about you," Estafette whispered, hauling himself up into the driver's seat. "I told them you were my son."

Jimmy nodded his approval. "Let's get out of here," he said, then quickly added, "Dad."

Estafette grinned another black grin and pulled out of the service station. "You did well," he remarked quietly. Jimmy nodded again, playing innocent. Estafette could have no idea that Jimmy was moved to say the same thing.

"You know," Estafette went on, a note of annoyance in his voice, "I do actually have to deliver that meat. They'll notice if it's been nibbled."

"Tell them it was rats," Jimmy replied without hesitation.

"Rats? That stuff's hanging half a meter off the floor."

"Flying rats."

"Flying rats?" Estafette couldn't help but laugh. At last, his frosty demeanor was melting.

"Okay then—bats," joked Jimmy.

"Bats?" cried Estafette. "In a refrigerated truck?"

"Um, arctic bats?"

At that, they both burst out hysterically. Estafette roared,

"Arctic bats it is, Michael Vargas. Arctic bats."

The truck rumbled on up the expressway, nearing London all the time. A few cars back, two policemen, eager for promotion, debated whether to turn on their siren.

HOMECOMING

A flash of blue in the side mirror alerted Jimmy. He felt it like a twist in his stomach.

"Get this thing moving." His voice was stern, businesslike.

"What?" Estafette looked in the mirror and saw it too. "It might be nothing to do with us."

"No," Jimmy countered. "They're after me."

Estafette glanced across. The wail of the siren was loud now, filling the truck. Jimmy leaned forward so he could see in the mirror exactly what was behind them. He picked out one police car in the forest of other headlights. Then, out of nowhere, another appeared.

"Get moving now!" Jimmy shouted. "Before they set up a roadblock."

"We're getting into London now," Estafette protested. "It might be a routine check. Maybe I should pull over."

Jimmy considered it. Perhaps he was right. Perhaps it was something totally innocent. Jimmy studied the side mirror as if it were a famous work of art. It was a constellation of head-lights. He rolled down the window and stuck his head out. The wind blasted into him. That's when he saw it. He didn't know how it had gotten onto the expressway because they hadn't passed an exit. But it was there: a long, black car, with no maker's mark and no license plate, but next to the front grille was a green stripe.

"It's them," Jimmy gasped.

"Who?"

"You don't want to know. But if they see me, they'll kill me."

Estafette checked to see if Jimmy was being serious. When he saw the boy's expression, he slammed down the accelerator and veered into the outside lane. The truck swallowed up the road ahead.

"Keep driving," Jimmy shouted over the whir of the road. "Is there a way into the trailer from here?"

"The only way in is through the doors at the back."

"That won't do." Jimmy's mind was storming on as fast as the truck. "Listen, I have to get out of here." He reached down to the floor and grabbed the old street atlas at his feet. "As long as they see me leave the truck, you should be okay. They'll send all their resources after me."

Jimmy rapidly flicked through the atlas. Then he ripped out one of the pages and stuffed it into his pocket.

"You're going to jump out?" Estafette shouted. "That's crazy."

"Thanks for everything," cried Jimmy, undoing his seat belt and pulling himself up toward the window. Then he added, "I need to borrow some of your meat."

Jimmy looked around one last time and was astonished to

see a fat smile creasing Estafette's beard. "That's okay." The man leered. "Arctic bats—remember?"

"Yeah," replied Jimmy. "Arctic bats."

With an unexpected smile, he pulled himself out of the window. The wind rushed into him, almost blasting his eyes out of their sockets. In one swift action, he twisted around and dropped between the cabin and the trailer, balanced on the metal tread that joined the two. There was a little shelter here, but a huge amount of noise. It was nothing, though, to the noise inside Jimmy's head. That's where his programming was issuing millions of instructions every second, awakening every muscle.

Jimmy knelt down. The asphalt flew by beneath him. The wheels threw grit into his face, forcing him to squint. Mustering all his strength, he took hold of the metal tread and lowered himself down. Always holding himself just above the road, Jimmy maneuvered himself until he was horizontal, underneath the truck.

Grime accumulated in his mouth. Every arm's length of his upside-down crawl, he spat out a black globule. He tried to shut out the noise, the strain on his forearms, the flash of the police lights reflected on the asphalt. He gripped the undercarriage, feeling for where there was a slight drop in temperature. That's where the insulation was at its thinnest.

With one last look up and down, checking his position in the center of the trailer, he hooked his legs into the metalwork to spread some of the weight. Then he drove his hand upward, slamming into the floor of the trailer. The second time, the metal dented. Jimmy gave another punch, then one more. That did it. His fist burst right into the compartment where he had been hiding only hours before.

The trailer floor couldn't keep him out. He ripped through the metal, widening the hole until it was just big enough for him to haul himself through. One sharp shove opened the hatch of the hiding place. Refrigerated air rushed into Jimmy's face. Even with the smell, it came as welcome relief from the cauldron below.

Jimmy wriggled through the hole in the floor, holding his breath. At last, he flopped down beneath the hanging hams. This was just the beginning. Without a moment to catch his breath, Jimmy jumped up and kicked open the trailer door. Immediately, he dodged to the side, minimizing the target if his pursuers decided to shoot.

There they were—a trail of cars was following them now, and they were close. Jimmy picked them out: three police cars and two from NJ7. He didn't waste a second. He reached up to the ceiling and carefully unhooked a whole ham. It was more than half Jimmy's size and surprisingly heavy. Jimmy wrapped his arms around it and flung it out the door, right into the path of a police car.

The car swerved wildly to avoid the lump of meat that rolled along the road. Behind it, other cars honked and dodged. Jimmy wasn't even watching. He had gone straight for the next ham. Unhooking that one too, he stumbled to the edge of the trailer and dropped it to the road. Like bouncing bombs, the hams kept coming, making it impossible to follow the truck except at a distance.

When enough of a gap had opened up, Jimmy threw one last ham. It punched into the headlights of the car behind, smashing it to splinters, and wedged itself between the car and the road. Hm, thought Jimmy, ham sandwich.

He pulled himself out the trailer door and up onto the roof. He lay there, flat on his stomach. The expressway had reached London now. Every few hundred meters there was another overpass crossing the road.

Jimmy glanced behind. Only the NJ7 cars were still in pursuit. A little cold meat wasn't enough to stop them. They were gaining ground. Ever so slowly, rocking as the truck thundered onward, Jimmy pushed himself onto his hands and knees. The next overpass zoomed toward him. Then, at the crucial moment, Jimmy sprang upward.

The side of the overpass smacked into him. The impact juddered through his body. It knocked the wind from his chest, but he didn't fall. His fingers locked on to the top of the overpass. He heaved himself up. He landed on his feet just in time to see the NJ7 cars screech over to the side of the road. Jimmy stood absolutely still for a second, traffic careering past in front of him on the overpass. He waited for an NJ7 agent to step out of his car and look up at Jimmy. Estafette had already driven out of view without anyone following him.

He's going to have some explaining to do, Jimmy thought. Then he pelted into the night, heading for the heart of the city. He was in the country he called home, but what was out there waiting for him?

Miss Bennett slammed down the phone. "It's confirmed," she hissed. She stood up from her desk and turned to face the window. The shutters were closed though—it was the middle of the night. Despite that, Miss Bennett was still in her suit and Paduk was standing to attention in his uniform.

Did they never go to bed? Mitchell wondered. He was in his pajamas, having been dragged out of bed to face this inquisition. He stared at the back of her head, mesmerized by her thin green hair clip. It seemed like several minutes before Miss Bennett finally spun around.

"I need to know exactly what happened when you *thought* Jimmy Coates was killed."

"What do you mean?" Mitchell's voice betrayed his panic. He looked desperately from Miss Bennett to Paduk and back.

Then Miss Bennett confirmed it. "He's alive and he's back in Britain."

"But that's impossible," Mitchell protested, "I told you: I pushed him down. I held him in the shredder. He could never have survived."

Miss Bennett held up a hand to stop him. Mitchell's mouth remained open. Inside, his stomach seemed to be swirling. It was his programming, distraught at the news. Then Miss Bennett glanced at Paduk. "Bring her in," she muttered.

Paduk marched to the door and nodded his head to Eva, who had been waiting in the hallway. She yawned, then smiled sheepishly at Mitchell because her borrowed pajamas were slightly too large. He didn't smile back. Had he even noticed her coming in?

"What's going on?" Eva asked.

Miss Bennett answered without ceremony. "You witnessed the accident in France, Eva. Tell me what happened."

Eva hesitated, searching the other faces in the room for clues as to what disaster had hit Britain. She had accommodation at the French embassy now, and at night it seemed quiet. But when she'd been woken up tonight and pulled from her bed by an agent, the corridors had been in a flurry of activity.

"The machine . . . ," she began, hesitantly. "The machine was on. . . ."

"Think back," Miss Bennett suggested softly. "Try to think of any details you may have forgotten when you told us the first time."

It was the last thing Eva wanted to do. The horror of Jimmy's death still dogged her. Every time she closed her eyes she saw the blood splashing up from the shredder. When she tried to sleep, she heard the crash of the machinery. She longed for the security of home. To be with her family again . . .

No, Eva told herself. I must stay here. This is important.

"I saw Mitchell reaching for Jimmy," she continued. "He was reaching down into the machine, but . . ."

Then Paduk interrupted, his voice even deeper than usual. "Is there any way Jimmy could have survived?" he asked.

Eva felt suddenly cold, as if there was no blood in her body at all. She thought if she spoke, her lips might disintegrate. Before she could try, Miss Bennett cut in.

"What a ridiculous question, Paduk. We know there's no way he could have survived, and yet we know he *did* survive."

Eva jolted back to life. She couldn't believe what she'd just heard. She felt her cheeks flush. Jimmy was still alive. A wave of joy exploded from her insides, but just as quickly, she threw her hands to her face and faked a crying fit.

"Oh no!" she wailed. "They'll come to get me again. . . ." The tears were real—all Eva did was act despair instead of the elation she really felt.

"Oh, look what you've done." Miss Bennett shook her head at Paduk. "That's enough, you two. Go back to bed."

114

She dismissed Eva and Mitchell with a flick of the wrist. Eva didn't hesitate. She scurried out, hiding her face and sobbing. Mitchell followed, his whole body tensed up. There was no chance of him getting to sleep tonight.

"Why didn't you tell the girl the truth?" Paduk asked when the two children were gone. "Why pretend it was an accident?"

"She's just started here, Paduk," Miss Bennett replied. "She doesn't need to be confronted with the most . . . unfortunate aspects of our work. When she's more comfortable, we can educate her bit by bit."

"So you're planning on keeping her here?" Paduk was astonished. "Do you know what sort of security risk—"

Miss Bennett cut him off. "If we can train child assassins," she snapped, "I don't see why we can't take on a bright young girl and teach her to be a first-class administrator."

"But the assassins are guaranteed by their genetics," Paduk protested.

"Yes, and we all saw how well that worked, didn't we?" Miss Bennett sneered. "I prefer to rely on simple judgment of character, Paduk, and Eva's just the sort of character this organization needs. You saw her reaction just now. She was genuinely shocked. That's patriotism, Paduk, and it comes with a good upbringing." Miss Bennett let herself fall into her chair, yawned, and lowered her voice. "She'll go far. I can even see her replacing me in twenty years. Don't you worry about Eva, Paduk—I'll vouch for her."

Jimmy reached Kensington before dawn. By now the sun was threatening to come up, and Jimmy was exhausted. His hands were shaking. The wind cut into his skin, and his lungs sent a bitter taste into his mouth. He pushed himself to keep running. The dressings on his leg were sodden with sweat. While his programming had once again shut off any pain, it was now seeping through his mental barrier. He had to stop.

Reluctantly, he threw himself into a doorway and slumped forward, his hands on his knees. One last time he consulted the map he had torn from the book in the truck. He was close now, but the rest of the way he had to walk.

The safe house was perfectly located, no more than a few hundred meters from the French embassy in South Kensington. This area of London had once been full of smart boutiques, but now that only British designers were allowed to trade, it had become as dilapidated as everywhere else in the city.

Jimmy rounded the last corner and surveyed the run-down blocks of apartments. It seemed as if a million windows stared down at him. What if another police patrol spotted him and alerted the secret service?

He pushed through his fear and marched the last few strides of his journey with only one thing on his mind—fierce determination to complete the tasks facing him. It might mean walking for miles on an empty stomach in the freezing cold, but nothing was going to stop him. His head throbbed with the pressure. He had to find Viggo and Saffron, and rescue Felix's parents from wherever they were imprisoned. But first, he would wait for his mother and Stovorsky to make contact.

Jimmy looked the building up and down. It was just the same as every other on the street—a shabby Georgian town house that had been converted into apartments many years ago. Jimmy trotted up the front steps, glancing over his shoulder. By the side of the front door was a silver panel. There were no buzzers though, just a number keypad. He'd been expecting that. He tapped in the entry code to the building: 311#279. He and his mother had both memorized it from the scrap of paper that had long since been destroyed.

The door let out a faint click. Jimmy pushed it gingerly and stepped in. The environment he found himself in was quite old-fashioned. The floor was covered in what looked like original tiles; many of them were cracked. There was a hallway leading down one side of a rickety staircase, with doors leading off it to other people's rooms. Other safe houses, Jimmy wondered, or just homes? He brushed past the coats hanging by the door and tiptoed up the stairs. His instructions were to proceed directly to the top floor.

At the top of the stairs was another door. Jimmy tapped the entry code into another keypad and pushed the door open. He found himself in a dingy one-room apartment. The whole place was grimy and smelled as if the windows hadn't been opened in a decade.

The first thing Jimmy did was search the room. He didn't know why and he didn't know what he was looking for, but an overwhelming instinct wouldn't let him do anything else until the whole room had been stripped and inspected, top to bottom. It didn't take long. The room was small, with only two beds and an empty chest of drawers. One corner of it had been converted into a kitchen. There was a little cash in one of the kitchen drawers and a small fridge containing a few basic items obviously left for Jimmy and his mother. Jimmy ate alone while he dismantled the fridge and put it back together piece by piece. He found nothing out of the ordinary.

There was a tiny bathroom too. Just a toilet, a sink, and a

shower—more like a cupboard, really. Jimmy's head was spinning. He hadn't slept and it was dawn already. He had to stay awake until he knew he was secure, then he could sit tight and wait for Stovorsky and his mother to come and meet him.

He stripped, laying his clothes over the radiator, and gently pulled the Band-Aid off his neck, then the bandage from his leg. The flesh had knitted together, but there were still thick red lines where the skin hadn't healed. And the whole area was tinged with the blue-gray that lived under the surface. Without that, Jimmy knew he would have lost his leg.

He stood in the shower, trying to refresh and refocus. It took a minute for the water to heat up, but as soon as it did, Jimmy wished he never had to leave it. Despite his programming doing its best to control his temperature, his fingers and toes had severely needed the circulation of warm blood.

That was it—his toes. Jimmy looked down at his feet. Water lapped around his ankles. Something was blocking the drain. He knelt down and carefully unscrewed the covering of the plug hole. A tile was loose. But it wasn't just one tile; it was a block of them grouted together to give the shower a false bottom. Jimmy lifted it up to reveal a sealed plastic bag. In it was a laptop computer and a gun.

In a few minutes Jimmy had toweled off and found that the laptop had a fully charged battery, but no data on it at all. It had a built-in modem. Jimmy wondered whether the signal would be scrambled. If he used it, would it give away his location?

The gun was another Beretta 99G pistol—the type used by the French secret service when they raided the farmhouse. Jimmy slipped the laptop back into its hiding place under the shower. He kept the pistol.

He had never held one before, but it was eerie how naturally it seemed to fit in his hand. Jimmy turned it over, examining it. Should he be afraid of it? he wondered. Or should it make him feel powerful? The longer he studied it, the more it became just a lump of metal. The gun was certainly dangerous, but there was a different kind of danger everywhere else: it was wherever the prime minister had agents operating and it was inside Jimmy.

With a shudder of disgust, he dropped the gun onto the mattress. He couldn't bear to hold it anymore. He rummaged in a kitchen drawer and found a spoon. With it, he began to dismantle the weapon, painstakingly tweaking at all the tiny screws until the whole thing began to come apart. Minutes later, he clattered its metal bones to the floor. That's safer, he thought. Only killers need guns.

Before Jimmy climbed into bed he suddenly stopped, staring at his hands. He couldn't look away, and fear crept over him like a storm cloud. What if these are even more lethal than that gun? he thought, laying his head on the pillow. At last he closed his eyes.

An ache returned to his leg. His fists were trembling.

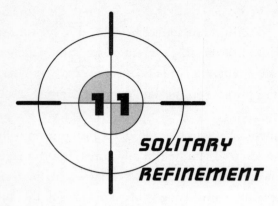

SOLITARY REFINEMENT

"Come in." Miss Bennett's voice penetrated the solid door with ease. Eva tentatively pushed it open and shuffled in, clasping a brown envelope marked TOP SECRET.

"The Ministry of Defense thought you would want to read this report immediately, Miss Bennett."

Eva stepped carefully forward under Miss Bennett's expectant gaze. Miss Bennett took the brown envelope without a word of thanks but examined Eva closely. "You know you're not a prisoner here, Eva?" she asked in a steady tone. "You can go home at any time."

Eva nodded, her face impassive. "As soon as I'm ready."

"I understand." Miss Bennett smiled at last. "You've been through a lot." She paused, fingering the envelope. "You know, I was young when I started working for the secret service too. Not as young as you, but still very young." Eva tried to push her lips into a smile. They twitched.

"There's a lot that I want to teach you," Miss Bennett went

on. "Why don't you start by taking breakfast to our guests?"

Eva nodded again and quickly left the room, pulling the door shut tight behind her. She didn't even linger to try and hear what Miss Bennett might be doing. She didn't need to. She knew Miss Bennett would be phoning the prime minister directly.

Eva had already read the report that was now in Miss Bennett's hands. She could recite it almost word for word: *Navy offshore patrol vessel intercepted and sank small craft off southeast coast. All crew and passengers apprehended. Those in custody include one woman. She appears to have Special Forces training and fits Helen Coates's description.*

Eva let the information wash around her head. They had Jimmy's mother. But it was a different world for Eva now. One with hope—Jimmy was alive.

She walked sedately through the plush corridors—blood-red carpet under her feet, ancient French tapestries on the walls around her. So this is what the inside of an embassy is like, she thought. She continued down a grand flight of stairs, avoiding a cleaner who was furiously vacuuming. At the lobby, three floors below, Eva paused to pick up a tray of food from the security guard at reception.

"Miss Bennett asked me to take this down," she said.

She crossed the lobby, and another security guard tapped the brim of his cap. He pressed the button that would call the elevator for her. After a wait of a few seconds, the light above the doors pinged to indicate that the carriage had reached the lobby, but the doors didn't open. The guard jangled his key chain and pulled a small golden key toward a panel by the elevator doors. When he turned the key in the lock, the doors slid open.

It took almost a minute for Eva to reach the basement. When the elevator doors opened again, Eva could have been in a completely different building. All the grandeur was gone. In front of her was a cavernous concrete hall that looked more like the basement of a multistory parking garage than the French embassy. It was about the size of a soccer field, and at one end an excavator was blasting through the wall. Men in hard hats and black suits milled around, helping with the construction job.

Eva walked steadily across to the other end of the hall, toward a line of cells. As she approached the bars, she stopped first at a wall of bulletproof glass. One security guard checked the pass clipped to her shirt, while another tapped a password into a computer, which opened a sliding door to allow her through.

That was as close as she came to the prisoners though. The security guard took the tray from her and waited until she was on the other side of the door again. Before heading back to the elevator she looked at the figures huddled in the cell. Two of the prisoners had been there for three days: Christopher Viggo and Saffron Walden. Then there was a third who had been arrested the night before on charges of espionage and was due for interrogation that day: Uno Stovorsky.

Jimmy burst into life and sprang off the bed. He kicked at the gun parts, which rumbled across the floorboards. He scanned the room. What time was it? The lights on the microwave glowed at him: 5:34. Could that be right? Had he slept all day? Why hadn't Stovorsky arrived and woken him? Where was his mother? They should both have arrived by now.

The fog of a nightmare still stifled his mind. He could never remember anything he had dreamed, and this was no different. All that remained was that intense anxiety clutching at his muscles. On this evening, he couldn't shake it off.

Something must have gone wrong. A few days ago the only people that needed rescuing were his best friend's parents. Now Jimmy felt like the only one who *wasn't* locked up somewhere.

Were Viggo and Saffron even still alive? And what about his mother? It took several minutes for Jimmy to clear his head. There was nothing to panic about. They were just late—that's all. But in his gut, the worry spread into a bubbling turmoil. All he could do was wait.

Jimmy assembled some scraps of food into a sandwich and paced the room. He peered out between the curtains. Every noise alerted in him some kind of hope that his mother was coming up the stairs. But nobody came.

I'm on my own, Jimmy heard in his head. He refused to believe it. But with every second that ticked by, he knew that he had to face the truth. He had no idea where his mother was. He had no idea where Stovorsky was. And they weren't coming.

Jimmy slumped onto one of the beds, staring at the cobwebs in the corner. She'll be OK, he assured himself. She told me she would be. He didn't stop to examine whether he believed his mother's promise. It would be far too frightening.

He jumped up and stormed around the room, kicking at the furniture. "Why did it have to go wrong?" he shouted aloud, surprising himself with the vehemence in his voice. He clenched his fists. There was a heat rising in his chest. His fist lunged toward the wall. But he stopped himself. This is no good, he thought. Keep control.

123

He realized then that there was one thing he desperately needed. His friends. Jimmy pictured Felix and Georgie stuck at the farmhouse. Should he try to contact them using the laptop? It was risky, but if he knew his sister, she was bound to spend time at the Internet café in the village. She would never risk giving herself away by checking her e-mails, but there were other ways of communicating.

Jimmy turned it over and over in his mind. As the time passed, it became increasingly clear that Stovorsky and his mother weren't coming. Jimmy was definitely on his own. But he didn't need to be. If there was any chance that Georgie and Felix could help him, he should take it. It soothed him just thinking about them coming to join him. Yannick's face would be all over security lists, but surely there was no reason for Immigration to stop two kids, was there?

Jimmy felt a spark of excitement. But could he leave them a message that wouldn't be intercepted? Jimmy tried to remember all the websites his sister might visit. Most of the Internet was restricted in the UK because of the government's censorship, so there weren't that many.

He set about the task methodically, posting in every chat room and blog he could think of that his sister might stumble across. It wasn't easy putting himself into the mind of a thirteen-year-old girl—some of the sites made him cringe. Eventually, he found himself in a rhythm, flitting from site to site, creating dozens of identities to register and post a message. He always registered with the same user name: JawG, and the message he left was always the same: *Get 2 London. Feel icks too? Then leave the cook.*

Jimmy was quite pleased with it. He thought it sounded

enough like a girl that most people wouldn't mind that it seemed irrelevant to whatever topic was being discussed. As for it not making sense, well—girls never made sense anyway, did they?

After a while, Jimmy found his eyes tiring, and his imagination running out of ideas of which websites to visit. He shut down the laptop. If Georgie saw the message and understood it, she and Felix would turn up at the safe house. It could take days, though, before that happened—if it happened at all. For the time being, Jimmy had to carry on as if they weren't coming.

There was only one obvious place to start investigating: the French embassy.

Jimmy went to the bathroom and stared at himself in the mirror above the sink. A crack in the glass ran down one side of his face. He took the thin bar of soap in his hands and squeezed off two small pieces, molding them into long cup shapes. He placed them just over each eyebrow and pressed them on to his forehead. He repeated the process, this time pressing more soap onto his cheeks.

His hands were moving confidently, as if they had performed this routine a thousand times before. Slowly, Jimmy began to understand what his programming was helping him do—create a disguise.

Next he made a roll out of toilet paper and stuffed it under his upper lip. More went between his teeth and his cheeks. He ran his hands under the tap for a few seconds, then rubbed them on the rusty pipe underneath the sink. They came away covered in muck, which Jimmy smoothed over his face and neck, blending the pieces of soap into this new skin color.

Finally, he needed to disguise his hair. He ripped off a corner of wood that was loose in the window sill and placed it in the sink. There was a box of matches in the kitchen drawer, and in a few seconds the wood was alight. A couple of minutes later it had burned away. Jimmy gathered the ashes and spread them through his hair with his fingers.

When he saw himself in the mirror again, he almost wanted to laugh. The shape and coloring of his face had completely changed. He looked more like an old man than a boy. But this old man was ready for his mission.

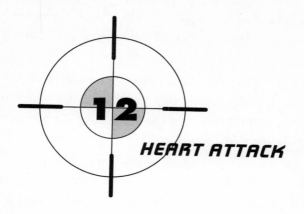

12

HEART ATTACK

Felix drummed his fingers on the old oak of the kitchen table. A book lay open in front of him, but he had hardly glanced at it in the last half hour. It was all in French. Opposite him, Georgie was making a better job of pretending to read. Every now and again she would flick her eyes up at him as a reminder that they had to look like they were studying.

Yannick's mother was puttering about the kitchen, mumbling to herself and scowling at Felix. At last, she left the room. Felix sprang up and pushed a chair against the door.

"I thought she'd never go!" he shouted.

"Shhh!" Georgie jumped out of her seat too. "What if she tries to come back?"

"No chance. She's gone for a nap. I slipped some cognac into her hot chocolate." Felix's grin was wider than ever, and Georgie couldn't stop herself from laughing.

"Great—so we've got about an hour before Yannick's back

from the village. Let's go." She leaped up onto the table. "You first."

Felix bounced on the balls of his feet and stretched a random selection of muscles. He took a three-step run-up, then launched himself straight at Georgie. She was quick on her feet too. She swiveled and parried Felix away. He crashed to the floor, then he was up again, this time attacking with an attempted swivel kick. Georgie caught his foot and pushed him over. He fell on his front.

"Looks like you need to practice that one." She giggled. Felix didn't mind. Without looking up, he hooked his foot around the leg of the table and wrenched it out from under Georgie. She gave a muted shriek and clattered to the floor. Felix was laughing his head off.

"Do you think this is what your mum meant when she told us to study while she was away?"

"We're studying the delicate art of hand-to-hand combat." Georgie giggled.

"Looks like you're studying the insect life of the kitchen floor." Felix hopped to his feet, set the table upright, and took his position standing on it. "Your turn."

They went on like this for nearly an hour, just as they had at every opportunity since Jimmy and his mother had left for England.

"How do you think we'd do against adults?" Felix panted, slumping into a chair by the stove.

"Let's hope we never have to find out." Georgie was exhausted too, but neither of them was laughing anymore. They knew that if they ever did need to defend themselves, it would be from a very serious threat. NJ7 was constantly on their minds.

Jimmy shuffled through the London streets with a deliberate stoop. He kept his face turned down to the sidewalk while his eyes darted about, taking in everything around him. His only clothes were the ones he had arrived in—jeans and an old sweater. But he covered them with an overcoat that had been hanging at the bottom of the stairs in the safe-house building.

The streets were dirtier than the last time Jimmy had been here, as if the city was disintegrating day by day. More shops were boarded up, and people hurried along, reluctant to linger out of doors after dark. That suited Jimmy. It meant he was less likely to be noticed.

He stopped at the corner, across the road from the French embassy, a grand Regency building. Outside the front door stood two security guards armed with machine guns. Above them was the empty pole where the French flag should have been flying. On the doorpost was nailed a judiciously small green stripe.

Jimmy stepped forward slowly, his heart pounding, reminding himself all the time that he was an old man. If they saw through the disguise, he might be killed on the spot. He stepped out of the shadows and crossed the road, knowing the guards would stop him, but careful not to make eye contact. His disguise wouldn't be so convincing up close.

"Sorry, sir," one of the guards said abruptly, barring Jimmy's way. "The embassy is closed."

Jimmy hesitated, pretending to shake a little. He tried to

move toward the front door, but again the guard stopped him. "I said the embassy is closed," the man repeated, louder and slower than the first time. Jimmy increased his shaking and clutched his left breast with his right hand.

"Are you okay, sir?" asked the other guard. Jimmy didn't respond. He pitched to one side and lost his balance, gasping for air. The guard caught him and lifted him back to his feet.

"Are you okay? Do you need a glass of water?" Jimmy nodded weakly. The guards took his weight and guided him through the doors of the embassy—just as Jimmy had hoped they would. They stopped at the staircase, and one of the guards eased Jimmy down gently. The other strode to the reception desk.

"Better call an ambulance, just in case," he called out. Jimmy was sitting on the bottom step, still staring at the floor, as he had been the whole time. But now he gestured to the guard, clutching his chest.

"Water," he panted, pointing at the jug on the reception desk. He was banking on the guard taking his voice to be the thinning tones of an old man. It worked. The guard nodded and turned to reception. For less than thirty seconds nobody had their eyes on Jimmy. But thirty seconds was enough. Jimmy sprinted up the stairs. The guard turned around, holding a glass of water. The old man was gone.

Jimmy heard the alarm being raised downstairs, but he didn't stop. He knew that security would immediately examine the CCTV footage of the lobby and see which way he went; cameras covered every inch of the building, inside and out. But Jimmy had to use whatever seconds he could to find out what had happened to Viggo and Saffron.

He bounded up the stairs, not even knowing what he was looking for. He could hear guards pounding after him. He reached the third floor and smashed his elbow into the fire alarm. A siren burst into life immediately and people stepped out of their offices, filling the previously empty corridors.

Jimmy smiled for a second—the confusion would slow down anybody who was trying to follow him. But before the thought was even through his head, he was shocked into panic. Every single person moving through the corridor toward him was a tall, broad man with close-cropped hair, wearing a black suit. Jimmy had stumbled into a nest of Green Stripes.

Jimmy's programming lurched up a gear to compensate for his moment of terror. He was almost knocked off his feet by it. As if someone had grabbed him by the shoulder, it threw him into one of the rooms he had just seen people leaving. By a stroke of luck, the room was now empty. He wondered whether anyone had seen him.

He knelt down and pressed his hand flat on the carpet, right by the door. This way he could feel when the reverberation of footsteps subsided. He glanced over his shoulder at the empty office. He could see immediately that he'd find no information here. There was obviously some kind of security procedure for evacuation. Everything was locked away.

Jimmy's eyes lingered on the window. He was suddenly aware of a strategy running through his head—abandon the mission, it reasoned. Escape while you can. Jimmy knew it was the right decision. But the window wasn't the answer. As soon as he was spotted on the outside of the building, he would be an easy target. Reach the roof, he told himself. Escape from there.

Jimmy opened the door a crack. The corridor was empty. Had they found him on the CCTV yet? He slipped out, then immediately had to jump across into the doorway opposite. There was someone leaving an office farther down the hall. Jimmy couldn't believe it—it was Miss Bennett.

The sound of her voice stifled his breathing. It was the voice that had assigned him his original mission, and the voice that in a previous existence had belonged to his teacher. He had to focus to pull himself together. Gently, he tried the handle of the door where he was hiding. It was locked.

Miss Bennett and whoever she was talking to were between him and the staircase, walking toward him. Then he heard the voice of the other person—Mitchell.

"But I'm ready to try again, Miss Bennett," he was saying.

They were only meters away now and approaching Jimmy. Jamming a foot against either side of the door frame, he climbed off the ground. Wedged in that position, near the top of the doorway, he yanked a button off his coat. With a flick of his wrist he sent it flying up the corridor toward Miss Bennett and Mitchell. They didn't see it soaring over their heads, but they heard it ricochet off the wall behind them.

"What was that?" snapped Miss Bennett. They both swiveled around for an instant. In that moment, Jimmy swung himself out of the doorway and reached up. The wall was covered with a giant tapestry that hung off what looked like a curtain rod. That's what Jimmy grabbed hold of now.

As Miss Bennett and Mitchell turned again to continue walking, Jimmy pulled himself up and slipped behind the tapestry. The only evidence that he was there was a slight swaying of the ancient wall hanging.

"Hadn't we better evacuate with the others?" Mitchell asked. He was standing right next to where Jimmy hung. Only a thin layer of fabric separated them. Jimmy held his breath. In his belly stirred a genuine fear. He tried to hold on to the thought that he'd beaten Mitchell in a fight before, but it was no good. He knew that had been at a time before Mitchell's killer instinct had been roused. Jimmy no longer had that advantage.

"Oh, please." Miss Bennett sighed. "Is the building on fire?" Jimmy made out a slight mumbling from Mitchell, but nothing more before Miss Bennett continued. "Jimmy Coates has arrived in England—just as we expected. I want you here so that you can kill him. Again."

They carried on walking, and Jimmy made his way steadily down the corridor, hand to hand along the wooden rod. He knew he was behind Miss Bennett and Mitchell now, but the staircase was still a couple of meters away. Then he reached the end of the tapestry.

There was no choice. He had to jump out and make a run for it.

He gathered his thoughts once more, urging his programming to give him a burst of silent speed. With any luck he would be halfway up the stairs before Mitchell or Miss Bennett turned around. The fire alarm still rang out, piercing his brain as if expressing the tension in Jimmy's heart. Then he went for it.

His fingers let go of the rod and he dropped to the carpet. As soon as his foot touched the floor, he was bounding off it again in a sprint. Security guards were already dashing up from the floor below, leading with their machine guns.

At the stairs Jimmy stopped dead. He had been so focused on Miss Bennett and Mitchell that he hadn't sensed the person walking with them, a few paces behind. Now Jimmy was face to face with that third person. It was Eva.

It seemed like all the world had slipped into slow motion. Any second machine-gun fire would tear into Jimmy's back. Eva and Jimmy stared at each other. What was it that Jimmy saw in her eyes? There was a cunning there, in this moment of crisis, that he had never seen in her before. Was she a friend or an enemy?

Then she moved, but she didn't run away. Instead, she threw herself into Jimmy's stunned arms, turning so that she was facing the same way as him. She grabbed Jimmy's arm and placed it around her neck. At last, Jimmy realized what she was doing. He tensed his hand, ready for a fatal chop, and pressed the tips of his fingers against Eva's temple. He spun her around to face his foe, her body shielding him from the security guards.

Eva screamed. Jimmy's voice emerged calm, but ferocious: "Come any closer and her brains redecorate the wall."

CORTES UNCORTED

Jimmy backed toward the stairs, dragging Eva by the neck. The security guards held their positions but trained their machine guns on Jimmy's head. At last, Jimmy reached the first step. He backed up it, keeping Eva directly between him and the guards. It was only four steps before the staircase reached a landing. If he made it that far, Jimmy would be able to run. But Miss Bennett wasn't going to allow that to happen.

"Shoot them both," she stated calmly. The gunmen adjusted their aim. Then a bloodcurdling yell made them hesitate.

"No!" It was Mitchell. He leaped up the corridor, kicking out with both legs in midair. His feet slammed into two of the guards, knocking them over. Jimmy took his chance to escape. It wasn't much, but it was a head start.

"Leave him to me," Mitchell shouted, sprinting forward.

Jimmy raced up the stairs, Eva close behind him. "NJ7 has taken over the building," she panted.

"Thanks, I worked that out," Jimmy replied.

"But Felix's parents were never here."

"What?"

"It was a trap." Jimmy couldn't let the shock of this revelation stop his legs from driving him upward. "Chris and Saffron were captured a few days ago when they came here," Eva went on, panting more and more. "They're in the basement, being interrogated."

They tore past another landing. Jimmy didn't dare look down. Even with the thick carpet, he could hear Mitchell pounding after them.

"So where *are* Felix's parents?" Jimmy blurted out.

"Somewhere called Fort Einsmoor. But I don't know where that is." The name meant nothing to Jimmy, but it was a start. He kept running up and up. Eva lagged farther behind with every step.

"Have you heard anything about Stovorsky?" Jimmy demanded.

"Yes. He was arrested yesterday. And Jimmy . . ." Eva stopped running, out of breath. She whispered after Jimmy, "They have your mother."

The words reached Jimmy just as Eva dropped out of view. They stabbed into him, but he couldn't let them slow him down. Then he heard Eva again. This time her voice was more distant and her tone had changed.

"Oh, Mitchell, I was so scared," she sobbed. "Thank you for saving me."

At the top floor, Jimmy burst through a metal fire door. The wind buffeted him, knocking one of the pieces of soap off his face. He didn't care about that now. He could already hear the roar of the helicopters coming to kill him. He dashed across the roof and vaulted onto the top of the next building, landing with a roll. A few seconds later he heard someone do exactly the same behind him. Without looking around, he knew who it had to be.

Jimmy's muscles burned with power, propelling him forward at a pace he'd never experienced before on foot. The helicopters were overhead now. Instinctively, Jimmy scooped up a handful of gravel. In his hands it could be lethal. Please don't kill anybody, Jimmy begged himself. Nobody has to die. But his programming was pumping through him, and he knew that Mitchell probably wasn't armed.

Jimmy sprang across to the next building, this time a jump of nearly five meters over a drop of fifty. Just before he landed, he hurled out a stone. The power in his shoulder lent it the momentum of a bullet. Suddenly, a high-pressure burst of steam erupted into the sky. Jimmy hadn't aimed at Mitchell, or even at the helicopters above him, but at one of the many pipes that snaked over the rooftops.

As he ran, he let fly with more stones. The pipes he hit blasted steam and water high into the air, making it impossible for the helicopters to see him. They couldn't shoot because they wouldn't know what they were shooting at. Even if they had thermal imagery, the heat from the steam would mask Jimmy.

He climbed out over the side of the building, listening for the helicopter rotors fading. Jimmy didn't dare look to see how close Mitchell was. He climbed out over the side of the building until only his fingertips clung to the rooftop. His body swayed in the wind. Between him and the ground were six stories.

He felt the tiny vibrations of Mitchell pounding closer. No time to think. He let go. The building lurched away from him. His stomach leaped. But before he even had the chance to take in a gulp of air, he halted his fall by catching hold of the top-floor window ledge. Then in one athletic heave, he flipped himself up and over, through the window. He landed in a shower of glass in an empty office.

Without wasting a second, he tore off his coat and wrapped it around the desk chair. He heaved it out the window then lifted the desk into the shattered hole to make it look as if it had been boarded up.

It was the chair that Mitchell saw hitting the pavement when he reached the edge of the roof, and in the poor light, that was what he took to be the body of Jimmy Coates. He peered down at it, then climbed over the edge of the building. He had already assumed Jimmy was dead once—this time he was going to check.

In very little time Mitchell had climbed down to the street. Jimmy, however, had taken the stairs to the ground floor. When Mitchell kicked over the bent limbs of the chair, he wasn't to know that, on the other side of the building, Jimmy was bursting out of the office and into the street.

Jimmy twisted back to the safe house through all the side roads, staying in the darkest corners. The sooner he was off the streets, the better. He quickly tapped in the door code and slipped into the safe-house building, sighing with relief.

When he reached his room, he bent down and removed a hair from across the crack in the door. He had secured it there with saliva when he went out. The fact that it was still there, intact, assured him that nobody had entered while he was gone.

Inside, Jimmy went straight to the laptop. One thing had been on his mind more than anything else as he had been running through London: Fort Einsmoor. There was still a risk involved in connecting to the Internet, but he decided it was definitely worth it. He knelt on the floor and set the computer on the bed. But however he searched, he found nothing.

Jimmy knew he shouldn't have been disappointed—did he expect to find a top-secret detention facility with ease? But he was. He shut off the laptop, defeated, and slammed his hand onto the mattress. At that moment, he was overcome with despair. His hands trembled. A lump rose in his throat. His mind refused to accept what he knew to be true—that the only possible next step was to go to NJ7 headquarters. That was the only place where he would find out about Fort Einsmoor.

Jimmy buried his head in the bedsheets. He was sick with worry for his friends. Not just Felix's parents, but Viggo and Saffron, locked up at the French embassy. And then there was his mother. He imagined all the things she might have gone through. He tried to work out rationally whether she would be OK. But the more he tried, the more he realized he didn't know. The mother he had known had been an act, a job to make it look as if the Coateses were a regular family. Then as soon as the real woman had begun to emerge, Jimmy had been separated from her again.

Focus, he told himself. One mission at a time. All Felix's parents had done was try to help him, and now they were locked up. They weren't equipped to cope with that. His top priority should be finding and freeing them. He felt the crushing weight of responsibility. His muscles were like bricks, they were so tense. Even to see the faces of Felix and Georgie would have been a comfort. Were they on their way?

Then, without wanting to, Jimmy pictured his father's face. If he was going back to NJ7, Ian Coates was likely to be there. Jimmy's heart seemed to soften, still imbued with love for his father. But the same man had chosen loyalty to the government over his family. How could he support Hollingdale? Jimmy still couldn't believe it. If he sees me again, maybe he'll change his mind. Jimmy longed for that chance, but at the same time he dreaded what might happen.

It took only half an hour for Jimmy to be out on the streets again with a new disguise. He "borrowed" another overcoat from the hallway of the safe-house building and trudged through the shadows, careful to make sure that his gait matched his appearance. Police patrol cars did pass, but they had no reason to stop the small Chinese gentleman hurrying through the darkness. Helicopters crisscrossed the sky, peppering London with pillars of light. They would search all night; it was as if Jimmy Coates had disappeared.

At each corner Jimmy trusted his sense of direction, following his first instinct every time. It felt as if his programming was pulling him to Westminster, desperate to return to its home. All Jimmy needed was a way in.

When he had rescued his parents from NJ7 with Christopher Viggo, they had gone in via an entrance at Holborn subway station. Jimmy knew that route was impassable now—the disused section of tunnel connecting the subway system to NJ7 had flooded. But Jimmy remembered that

Viggo's first idea had been to enter through a manhole. Apparently, not all of them led to the drains.

Jimmy rushed to the first one he saw. He heaved it open. Straightaway the stench of the sewer smacked him in the face. He dropped the cast-iron seal back in its place. Now he knew exactly what to look for. All he needed was a manhole that didn't smell.

He walked on, into the heart of Westminster, and found another of the iron covers. A light rain had formed a puddle that reflected Jimmy's face as he stared into it. He kicked away the water and strained to lift the cover. The sound of iron scraping against concrete echoed off the buildings. Jimmy put his face to the opening. No smell. He lowered himself into the concrete tube, balancing on the metal bars that passed for steps down the side. When he was low enough, he dragged the cover back across the hole. It was an incredible weight. Jimmy was breathless before his journey underground had even started.

The shaft dropped for several meters below him, but there was light at the bottom. A real drain wouldn't look like this, Jimmy thought. He felt around the rim of the manhole for any wiring—if he'd set off an alarm he wanted to know about it— but there was only the cold of the concrete.

Steadily and silently he made his way down. The deeper he climbed, the more his insides hummed. He had to be ready for action. No disguise in the world could keep him alive down here. At the bottom Jimmy paused to listen. There were no footsteps, but that wasn't what he was listening for. Then he heard it—the thin fizz of a security camera scanning the corridor. He waited there, learning the rhythm of its movement, deciphering which way its eye was trained.

Jimmy picked his moment perfectly. With split-second timing, he swung out of the shaft. He clasped his knees around the steel girder that ran along the ceiling of the tunnel. As the camera turned, Jimmy twisted, keeping pace with it so he was always just out of its range. He was in. As long as he stayed on the ceiling and kept moving, he would avoid the surveillance cameras.

All the blood rushed to his head, and the muscles in his stomach wrenched tight, but Jimmy held on to the girder. He crawled along upside down as fast as he could. The tunnels were deathly quiet. Only occasional voices echoed through to Jimmy.

The first place he thought to look was Dr. Higgins's office. He remembered the computer technicians who had been working in there when Jimmy had first been briefed by NJ7. If he could somehow get access to one of those computers, surely everything he needed to know about Fort Einsmoor would be on it.

As he approached, he heard exactly what he was afraid of—the tapping of fingers on a computer keyboard. Somebody was still working in there. But Jimmy didn't have time to wait for the room to be empty.

Straining all his muscles once more, he pulled himself around the corner. Here, the corridor widened out, becoming an office space, and the ceiling was a little higher. Below him was a bank of computers, but he couldn't get to work until he had made sure the surveillance cameras weren't going to pick him up.

He crawled toward one, sweat dripping down the side of his face. He did all he could to breathe silently. The effort of holding himself upside down for so long was beginning to tell. Then, just as he came close, Jimmy heard footsteps tapping closer, and the mumbling of a faint conversation. Two people were approaching. Walk past, Jimmy urged them in his head. But they didn't. Together, two men marched into the office. The first was Dr. Higgins. He stood directly below Jimmy, who looked down on his thin hair and protruding nose. If Jimmy so much as breathed too loud, he was done for.

Next to Dr. Higgins was a man in a suit, carrying a briefcase. It wasn't the black suit of an NJ7 agent though; it was a faded blue business suit. And when Jimmy saw who it was, his fingers nearly lost their grip. His head spun. It was Ian Coates, his father.

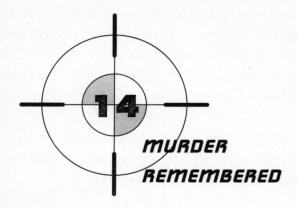

MURDER
REMEMBERED

Jimmy clung to the steel girder, his arms vibrating with the strain, sweat dripping into his eyes. A part of him longed to give up. He was suddenly tired of hanging upside down, tired of disguises, tired of the whole affair. He almost expected his father to look up at him, smile, and reveal that it had all been a game. What if he did look up? Would Jimmy's own father betray him again? Have him killed? Jimmy refused to believe it. And yet he had no idea what his father *would* do.

"Has Ares taken his pills?" Dr. Higgins's voice was distinctive. It was an old voice, but the authority of experience gave it a richness.

"Yes, but he still refuses to leave his bunker."

"That puts you in a powerful position, doesn't it, Ian?" Dr. Higgins busied himself at his desk. Jimmy noticed for the first time that it was covered by a sheet of black tarpaulin. Dr. Higgins pulled it back with a flourish to reveal the body of a young man.

The open eyes stared up at Jimmy. He looked away, horrified. But when he looked back, he realized that whoever the man was, he wasn't dead. Though his skin was pale, his chest rose and fell with his breath. There was no life in his eyes though. He was nothing but a living corpse.

"Who's this poor soul?" asked Jimmy's father as Dr. Higgins wheeled a large silver contraption into position over the young man's head.

"Ian Coates, meet Leonard Glenthorne. Mitchell's brother," the doctor announced with a hideous grin.

"You're keeping him alive?"

"Of course. He wasn't badly injured. It was necessary only to make Mitchell *think* he'd killed his brother. And so long as he makes no trouble, we'll keep it that way." Dr. Higgins lowered a metal nozzle until it was directly over Lenny's left eye. "Meanwhile, I can carry out valuable tests using some of our latest technology."

With the flick of a switch, a blue laser shot out of the nozzle directly into Lenny's pupil. The body convulsed, but it could have been the vibrations from the laser machine. Jimmy didn't want to look any closer.

"So now that you're the PM's right-hand man, so to speak," Dr. Higgins continued, still engrossed in his experiment, "what has he sent you here to ask me?"

Ian Coates paced the room as if unwilling to answer. "You won't like it, Kasimit," he began.

"I never do, but it keeps me busy." Dr. Higgins smirked at his own response.

145

"The prime minister is worried."

"Worried? He's paranoid. Not leaving his bunker? Sending you to carry out even his most basic duties?" Jimmy's mind whirled—since when was his own father the prime minister's most trusted man? Jimmy felt a pain where in a different world there might have been pride.

Ian Coates ignored Dr. Higgins's outburst and carried on. He was clearly agitated about something. "When Memnon Sauvage left NJ7, he passed top-secret British technology to a French agency known as ZAF-1."

"Rubbish," scoffed Dr. Higgins. "Memnon was my closest friend. He wasn't interested in selling secrets to the French. He just didn't want Hollingdale taking the credit for his genius."

"Is that why he sabotaged the second chip?"

Jimmy was startled. He remembered what his mother had told him about each assassin being programmed by a computer chip. Surely the second chip meant *him*, Jimmy Coates? He didn't know what to be more upset about—the suggestion that he had been sabotaged or the fact that his father hadn't referred to him by name.

Dr. Higgins looked up from his laser experiment. He stared at Jimmy's father. "Sabotage? *He* was the true genius behind the assassin technology. He loved the project too much to damage it. All he did was add his own flourishes. Typically French ones, I might add—like fencing." Dr. Higgins was reminiscing now, with a fondness in his eyes. "Whoever heard of giving a twenty-first-century assassin the ability to fence? But that was typical of Memnon. I wonder what he's up to now, eh?"

Jimmy couldn't help shuddering. They were talking about

him. And he had been sabotaged. He started piecing everything together in his head. Eleven years ago, a French
doctor, working for NJ7, had grown frustrated at Hollingdale
taking all the credit, so he'd tinkered with the project they were
working on at the time—Jimmy Coates, assassin. Jimmy
remembered fencing with Viggo and also Higgins's surprise
when he found out. Was it the same French touch that gave
him the ability to speak the language? And what about his
cooking? Were all his extra skills the product of a proud scientist showing off?

"I'm not here to argue about whether Dr. Sauvage was an
eccentric rogue or a traitor," snapped Ian Coates. "I need you
to stop everything you're working on and decipher these." He
opened his briefcase and threw down the contents onto the
body of Lenny Glenthorne: an orange folder marked *ZAF-1*
and a clear ziplock bag containing a bloodstained orange flash
drive.

"What's this?" asked Dr. Higgins, mystified.

"Memnon Sauvage's files. You were his closest friend.
You're the only man who could possibly crack his codes."

Dr. Higgins seemed to move in slow motion now. "Where
did you get these?" His voice trembled. "Whose blood is this?"

"I'm sorry, Kasimit." Ian Coates cleared his throat. "We've
had these for eleven years."

"Memnon is . . . dead?" gasped the doctor. "He's been dead
for eleven years, and nobody told me?" His eyes bulged and he
seemed to age visibly. His temples were flushed purple. "You're
telling me the French killed him because he wouldn't give
away Britain's secrets?"

"No, Kasimit," replied Ian Coates, calmer now that the truth was at last emerging. "*I* killed him because he *did* give away our secrets." Jimmy's father said no more. Only the hum of the laser accompanied his footsteps as he turned and strode away down the corridor. Dr. Higgins didn't move. He just stared at the folder and the flash drive.

Jimmy could only do the same. He hadn't known Dr. Memnon Sauvage. He had never even heard the name before, but suddenly he wished more than anything else that the man was still alive. Because his death made Jimmy's father a murderer. Ian Coates had just confessed, and Jimmy had heard every word, spoken all too calmly.

Rage began to simmer inside him. His father had not only worked for the British secret service, he'd killed for them. And he talked about it now as if it had been the most natural thing in the world. How many times had he done it? How many people had Jimmy's father killed just because they stood in the way of Ares Hollingdale's rise to power?

A tear trickled across Jimmy's cheek. He was so confused, he didn't even notice when it hung from his earlobe. Eleven years, he thought. Has my father been a killer all my life?

The tear fell. Like the first raindrop of a storm, it splashed onto the concrete floor. Jimmy froze. He realized what had happened. Dr. Higgins looked at the spot it had hit. There was a single speck of salt water on the floor. If the doctor looked up . . .

Jimmy's chest rumbled and something itched in his throat. Then he felt his mouth open against his own will. A noise pushed out from his chest. "Doctor," he called out, but it wasn't Jimmy's voice—it was his father's. Somehow, Jimmy had managed to imitate perfectly the voice of Ian Coates and throw it across the room to make it sound as if it came from somewhere else. The sound distracted Dr. Higgins.

"The files, Doctor," Jimmy shouted, in the same voice. "What is ZAF-1?"

Jimmy was as bewildered as Dr. Higgins. It felt like his own father was inside him, shouting to get out. The doctor half turned to where he thought the voice was coming from—the opposite direction from where Jimmy was hanging. Then he snatched up the flash drive and threw it to the floor. With an efficient stab of his heel, he crushed it and stamped on its remains with venom.

For all the confusion and anger Jimmy felt toward his father, it was tempered by a sliver of pity for Dr. Higgins—he suddenly looked every bit the frail old man, betrayed by the country he had served so loyally.

When the flash drive was crunched into a thousand pieces, Dr. Higgins turned to the file marked ZAF-1. He held it in his hands for a moment, trembling. He never opened it. Instead, he redirected the laser from Lenny Glenthorne's eye onto the file and turned a dial on the machine. The file erupted into flames. Dr. Higgins held it there until every scrap had disintegrated to ash. Then he screamed with pain and pulled his hand away. Tears cascaded through the wrinkles on his face. He ran from the room, clutching his hand in distress.

Jimmy was too shocked to do anything at first. He couldn't rid his mind of the image of Dr. Higgins burning his hand on the laser. There was ash all over Lenny Glenthorne's face now, though he wasn't conscious of it of course. That was all that remained of ZAF-1—NJ7's knowledge of it at least.

Jimmy eventually gathered his thoughts once more. He had come here for one reason: to find Fort Einsmoor. But he couldn't just drop to the floor and set to work at a computer. First, he carefully loosened one of the screws that fixed the surveillance camera to the iron girder. The camera was still working, of course, but now it wasn't attached to the mechanism that revolved it. It could no longer sweep the room. Instead, it remained focused only on the far corner.

Jimmy jumped to the floor, confident that he wasn't being observed, and sat at a desk. He immediately felt something on his leg. He jumped up. His heart nearly stopped. Then a black cat padded out from under the desk. Jimmy breathed again.

He didn't waste any more time. He placed his fingers on the keyboard and let his programming guide him around the operating system. His hands were sore from holding his body weight to the ceiling for so long, but that didn't slow him down. He didn't know how long he had before Dr. Higgins came back to his office.

This computer had access to Milnet—the military version of the Internet—so Jimmy tracked down Fort Einsmoor very easily. There were schematics of the compound and details of the security surrounding it. It was perfect. There was even information on Neil and Olivia Muzbeke, including the false names under which they were being held. Jimmy studied for as long as he dared, committing to memory as much as he could.

Then he heard footsteps in the hall. He took one last look

at the location of Fort Einsmoor on the map, closed the page, and climbed back up the wall. Five minutes later he was aboveground, once more transformed into an insignificant Chinese man shuffling through London's nighttime streets.

FORT EINSMOOR

Georgie rushed into the farmhouse and let the door slam behind her. Her cheeks were flushed.

"Felix!" she shouted, not waiting to catch her breath. "We have to get to London!"

Felix burst out of the kitchen. "What?"

Georgie barely knew where to start. "I printed this out at the Internet café in the village." She thrust a piece of paper into Felix's hands while she caught her breath. "I found it on a Louise Rennison message board."

"Who's that?"

"It doesn't matter," Georgie panted. "When I started looking, I found loads of messages that were identical, all on different sites."

Felix studied the printout, a smile creeping onto his face: *Get 2 London. Feel icks too? Then leave the cook.* "It's Jimmy!" he exclaimed. "It has to be."

"I know. And look at the user name—'JawG.' He's talking to me."

"He knows it's dangerous to use e-mail, so he found another way of getting in touch with us." Felix read the message again. "*Feel icks*—that's me, isn't it?"

"You know, for such an idiot, he's pretty clever sometimes—there's nothing in this message NJ7 could pick up." Georgie thought for a second, then added, "Do you think this means Mum's in trouble? And what's happened to the others?"

For a second she was almost talking to herself. Then she snapped back to Felix. "So, what's the plan?" she asked.

Felix looked at her with thinly disguised disappointment. "Isn't it obvious?" he asked, bubbling over with energy. "Pack light. Don't wear anything that might attract attention. Do you have a hat? Maybe wear something that will cover your eyes just in case. Not that NJ7 will be looking for us, or Jimmy wouldn't have told us to come. That's why he says to leave the cook behind. He means Yannick. Did you get that bit?"

Georgie rolled her eyes. "Duh!"

"What about me?" Yannick had appeared at the bottom of the stairs, alerted by the excitable conversation and then the sound of his name.

"We have to go to London." Georgie's mind was made up. "Not you though. Drive us to the station and we'll explain on the way. Oh, and we'll need some cash." Her voice was firm, but Yannick was startled.

"Are you mad?" he whispered, peering up the stairs to make sure his mother wasn't listening. "Look," he started, "I'm responsible for you while the others are away. I can't let . . ."

Felix and Georgie already had their coats on. Georgie dangled the key to the truck in front of Yannick. "You can come back here and look after your mother," she ordered. "But we need a lift to the station." She held up the printout of Jimmy's message in front of Yannick's nose.

The chef read it several times, then sighed and rubbed his face. "Okay," he groaned.

Felix's face lit up. He beamed at Georgie, and under his breath he quipped, "Time to put our training into action."

Along with places like Fort Monckton in Hampshire and Fort Monmouth in Yorkshire, Fort Einsmoor's existence was officially denied by the British government. It always had been. But Monckton and Monmouth were relatively innocent establishments. One was the principal MI6 training center; the other housed eleven underground floors of computers analyzing and eavesdropping on the world's electronic communications. Jimmy had learned that Fort Einsmoor was Britain's Siberia. Where the government sent people to disappear.

Jimmy lay on his front, hidden by the grass. Fort Einsmoor glowed against the dark of the sea. He was just out of range of the floodlights, which meant he was still more than two hundred meters away. The fort consisted of a group of simple but sturdy buildings, surrounded by a high fence of corrugated metal, barbed wire, and more security guards than Jimmy had ever seen in a single place. They had guard dogs too, but Jimmy wasn't worried about those. They couldn't smell him. Jimmy knew from the computer at NJ7 that Neil and Olivia Muzbeke were being held in separate buildings within the complex.

The rain lashed against his back; he didn't mind. It would

only make his job easier by reducing visibility for the guards. Besides, he had already hiked for two hours through the rain from the station.

The only other building for miles was the small concrete hut that Jimmy was studying now—the hut that contained the transformer for the fort's power supply. Jimmy knew that if he knocked out the electricity, the fort's backup generator would kick in. But all he needed was the slight delay before that happened. In those seconds, the lights would be out, and Jimmy would be the only person there able to see. That would be enough to get him to the main gate.

He crawled on his front, digging his elbows into the mud and dragging himself onward. The power supply was guarded, but nowhere near as heavily as the main complex of the fort. Jimmy was close now. There were two guards, both heavily armed and covered from head to toe in bulletproof body armor.

Jimmy took two deep breaths. This was the last moment before the assault began. Once he revealed his presence, there was no going back. But he was determined—before the end of the night, he would have freed Felix's parents from Fort Einsmoor.

He sprang up from the ground and sprinted toward the first guard. Before the man could aim his gun, Jimmy was on him. He spun full circle, kicking the guard first with his right leg then with his left. The second guard turned in time to see his colleague crumple to the ground. He didn't have time to raise the alarm. Jimmy rolled through the grass and hacked him down at the knee. Then he slammed his hand onto the back of the man's head with a sharp chop.

Both guards were knocked unconscious. Jimmy grabbed the

padlock on the door to the hut. Focus, he told himself. His programming was already on high alert. It surged through his fingers. The padlock snapped with apparent ease.

Inside, Jimmy was met by a baffling piece of machinery: a large gray box with dials on every surface and spindles of wire coming out of the top. There were dramatic warning signs that depicted the figure of a man being struck by lightning. Jimmy could only ignore them.

He scuttled back to one of the guards, who was still lying in the mud. Gently, Jimmy lifted the machine gun from the man's hands. Then his eye caught on a weapon he preferred — there was a knife tucked into the guard's belt. Jimmy took it delicately and crawled back to the transformer.

He set about his work efficiently, using the blade of the knife like a screwdriver to open up more of the machine's panels. This exposed even more wiring. Fortunately, Jimmy didn't need to know how this thing worked. He just needed to stop it from working. He slipped the knife between the wires in different places around the machine and slit right through them. Sparks rained around the concrete in a series of tiny explosions. The noise attracted the attention of every security guard in the fort. Jimmy peeked his head out of the bunker. Dogs pounded toward him, slavering at the mouth. Then the lights went out and Jimmy ran.

Suddenly, the barking turned to a howling. The dogs had nothing to chase. Jimmy tore across the field, pumping his legs harder than even he realized he could. Flashlight beams shone in every direction, but only Jimmy had night vision. Seconds later, he was thrown forward by a massive explosion. The transformer. Flames lit up the whole area. In the confusion, nobody noticed Jimmy.

He made it to the gate just as the backup generator brought the floodlights back to life. Jimmy sprinted to the main building. As one, an entire unit turned to aim their weapons at him. From guard towers fifty meters up came a hail of bullets, fired in panic.

Jimmy burst into the entrance hall, never letting up in his pace. He brushed aside four guards with efficient karate moves. From the last to fall, he snatched an ID card-key, snapping it off the man's belt. In the same movement he swiped it and slipped through the metal door beside the reception desk. There, a single jab flattened the waiting guard. At the desk, a single button released the doors of the cells.

Chaos descended on Fort Einsmoor. A siren exploded into life. Beneath it, Jimmy heard the pounding of feet rushing down the corridors toward him. Their boots squeaked on the linoleum. The sound of the siren was drowned out by the scores of inmates hollering with excitement. They had been forewarned that something was about to happen when the lights went out. Now they were each attempting their own escape.

Jimmy needed just a glance at the register on the computer to check where Neil Muzbeke would be. Then he ran through the commotion. He could have found the correct cell with his eyes closed—since leaving NJ7 he had thought of nothing but the schematics of the fort. He raced along the rows of cells, counting the doors. He dodged guards and inmates alike, battling it out between themselves. Then he slid to a stop and swung into the next cell.

"Jimmy!" exclaimed Neil Muzbeke, sitting calmly on the edge of his bunk. Prison had worn him down. His face looked thin and his stubble was silver. The gray uniform drained the color from his skin. But there was a smile on his face. It seemed like the first smile his face had ever attempted. Jimmy dropped his knife and went to embrace his best friend's father. "How's Felix?" the man asked.

"He's fine," Jimmy shouted over the din. "Now let's get out of here." But Neil Muzbeke was not alone in his cell. Leaning against the wall, perfectly still, was a man whose lean physique could have been all muscle. His bright blue stare pierced the disorder. Then, in a flash, he pulled out a gun from under the sink.

"Don't move," he snarled. Neil Muzbeke shot to his feet, amazed.

Jimmy stayed perfectly still. He hadn't expected to find an NJ7 agent undercover in Neil Muzbeke's cell. But this wasn't the first time he'd faced the business end of a gun. He steadily raised his hands. Then, in a sudden burst of movement, Jimmy twisted and ducked. The agent fired, but Jimmy was too quick. He ripped a sheet from the bunk and whipped it at the agent's arm. The agent tried to adjust his aim, but the sheet had wrapped itself around his wrist. Jimmy had control and he pulled the sheet downward. The agent made a move to switch hands, but Jimmy brought him to the floor with an explosive roundhouse kick.

Outside the cell the confusion was still growing. Jimmy peeked out of the door. The prison security guards were busy quelling the disquiet among the inmates. Then Jimmy saw a different team of soldiers at the end of the corridor: the SAS had arrived. With devastating efficiency, they were searching and securing every cell. They were looking for Jimmy.

"There's no time," Jimmy muttered, almost to himself.

"How are we going to get out of here?" whispered Neil Muzbeke. Jimmy had no answer. He had lost vital seconds dealing with the undercover NJ7 agent. Fort security was one thing, but now the SAS was here. . . .

Neil realized what Jimmy's silence signified. He whispered, "Jimmy, leave me here. You'll be able to get out alone."

Jimmy felt a dark anger squeezing him from the inside. He couldn't fail. But he knew that Neil was right. Alone he would probably be able to make it, but Neil wouldn't last ten seconds. Jimmy's infiltration of Fort Einsmoor had been a total waste of time. Tears of fury welled up in his eyes. He turned back to the NJ7 agent lying on the floor, just starting to come around again.

You did this, thought Jimmy. You and your whole organization. Jimmy strode over to him and heaved his foot into the man's side. The agent clutched at his ribs. Jimmy couldn't hold it in anymore. "You did this!" he shouted, overwhelmed by the bitter power of his anger. "You and my father! How could you do this?"

"Jimmy, what should we do?" Neil whispered frantically. "Those men are getting closer."

Jimmy brushed off Neil's consoling hand and screamed at the agent, "How could you let your friend be locked up?" His feet rained blows onto the agent's body. "How could you do this to your own friend? How could you do this to your son?" Tears streamed down his cheeks. Finally Neil Muzbeke pulled

Jimmy away, holding him in a tight hug. Jimmy heaved in wretched sobs.

He closed his eyes and wished the darkness would swallow him. Still, the sounds of the prison invaded his head. He pulled away from Neil and turned once again to the NJ7 agent. But the man on the floor wasn't moving; a trickle of blood drained from his mouth. Somewhere deep beneath his anger, stifled by the violent rage, Jimmy heard a small voice in his head. What have I done?

COUNTRY RETREAT

"It's okay," Neil said softly, holding Jimmy back from the blood that seeped toward them. "We have to get out of here—now!"

Jimmy snapped around. If the man at his feet was dead, he didn't want to know right now. "Okay, I'll go," he choked. "You stay." His programming blew a path through the fog in his head, and he grasped the spark of an idea. "You have to be him." He pointed at the crumpled agent.

"What?"

"There's a river six miles east of here . . ." Jimmy had trouble finishing his sentence. Neil clasped him by the shoulders, and Jimmy marshaled his thoughts. "I'll meet you there. Here's what you do . . ."

Jimmy explained everything in a rush. There was no time for Neil to ask questions. The SAS was searching the cell next door.

"Got that?" Jimmy asked. Neil Muzbeke nodded. Jimmy collected his energy for the fights to come, shutting out the body at his feet.

"Go," Neil whispered. Jimmy burst out of the cell, just as an SAS soldier stepped out of the one next door. "In here, quickly!" The SAS man peered through the turmoil, but whatever it was he had seen, it was gone. In seconds the SAS filled Neil's cell.

"Secret service!" Neil shouted to identify himself before the commanding officer could say anything. "I'm undercover. Jimmy Coates was in here, so I killed the prisoner he came for." He indicated the NJ7 agent lying at his feet.

"Do you have ID?" barked the soldier.

"ID?" scoffed Neil. "This is an attempted jailbreak, not a post office. Now do as I say." The SAS team looked unsure whether to shoot or listen to orders. Their commanding officer leaned his mouth down to a walkie-talkie on his shoulder.

"Warden," he muttered, "please confirm—is there a government agent undercover in cell two-one-seven-four? Out." A moment later the response crackled through:

"Affirmative. Repeat: There *is* an agent of the secret service posted in two-one-seven-four. Out."

Immediately, the soldier's body language changed. He stood to attention and saluted. "Saber Squadron G, Mobility Troop under your command, sir."

Only Neil's fear stopped him from smiling. His adrenaline lent his voice authority. "Jimmy Coates is heading for cell block D. He's leading a team of at least a dozen men. Inform the warden. Take your troop to that block; bring the prisoner Olivia Muzbeke away from the enemy. Fort Einsmoor is compromised. I need the prisoner alive, in a prison van at the main gate, where I—and I alone—will escort her to a secure location."

The SAS commander saluted again and led the troop away. Neil was about to jog after them, but the NJ7 agent on the floor rolled over and groaned. Relieved that the man was alive, Neil used the bedsheets to tie him up and gag him, making sure he wouldn't ruin the plan. Then Felix's father caught up with the SAS.

As soon as he was outside, he couldn't help it. A broad smile split his face and he pulled the rain-soaked air into his lungs. He saluted the SAS and peeled away toward the main gate. Nobody stopped him; a few even saluted.

Jimmy didn't waste time looking back. He jumped through the crowds of inmates, weaving a path that was impossible to shoot at, ducking below the sights of anybody behind him. It came naturally to him now—his programming was conveying him to safety.

But had it been his programming at work in the cell? Once the NJ7 agent had been incapacitated, there had been no reason to continue with the assault. Jimmy feared that even without his programming, he would have lost his temper and kept on kicking the agent. Was the man still alive?

Jimmy tried to remember exactly what he had done to the NJ7 agent, blow by blow, but he couldn't. Did he kick him in the head? When he thought back, all he saw was a confused haze. Just as anger threatened to swamp him again, a bullet screamed past his ear. That refocused Jimmy's attention.

He used the ID card to slip through a supposedly secure door. A guard spun around, surprised, but Jimmy nailed him with a kick to the solar plexus. A backhand slap knocked the guard out, and Jimmy was back at the main desk. From here he could control what happened throughout the whole of the fort. For a start, on a bank of a dozen monitors, he could see the coverage of every CCTV camera. Now he knew exactly where security was heaviest and, more importantly, where it wasn't.

From the grainy images on the screens in front of him, it looked like the plan was working. The army had brought in backup and established a cordon around cell block D—the block where Olivia Muzbeke was being held. Then the SAS expertly stormed the building. Jimmy had no chance of getting her out himself. But Jimmy didn't need to. The SAS was doing it for him—when you need the best, employ the best. Jimmy watched as they moved in waves around each corner, secured the route from the cell, and gently pulled Olivia Muzbeke from her bunk.

Jimmy's block was virtually unguarded now. He plotted a path in his head, based on what he could see on the screens. Then he hit the lights. This time it would be much longer before they came on again—Jimmy didn't just flick the switch, he smashed the whole control desk out of recognition. He ripped off the metal casing and tore through wiring with his fists. First the surveillance monitors died, then the lights went out across the whole of Fort Einsmoor.

Jimmy ran through the rain without a single obstacle. Soon he was out of the fort complex, steaming across the field. Ahead of him he caught sight of the silhouette of a prison van. As soon as he saw it, it rounded a corner and was gone. Jimmy smiled.

Jimmy was reunited with the Muzbekes at the river, as he'd arranged.

"Thank you, Jimmy," panted Neil Muzbeke. "Thank you so

much." He embraced Jimmy again, then took hold of his wife's hand. Jimmy grimaced against the rain. They were in open country now, with only the van to shield them from the wind. Jimmy looked at the smiling faces of Neil and Olivia, but couldn't bring himself to share their joy.

"It's okay, Jimmy," Neil said, reading his expression. "The agent in the cell was still alive. I had to knock him out again. You didn't do permanent harm to anybody."

Jimmy turned away. His insides heaved with relief—he still hadn't become the killer his body wanted him to be. But there was no satisfaction in that. He knew that this time it hadn't been his assassin's programming forcing him to kill. It had been *him*—the human Jimmy Coates. He had never before lost control over that part of himself. Whether the man had died or not didn't seem to matter anymore. That had just been luck. The fact was, from the position he'd been in, Jimmy could easily have killed him.

"How's Felix?" asked Olivia Muzbeke, pulling him out of his turmoil for the moment.

Jimmy wiped his eyes. "Don't worry. He's fine. And safe." He smiled and added, "He says hi."

"Thank you, Jimmy," declared Olivia. "That's wonderful."

Jimmy scanned the horizon, wondering how much time they had before they should move on. "I don't know where you can go," he said. "London's too dangerous. I can't take you to the safe house. We can use the van for now, but soon NJ7 will identify their agent and be after us."

"He'll identify himself, Jimmy," reprimanded Neil. "He's not dead—remember?" Jimmy nodded faintly, his brain torn between the military planning of the assassin and the terror of a normal boy. For an instant they united. Both knew that when the NJ7 agent raised the alarm, all of Britain's military resources would be searching the countryside for that prison van.

"Neil," started Olivia softly, "what about the bed-and-breakfast in that village we visited years ago? Do you remember the owners? I'd trust them. And nobody would ever think to look for us there." Neil nodded slowly.

"Where is this place?" Jimmy asked.

"I'll show you on the map," replied Neil.

There didn't seem to be many other options—they certainly couldn't seek out any family. NJ7 would be hot onto every obvious contact.

"As soon as you get there," Jimmy instructed, "repaint the van, remove the license plates, then get rid of it anyway." Felix's parents nodded solemnly.

The three of them hurried back into the van and sped across the fields to join the country roads. Soon they were back at Ulverston station, where Jimmy jumped out, still covered head to toe in mud. Neil and Olivia thanked him over and over, then drove on. Jimmy hoped they were right about being able to hide at that B and B. If not, all his efforts would be for nothing.

He found himself a seat on the train back to London—a four-hour journey—and tried to sleep. It was impossible. The anxiety tore at his brain until he thought he could hear it. Blood clogged the fibers of his sneakers. As it dried, Jimmy picked at it, diligently scratching at every speck.

"What do you mean?" raged Hollingdale, from his bunker deep beneath the streets of London. "Their location was top secret!"

Paduk dropped his eyes to his shoes and cracked his jaw. "I know that, sir," he said. "But the news has just been confirmed: the Muzbekes are in the open. We're doing all we can."

"Who did this?" Hollingdale's face was blistering red. His lips were raw and speckled with spit. Paduk looked into the prime minister's face. He knew he didn't need to answer the question. Hollingdale knew it too and didn't wait for an answer.

"That boy!" he fumed. "But how?"

There was an eerie silence. Hollingdale's eyes flicked all around the room as if the concrete walls were closing in on him. "Someone will suffer for this," he hissed. "Someone will suffer. And we *will* terminate Jimmy Coates."

Viggo, Saffron, Helen, and Stovorsky all slumped against the walls of the cell. For a few hours it would be too much effort to stand because of the small but painful operation to implant tracking chips in their heels. Their faces were twisted in concentration—blocking out the discomfort, and puzzling over what to do about their predicament.

They were silent until Helen Coates let out another blistering cough.

"They have to let you see a doctor," said Viggo, looking across at Helen's sickly coloring.

"I'll be fine," she replied with a slight smile. "Nobody can come out of the English Channel in perfect health."

"But you look terrible."

"Thanks." Helen chuckled.

"No, I mean . . ." Viggo was blushing.

"One of you knows where Jimmy Coates is," announced Paduk, appearing at the cell as if out of nowhere. "And it's time to tell me. I mean *you*, Viggo."

Paduk pointed, and another agent stepped in to drag Viggo to the end of the hall, back into the interrogation room. Viggo breathed deeply as they strapped him once again into a vast leather chair. It was similar to a dentist's chair, but this one had buckles to secure the arms, legs, and neck.

"Where is Jimmy Coates?" Paduk began. It was the question he had repeated over and over throughout every interrogation session. This time, however, there was an added ferocity in his eyes.

"This is a waste of time," Viggo replied. His voice didn't waver, but every one of his muscles was tensed. Then he felt the stab of a syringe in his lower back. He didn't wince.

"Where is Jimmy Coates?" Paduk asked again.

"How can I tell you," Viggo slurred, "when I don't know?"

Paduk bent down and placed his mouth next to Viggo's ear. "Be creative," he whispered.

"You're sure this is the street?" Georgie had been trying to think of some way to verify Felix's information.

"This is definitely the address," Felix replied. "Trust me." He cast his eyes around the apartment blocks. The place was deserted. "It's that one," he announced.

"It looks like a normal house."

"And you look like a normal human being. Just goes to show, doesn't it?"

Georgie realized she had no choice. She was completely in Felix's hands. She reached the doorway first. "There's no buzzer," she whispered. "Just a keypad."

"Oh yeah, the code." Felix scrunched up his brow and

mouthed a series of numbers.

"Tell me you remember the code," pleaded Georgie, her eyes to the sky.

"Got it!" Felix shoved Georgie to one side and pounded the keypad. Georgie felt herself tense up, half expecting a cage to come down on top of them. Instead, the door buzzed long enough for Felix to push it open. He welcomed Georgie in with a massive grin on his face.

"It's the top floor," he whispered before turning to bound up the stairs. Georgie didn't follow.

"Don't worry," Felix reassured her. "That Vostorsky guy wrote down very specific instructions."

"It's *Stovorsky*," Georgie responded, one eyebrow arching upward. "And you remembered every single detail when you only saw it for a second?"

"It's a vital skill. How else could I copy Jimmy's school-work?"

Jimmy's eyes burst open. The flash of a nightmare sizzled away. His programming zipped through his veins, stirring every sinew of his body. A creak on the stairs. Definitely. He knew that immediately, despite the fact that he had been asleep. A glance at the clock told him he hadn't been sleeping long.

There it was again. Then voices. Whoever it was, they were indiscreet. His programming made the judgment—the human in him overheard it, but hadn't yet woken up fully. He rolled off the bed and crept to the door.

He blinked fast. There was mumbling in the corridor. Somewhere in his head, he felt he knew who it was. But he couldn't trust that. It could be a trick.

In one movement, he unlocked the door and ripped it open. Two people. Moving with the speed of a machine, he twisted between them. He grabbed the smaller one by the neck and pressed him up against the doorpost. The other one, a girl, screamed and stepped away.

Jimmy caught her ankle with his foot. She crashed to the floor. Jimmy jammed his heel into the back of her neck.

POWER

"Jimmy, it's us!" the girl cried.

The boy in his grip was gurgling and spluttering. Jimmy lifted him off the ground by the throat.

"It's me, Georgie—your sister!"

Jimmy twitched. His sister? No, he heard inside his head, they could be assassins like you.

"You sent for us," the girl pleaded. Her eyes squeezed out a tear. "Jimmy!"

At last, Jimmy forced his sleepy human self to take control. There was a faint warmth in his brain. He focused on that, bringing it to life. He relaxed his grip on Felix, who staggered about, heaving in deep breaths.

"I'm so sorry," Jimmy gasped. "I didn't . . ." His voice trailed off. There was nothing he could say. Instead he let his sister squash him in a hug.

The three of them moved out of the hallway, and Jimmy closed the door, making sure to lock it again. "You woke me,"

Jimmy explained, still panting.

"That," Felix announced when he could speak, "was *so* cool."

Finally, Jimmy smiled and threw Felix a punch on the arm. "Good to see you," he said. "Thanks for coming."

"You look terrible," Felix replied.

"Where's Mum?" Georgie asked, still examining Jimmy with concern in her eyes.

Jimmy hesitated over his words, searching for the right way to explain things. "Mum's okay—," he started. Then Georgie interrupted.

"I didn't ask how she was—I asked *where* she was." Jimmy's momentary silence told Georgie all she needed to know. "NJ7 have her?" she asked quietly.

Jimmy nodded. "They're all being held in the basement of the French embassy. I'm on my own. That's why I sent you that message." Suddenly, a thought struck him. His mind was clicking into gear, throwing up what should have come to him immediately.

He smiled at Felix, and all his words tumbled out at once. "Your parents," he babbled, brushing his hair back. "They're okay. They weren't at the French embassy. That was a trap. But I found them in this detention center called Fort Einsmoor. I went there and I, like, broke them out. Well, I got the SAS to do it for me, sort of."

Felix jumped in, "My parents are free?" Jimmy nodded frantically. "Where are they?"

"Don't worry, they went to a safe place. Some B and B they used to go to."

"That's amazing!" Felix jumped on the spot then belted

around the room punching the air.

"That's brilliant, Jimmy," said Georgie, much calmer, but still thrilled. "Now we have to rescue all the others."

"I know," Jimmy replied.

Felix had stopped dancing around and found his way to the fridge. He didn't seem too perturbed by the prospect of having to rescue everybody else. He was more concerned with what he could put on his toast.

"I didn't realize the deputy prime minister had to stay at the office so late into the night." Dr. Higgins's voice was hoarse and his step was unusually shaky.

"Oh, it's you, Kasimit." Ian Coates looked up from his desk, taken aback. "I didn't hear you come in." He indicated the chair opposite his, but Dr. Higgins remained hovering at the door. "I'll stay in the office as late as the prime minister," Coates added with a dry chuckle. "Have you cracked the code already?"

The light from Coates's desk bounced up to catch the doctor's face as he entered the office. "I won't sit down, thank you," Dr. Higgins said slowly and carefully. He enunciated every syllable with a sinister clarity. "I came to talk about Memnon Sauvage."

Coates stood up and gathered himself to his full height. Being away from his family and a full-time agent once more had given him time to work out and retrain in the art of combat; his physique showed the benefit now. "Dr. Sauvage was a threat to national security," he said. "As such, he had to be neutralized. You know that."

Ian Coates tensed up again as the doctor approached.

Dr. Higgins's right hand was completely enveloped in bandages. But in his left, he held a gun.

"There's no point taking your grief out on me," Ian Coates said calmly. As he spoke, the blood rushed to his fingers. If persuasion failed, his own weapon was in the top drawer of his desk. Could he aim and fire fast enough? It was only then that he perceived the opportunity presenting itself to him.

"You have no grudge against me," he continued. "I was a soldier. I was following an order." Dr. Higgins crept closer. "The man who bears responsibility for this terrible deed is the man who gave that order." Ian Coates was almost frozen to the spot now, pierced by the stare of an elderly man whose world had been shattered.

"I came to kill you, Ian," stated the doctor. The hollows of his cheeks sucked the life from his face. "I came to kill *you*." By his hip, his fingers trembled around the handle of the gun.

Ian Coates felt his loyalty grappling with his sharklike desire to survive. "Kasimit, you're not thinking straight," he insisted. "You'd be killing the wrong man. What sort of revenge is that?"

Dr. Higgins held the gun level for one more second. Then, at last, his eyes wandered away and his hand relaxed. "What do you mean?" he gasped. "H-H-Hollingdale? I'll never get near him."

"Of course you can, Kasimit," Coates replied. The tension in his chest forced his voice out too loud. He reined it in. "You're his doctor. And if his personal security is ordered to let you treat him in private . . ."

The desperation in Higgins's eyes shifted now to something more—a glint revealed the workings of his immense intellect. "You're a smart man," he said. His voice wobbled with emotion.

"If I kill Hollingdale, who would take over as prime minister?"

Ian Coates let his smile answer the question. Dr. Higgins smiled back and mused, "Don't you think the British public will have something to say about the change?"

"They'll accept anything if it's presented to them right. For comfort, people will always cling to apathy." The two men stared at each other for a few seconds, each understanding the other's motives perfectly.

Then Dr. Higgins spun on his heels and hurried away. Ian Coates's eyes followed him out of the room. He found himself strangely calm. He picked up the telephone sitting on his desk and tapped a few keys. "Dr. Higgins is on his way," he said with authority. "He needs to see the prime minister alone—some . . . private treatment."

He replaced the handset with a bang. Was this wise? His hand wavered over the telephone for an instant. He could easily call back and warn the prime minister's security not to admit Dr. Higgins. But his hand dropped to his side. Then he sat down, staring at the documents on his desk, unable to work.

Ian Coates was still staring at the same meaningless document when his telephone rang shortly afterward. He lifted the receiver and waited for the news he had been expecting.

"Oh no," he said in response, "that's terrible. . . . Yes, send an agent over." He hung up. His hand was still on the receiver when a young NJ7 agent rushed into his office.

"It must have been in his pills—poison, sir," the agent announced, not sure where to look. "The PM died almost instantly. There was nothing we could do."

Ian Coates nodded slowly and rose from his desk. The

young agent searched his face for guidance. "What should we do, sir?" he ventured. "Dr. Higgins has fled. Should we send all units after him? Do you want air support?"

Jimmy's father ran his fingers along the edge of his desk in thought. He was silent for no more than a moment. "Let him go," he ordered suddenly.

"What?" gasped the agent.

Ian Coates glared at the younger man. "I gave you an order!" he shouted. "I do not repeat orders." He pulled his jacket from the back of his chair and smoothed his hair with his hands. "Call the television stations," he declared. "Issue a press release. I'm going to the French embassy. This afternoon I'll address the nation from there."

The young agent stood to attention. As Ian Coates marched past, the boy saluted and stuttered, "Y-yes, Prime Minister."

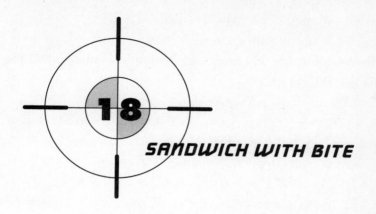

SANDWICH WITH BITE

The next morning, Jimmy woke up with Felix's feet in his face. They'd had to share a bed, head to toe. He jerked in horror and nearly fell out.

"What is it?" Felix gabbled, jolted awake. "What? What?"

"Nothing." Jimmy yawned, scrabbling to his feet. The floorboards were surprisingly cold. "It's just me." Georgie had already made the other bed and was buttering a slice of toast.

"Mmm, I'll have some of that." Felix was suddenly more awake than any of them. He dashed toward the food. "Nice one, Georgie—thanks. This is the real stuff—way better than baguette."

Jimmy scratched his head. He took a couple of deep breaths, bringing himself into the real world, not the twisted blackness of his nightmares.

"So what's the plan today then?" Felix piped up, his mouth already full. "Operation Thumbscrew—phase one."

"What?" Jimmy exclaimed.

"Operation Thumbscrew," Felix explained. "It's a cool name. All good operations have a cool name."

"Yeah, but—'Thumbscrew'?"

"You don't like it? How about Operation Thunderjam?" He looked at Georgie.

"I think you're both nuts." She shrugged.

"Whatever," Jimmy said with a shake of his head. "I need information, so I'm going to see Eva."

"Eva?" Felix stopped munching.

"But Eva . . ." Georgie trailed off.

Jimmy took a deep breath. "Look," he began, "I know she ran off with Mitchell and I know she's not my favorite person. But when I was in trouble, she helped me. It's complicated. I think she's still on our side."

There was a moment of silence while this sank in.

"Was she ever on our side?" Felix grumbled.

"She's not like her parents," Jimmy replied. "She helped me." Georgie looked away. "Be careful," she muttered.

"I thought Eva was your friend." Jimmy kept his eyes on his sister, but she wouldn't look at him. "Georgie, don't be upset with her just because of Mitchell. He's programmed to kill me. You can't fancy him."

"Shut up!" Georgie snapped. "It's nothing to do with Mitchell. Of course, Eva's still my friend. I just don't trust her, that's all."

Jimmy moved into the bathroom and methodically began the routine to create a new disguise—the soap, the toilet paper under his lip, the rust from the drainpipe to change the shade

178

of his skin, and the ashes in his hair. When he finally looked up, several minutes later, Felix was staring at him, his mouth wide open.

"That is . . ." He was so impressed he couldn't even finish his sentence. "Will you teach me how to do that?"

"Another time," Jimmy said, trying not to smile. "I have to go. Operation . . . whatever it is." He punched his friend on the arm, smiled at his sister, and strode to the door. Just before he left, he ordered, "Whatever happens, don't leave this room. Wait for me here. I'll come for you when I need you." He looked each of them in the eye in turn, gave a sharp nod, and left.

When the door closed after him, Georgie and Felix stood in silence for a few seconds. Both were amazed at Jimmy's transformation. Eventually, Felix realized something and gasped, "He looked like your dad!"

Ian Coates strode through the lobby of the French embassy. He glowed with pride, though there was still no smile on his face. Running the country was a serious business and there was a lot to worry about. For now, though, a line of staff waited to meet him. Right at the end were Eva and Mitchell.

By now Eva was beginning to adjust to playing the part of the appreciative little girl. She was growing sick of her own simpering gratitude. It was Miss Bennett she blamed, though. For Mitchell, she only felt pity. She knew he was as trapped at NJ7 as she was, albeit for different reasons. And, after all, he *had* saved her life—even though she hadn't really been in danger.

There was a part of her that longed to return home, but she knew that she was in a position too valuable to throw away. Miss Bennett had taken her under her wing. Eva had access to NJ7 intelligence, and when the time came, she might be able to help the prisoners escape.

As the new prime minister made his way down the line, Eva was thinking about everything she missed: Georgie, her other school friends, her brothers, and now perhaps even her parents. They may have been loyal to the government, but they had always treated *her* well, hadn't they? It seemed that, despite their beliefs, Eva loved them.

Eva had her hands firmly behind her back. She leaned forward slightly to keep the prime minister in view. She had met Ian Coates many times before, of course—but only when he had been nothing more than her best friend's father.

"What's he like?" whispered Mitchell.

"Stop fidgeting," Eva replied. She was trying to concentrate on what was going on at the other end of the line.

"This is the new French ambassador," Miss Bennett was saying quietly, acting as Ian Coates's guide. Eva couldn't make out every word, but the gist was obvious.

"Thank you for letting us take over your splendid building," Coates said in a deep tone.

"Of course, Prime Minister," gushed the ambassador. He was a small man with smooth gray hair molded into an elaborate forelock. "When I heard that security had been breached, it was the least I could do." He bowed his head and for a second his eyes flicked down to Eva. She pulled herself smartly back into line.

The prime minister continued steadily, greeting each member of staff with a handshake and a few words of reassurance that the government would soon return the building to the French ambassador's control. Eva wondered whether that could possibly be true. If that were the case, why was the excavator still tunneling in the basement? Eva suspected it wouldn't stop until it had connected with the maze of tunnels that comprised NJ7 HQ.

When Ian Coates had moved along the line, past the office staff, the NJ7 agents (most of whom he already knew), and finally the building cleaners, he reached Eva. Not a flicker of surprise showed on his face. Perhaps Miss Bennett had warned him that Eva would be there. He nodded slowly and held out his hand. Eva hesitated for less than a second, then took it.

"I'm glad you're on our side," Jimmy's father said carefully. In that moment, Eva thought she saw a hint of disappointment. Did he wish it were his own daughter standing in front of him?

"Ah, the man of the hour," said the prime minister, holding his hand out to Mitchell. But he didn't smile. Mitchell stood as tall as he could. Eva's heart went out to him for a second. She knew that Mitchell thought of himself as a soldier now, but in reality what was he? A boy? No, thought Eva, but he isn't a machine either. He's more confused than anyone I've ever met.

"Pleased to meet you, Prime Minister," Mitchell muttered.

The light cast deep shadows under Ian Coates's eyes, as if the weight of responsibility had aged him overnight. Or maybe he just hadn't slept. "I knew a boy a little younger than you," he whispered, almost talking to himself. "He could have been a soldier too." He turned away immediately and walked toward the staircase.

"Did I do okay?" whispered Mitchell, frantically fidgeting again. Eva tried to respond, but she couldn't speak. Her mouth was dry and her throat had closed up. Mitchell's fidgets melted away. He stood completely still now, staring out in front of him.

"I can't believe I just met the prime minister," he said, but he didn't sound happy, and the corners of his mouth were turned down. "You know, when someone meets the prime minister . . ." He paused as if he didn't want to carry on speaking. When he did, his voice was tremulous. "It's supposed to make people proud of you, isn't it? I mean, your . . . family and stuff. I think my brother would have been proud."

Eva could hardly hear what Mitchell was saying. At that moment, she felt so strongly that she should put her arm around him. But she couldn't do it. Her arm had frozen to her side. Suddenly, she was aware of Miss Bennett frantically clicking her fingers at her from the top of the stairs.

"Eva!" she snapped. "We're waiting for you." Eva shuddered. She hadn't even noticed that everyone else had gone back to work. "Where's your notebook?" Miss Bennett asked.

Eva pulled out a notebook and pencil from her pocket. She scurried up the stairs. Mitchell was left alone in the lobby. He dropped his head and walked away.

When Eva reached the top of the stairs, she almost tripped. Miss Bennett was waiting with the new prime minister. Following Miss Bennett around and taking notes had become one of Eva's primary duties.

"Sorry, Prime Minister," Miss Bennett cooed. "Do carry on."

They walked down the corridor, with Eva scribbling behind them, taking down the crucial pieces of information.

"The crew will be here soon," Ian Coates was saying. "I'm going to address the nation. My personal security staff will also be here. While Downing Street is still out of commission, I want this to be the safest building in the city. Paduk will need a full set of schematics."

Eva struggled to keep up—both with their furious walking pace through the corridors and Ian Coates's imperious speech. When she heard his next item, however, the world reeled about her.

"As for the prisoners"—Ian Coates sighed—"they have two hours to reveal the location of their safe house. That will be where Jimmy's hiding. Tell them that if they don't, you will execute one of them on the hour, every hour."

Miss Bennett nodded. "Do you want them killed in any particular order?" she asked. The PM seemed to hesitate. He couldn't answer.

Out of the corner of her eye, Miss Bennett glanced backward to check that Eva was still working. Gripping her pencil in her fist, Eva dug it into the page. She wrote, in fat capital letters: "TWO HOURS." She circled it, and her lead broke.

Eva elbowed her way through the lunchtime crowds. She kept her eyes down, not wishing to attract any more attention to herself. She already stood out as the only child in a street full of secretaries. This was the only time of day when she had a chance to be away from NJ7—away from Miss Bennett and Mitchell. Today, however, it was not a time to relax.

As she pushed her way to the counter of the sandwich bar to pay for her lunch, her mind was screaming. Two hours. What could she do in two hours? Where was Jimmy?

As she turned to leave, a small old man bustled into her. "Excuse me," she huffed, but the old man hurried on without even apologizing for walking straight into her.

Eva plunged her teeth into her sandwich. It was disgusting. There was something chewy inside it. She pulled it out of her mouth—a soggy piece of paper. She was about to return to the counter to complain, but the paper wasn't blank. There was a message on it: "Hyde Park boathouse. Five minutes."

She recognized that the handwriting was that of a child. She quickly stuffed the paper back into her mouth and swallowed. Eva looked around her. All she could see was a crowd of hungry workers on their lunch breaks.

Eva wolfed down another bite of sandwich, happy to take away the taste of the note. She hurried into the street, constantly checking for anybody who might be following her.

The park was fairly quiet—it was too cold and windy for anybody to be taking their lunch outdoors. Unsurprisingly, the area around the boathouse was almost deserted. Even the few tourists who were still allowed to come into Britain wouldn't have ventured into the park on a day like today. There were only closed-up ice-cream stalls and an old man sweeping the path.

Eva moved toward the ticket window of the boathouse, but the old man stepped in front of her. Eva was shocked as he brushed past, pushing something into her hand. "Pedal to the center of the lake," he whispered. Then he shuffled on.

Eva opened her palm to find a ticket for a paddleboat. She stepped toward the edge of the Serpentine, the lake that runs through the middle of Hyde Park. She stopped at the gate in the fence, where a scruffy young man was reading a newspaper. He took her ticket, showing no interest at all, and led her to the cluster of paddleboats that were tied up at the edge of the lake. He gruffly detached one with his pole and pulled it into position for Eva.

All the time she was looking about. The old man with the broom was nowhere to be seen. Eva kept telling herself that it must be Jimmy, but she couldn't believe it.

Pulling her coat tighter around her, she pedaled the boat toward the center of the lake. Hers was the only one out on the water today. Even the ducks kept their distance, happier to shelter near the banks.

Eva shivered. Suddenly, her doubts overcame her. What if it hadn't been Jimmy passing her notes? She'd never seen the man's face. This whole charade could be a trap. Then she felt something cold grab her hand. She almost jumped out of her seat—a clammy white arm reached out of the water and held tight to her wrist. Eva wanted to scream but she was too shocked. Then a head followed the arm: Jimmy.

He placed a finger on his lips but didn't ease his grip on Eva's arm. He had crept up on her silently, breaking the surface of the water with hardly a ripple. "Don't look at me," he whispered. "Keep your eyes straight ahead." Eva did as she was told. "I could pull you under in a second. You know that, don't you?" Eva's eyes were watering. Jimmy's fist was hurting her arm. She nodded.

"Now tell me the truth," Jimmy rasped. "What are you doing at NJ7? Why did you run off with Mitchell?"

Eva was almost in tears. Her words tumbled out. "I thought Mitchell killed you. I saw him holding you down in that machine. He pretended he was reaching in to help you, but I saw him pushing. He doesn't know that. He thinks I'm his friend."

"What about NJ7?"

"They think I'm working for them," she quivered. "I told them about Viggo and Saffron."

"*You* told them?" Jimmy hissed through his teeth, digging his fingers in even harder.

"They already knew," she added quickly. "But they had to think I was betraying you. Please! Let go of my arm!"

Jimmy released her and held on to the side of the boat instead. Eva immediately pulled her arm away and rubbed the red marks left by Jimmy's grasp.

"Sorry," mumbled Jimmy. "I had to make sure. Thanks for meeting me."

"It's okay," Eva said eventually.

"Don't look at me. They might be watching."

Eva nodded by dropping her head to her chest.

Jimmy continued. "Tell Viggo and the others that Felix's parents are safe."

Eva couldn't help herself. "That's brilliant!" She beamed. "How did you do it? Did you find Fort Einsmoor?"

"Turn away," Jimmy snapped. Eva did so. "I can't tell you everything now, but thank you—I couldn't have done it without knowing where they were being held." Eva held her joy in check. She forced herself not to look at Jimmy.

"I need to know about the prisoners," he went on. "Are they still alive?"

"Yes, they're alive," Eva quickly replied. Jimmy sighed with relief. "They're fine. But, Jimmy—"

"And my mum?" Jimmy butted in, not allowing any emotion to sneak into his voice.

"She's fine. They're all fine, Jimmy—but we have to get them out of there."

"I know," Jimmy snapped back. "That's why I'm here."

"You don't understand. They're going to be shot in less than an hour and a half."

"What?" Jimmy gasped.

"If they don't reveal where you are, they're going to be shot, one by one."

"When?" Jimmy was almost shouting. "How much time do I have—exactly?"

"I don't know." Eva was crying now, but holding herself together—just. "No time at all."

"Okay," Jimmy panted, desperately telling himself not to panic. "I need information. Anything you think could help. I'm going to get them out of there."

Jimmy immediately felt terrible for being so harsh with Eva. It was clear to him now that she was acting like a hero and in extreme danger. But the days of being alone had eaten into him. He felt less human every minute, and only humans had time for courtesy.

"I'm sorry," he murmured. "I'm just tense." Eva looked away, but placed her hand on Jimmy's. The touch seemed to warm his whole body.

"They're in the basement," Eva mumbled, her other hand hiding her mouth. "As far as I know, the only way down is the special elevator in the lobby. The doors are reinforced. You need a key to open them."

"Just a key?" Jimmy interrupted. "Nothing fancy or electronic?"

"I—I don't think so," Eva stuttered. "It's an old building. The only fancy security I've seen isn't until you reach the basement."

"Okay. I'll need that key. Can you get it?"

"I'll try."

"Good. On your way back, buy some chewing gum. Use it to stick the key right in the middle of the road outside the embassy."

"Okay." Eva sniffed and stared frantically in every direction except at Jimmy. "I thought things would be better," she sobbed. "But when your dad took over, he—"

"Wait," Jimmy interjected. "Took over? What do you mean?"

Eva was thrown for a moment. The surprise held her tears in check. "You know, when he became prime minister." The words sent a shudder through Jimmy's whole body. He couldn't speak.

"Didn't you know?" Eva asked. "Hollingdale died early this morning. Murdered." Jimmy looked around him. He couldn't believe what he was hearing.

"I thought you knew," Eva squeaked, still forcing herself not to look directly at Jimmy. She couldn't tell the effect of what she was saying on him of course, so she rattled on. "He came to the embassy. He's going to address the nation on TV any minute. He was with Miss Bennett. He said . . . Oh, it was terrible. Two hours, Jimmy! And how can I get that key?"

Only now did she look down, but too late—the face in the water was gone.

MANHUNT

Jimmy pulled himself out of the lake at a secluded part of the bank. He picked up his coat and pulled it over his dripping clothes. His disguise had disintegrated in the water. There was so much racing through his head. Had he really just heard Eva say that his father was prime minister of Great Britain? I must be more tired than I thought, Jimmy said to himself. He set off at a jog, too dazed to know where he was heading.

Piece by piece, snippets of information floated back to him, as if in a dream. Ares Hollingdale was dead. Could it be true, or had he imagined the whole thing?

He stumbled out of the park and stopped to look around. The world seemed to carry on as normal. How could that be if what he had heard from Eva was true? Shouldn't the whole world stop? Shouldn't everybody be screaming in the streets? He peered at people as they passed. He couldn't help himself. It was as if something in their faces would tell him whether Ian

Coates was prime minister, and what that meant.

Then, despite the mist inside his head, something seeped through to him. The people in the street were rushing with an unusual urgency. They were scurrying back to their cars or into the subway, bustling past Jimmy. A crowd formed around an electronics store, the window filled with television screens of all different sizes.

Jimmy bent over and barged his way through to the front. People let him through, pulling away from the stench of the Serpentine that still doused his clothes. The televisions were all showing the same thing, but it meant nothing to Jimmy as there was no sound to go with the pictures.

What could this be that was so important? Jimmy felt as if every muscle was urging him to find out what it was. He pushed against the door, but the shop was so packed that people had to shuffle out of the way for it to open. Eventually, Jimmy made it through. As he did, he heard a voice that froze his insides.

"Good afternoon, people of Britain," it announced.

It was his father. Ian Coates was repeated dozens of times around the shop. He appeared on every television screen—completely surrounding Jimmy. He was sitting behind a grand desk in an old-fashioned study. He waited a couple of seconds, breathed deeply, then continued.

"As I am sure you have heard by now," he said, his voice deeper than Jimmy remembered, "in the early hours of this morning, our prime minister, Ares Hollingdale, was the victim of a savage terrorist attack." Jimmy steadied himself and wiped his face with his hands. There was no time for him to absorb

191

the information as his father carried on.

"The prime minister died despite the best efforts of our medical emergency teams. I, Ian Coates, was his deputy and as such I have now taken over as prime minister of Great Britain."

So it was true.

There was a low chatter spreading through the crowd. Jimmy picked up a smattering of broken comments. Next to him, a woman muttered to her baby, "That man's a true patriot."

Jimmy let out a sharp laugh, then clamped his hands over his mouth. His father was the prime minister—surely that meant all Jimmy's troubles were over. He'll order NJ7 to leave me alone, thought Jimmy, then he'll let my friends go free. But Jimmy's joy was muted. His father had already put his loyalty to Hollingdale over the happiness of his family. If his political beliefs were that strong . . .

Even as the terrible thought ran through Jimmy's head, Ian Coates confirmed it. "I promise," he declared, "to continue the good work that Ares Hollingdale began with his neo-democratic project. At this time of crisis, I assure you that no ordinary member of the public will be called upon to make decisions regarding government business. None of you will have to vote for the foreseeable future."

"I should think not," nodded the woman next to Jimmy. He stared at the image of his father in disbelief. Every second that passed, the slight nervousness in Ian Coates's eyes dissipated. To Jimmy's shock, his father looked more and more like the leader of a nation.

"What's more," he went on, "I pledge to you now that no effort will be spared to bring to justice the cruel murderer of

Ares Hollingdale. I am working closely with the police and secret service to that end. We have one suspect."

A picture filled the screen. It was the school photograph of an eleven-year-old boy. Jimmy's face filled every screen in the shop. As each of them showed the camera zooming in on his eyes, he felt the world cave in around him.

"He may look like a child," Ian Coates continued, "but he is a threat to the security of the nation. If you see him, do not approach him. Alert the police at once."

Jimmy's father reappeared on the screen. He curled the corners of his lips upward and clasped his hands on the desk. "Otherwise, here at Westminster, it's business as usual."

Jimmy was unaware of anything happening around him. The rest of the world faded to black, and his father's eyes seared into his face. "A threat to the security of the nation." The words pounded through Jimmy's head, over and over. Surely his own father didn't want him dead. Jimmy felt that if only he could speak to him and explain that he didn't want to do any harm to the nation or anybody in it, surely his father would understand.

Jimmy wanted to cry out at the television screens, but he knew it was useless. Then he was jarred out of his thoughts by the growing murmur of the people around him. Everybody backed away from him. The woman with the baby was pointing at him, her mouth stretched wide in a silent scream.

Jimmy spun around. The clerk behind the desk edged his hand toward the phone. Jimmy didn't wait to find out who he was calling. He bolted out of the shop, bouncing off the strangers that still stood around the door. They pointed and shouted after him as he ran.

Jimmy's mind was racing as fast as his feet. Everybody in the country would now assume that he had killed Ares Hollingdale. Everybody would be out to get him. Surely his father didn't really believe that, though. Jimmy made a huge effort to keep his thoughts calm while his body strained to move him through the streets as quickly as possible.

It was enough of a shock that his father had just become prime minister and then announced that he wasn't going to let the country go back to being a proper democracy. On top of that, why had he proclaimed to the whole country that his own son was a murderer and needed to be arrested? Slowly, Jimmy began to suspect he knew the answer: his father wanted control. He already had control of the country, but he needed control of Jimmy.

Jimmy's legs thrust him forward. But something in his head prickled for his attention. It felt like there were daggers stabbing his eyes from the inside. His friends. His mother. Time was running out.

Ian Coates's steps echoed through the lobby as he approached the elevator. His eyes were downcast, betraying the concerns that weighed on his mind. Miss Bennett strode next to him and Eva scurried along behind, chewing gum. When they reached the elevator, the guard tipped his cap and slotted his key into the panel on the wall. Eva's teeth crunched together furiously. Just then, an NJ7 agent dashed up to Miss Bennett and handed her a note.

"Prime Minister," she said immediately, pulling him back. Then she stopped herself and looked around. Everyone's eyes were on her. "We'd better talk in here." The chrome doors slid open, and the pair of them stepped in. "Eva, wait here," she barked, without even looking at her.

Once they were alone, sealed into the elevator, Miss Bennett began again. "Prime Minister—"

"Please, Miss Bennett, you can still call me Ian," Jimmy's father interjected. He tried to soften his expression. "And I hope I may call you—"

"You can call me Miss Bennett."

Ian Coates tensed up at the frosty response. Miss Bennett talked on. "We've just identified two passengers who entered the country on Eurostar late last night."

"Don't beat about the bush, Miss Bennett; who are they?" He glared intensely into Miss Bennett's eyes. She was equal to him and didn't flinch.

"One is Felix Muzbeke, and the other is your daughter." Her tone was bold—almost challenging.

Ian Coates was thrown for only a second. "So they're in England?" he mused. "Do the prisoners know this?"

"No, the news only just reached me."

"They must be with Jimmy. Tell your agents that if we find them, we find Jimmy. But I don't want them harmed. And I don't want them brought here." His voice was hoarse, as if the words were reluctant to come out. "Have every agent looking for those three kids."

"Consider it done," Miss Bennett replied. "And shall I call off the aerial strike on the farm?"

"Not yet." Coates was deep in thought.

"But the place is empty now—it's only Yannick Ertegun and

his mother left there. Satellite surveillance shows that even they have gone into the local village. What's the point of bombing an empty farm?"

Coates held up his hand with a commanding silence. "Tell the pilot to hold off, but to be ready for my order," he said. "Let's give my wife something to think about."

Eva tapped her foot on the marble floor of the lobby. She threw an awkward smile at the security guard standing at his post by the elevator. He was a middle-aged man who had probably worked at the embassy when it was still an embassy—before NJ7 took over. His slightly bulging middle didn't look like the physique of an NJ7 agent or even an ex-agent. The lobby was secured by two real NJ7 agents at the reception desk and, of course, the armed guards outside the door. This man was an extra precaution—but also a weakness.

He smiled back tentatively. The creases in the corner of his eyes stretched to the graying temples beneath his cap. His keys hung tantalizingly from a chain on his belt. This is my only chance, Eva told herself. Miss Bennett could be back at any moment. Fortunately, Eva was prepared.

In the corner of her eye she picked out her target: a cleaner's bucket full of soapy water. It rested by the wall next to her—exactly where she had placed it on her return from Hyde Park. Time to perform, she thought with a deep breath. Then she spun around on her heels, kicking the bucket over. There was a crash of metal and marble. Soapy water poured out across the length of the lobby. Eva threw herself headlong into the ever-expanding pool. It was the finest fake trip she could have hoped for.

"Agh!" she yelped as she hit the marble. Soap splashed into her face. The whole of her front was soaked. "Help me!" She reached out in the direction of the elevator. Sure enough, the guard stumbled forward, being careful not to slip, and held out his hand. Eva grabbed his wrist.

"Oh, thank you," she squealed. She pulled the guard sharply downward. He wasn't expecting it. He lurched forward and tumbled. The *splat* as he hit the floor resounded throughout the lobby and splashed droplets of water a meter into the air. "Oh no!" Eva cried. "I'm so sorry!" She leaped to her feet. "Did it hurt?"

The guard groaned and began pushing himself up. Eva pretended to slip again and landed with a thud right across the man's torso.

"Oh no! Did I injure you?" she flustered, pulling herself to her knees. "Does it hurt when I do this?" She dropped her elbow into the small of the man's back. He let out a cry of agony. Eva fumbled for his key chain. One of the agents from behind the reception desk stood up and moved toward her.

Eva found the key that she needed. She threw herself to one side, pretending to slip, so that her back shielded her hands from view. She tore at the key chain. The key wouldn't come off.

"Are you okay?" asked the guard from behind the desk. The guard on the floor groaned again. Eva jabbed his thigh with her knee.

"You'd better call first aid," she babbled. "And don't come too close or you'll slip too!" Her nails dug into the metal chain, but the soap from the floor made it slippery. Her hands shook violently.

At last the guard on the floor rolled himself over. Eva couldn't keep him there any longer. He heaved himself up.

"Sorry about that," Eva whimpered, jumping to her feet. Behind her back she clutched a small golden key.

20

WAR

The closer Jimmy came to the French embassy, the more people bustled through the streets around him. He kept his head low. Any of them might recognize him. The Green Stripe had eyes everywhere. Suddenly his heart jolted into a quicker tempo. At the end of the street, glaring back, were two men whose brawn strained the seams of their black suits.

The two NJ7 agents hurtled toward him. Jimmy forced himself to a stop and tore back in the direction he had come from. He wove a path through the side streets, dodging pedestrians, bouncing at every angle. He hoped the agents couldn't follow him through the crowd.

But they didn't need to. As Jimmy rounded the corner, he felt another pang of panic. No more than a meter away were two more NJ7 agents. Jimmy didn't hesitate. He hopped on his toes, dashing off the sidewalk into the line of traffic. A bumper brushed his thigh. There was a furious blast of car horns. Drivers yelled at him out of their windows.

Jimmy made it to the other side of the road with an earful of insults and his nose full of traffic fumes. The agents were there a few seconds later. Even as he ran, his thoughts tormented him. He pictured his mother, Viggo, and Saffron trapped in the basement of the French embassy, waiting for him. Jimmy was so close to them now, but every time he turned to take the most direct route, NJ7 was there.

How much time had he wasted? How long had he been paralyzed by his shock? He gritted his teeth and cursed his frailty. If only the machine in him had been strong enough to compensate for his human weakness.

He had to confront Miss Bennett. Jimmy dreaded the prospect of breaking the prisoners out by force. He held on to the shred of hope that maybe Miss Bennett would see things differently now that Jimmy's father was Prime Minister. Somehow he had to find a way to convince her to release the prisoners.

Jimmy didn't realize his father was still at the embassy too.

Ian Coates and Miss Bennett exited the elevator in the basement. Security was waiting, and two agents escorted them across the vast space to where Viggo, Stovorsky, Saffron, and Helen Coates were still incarcerated. The workers manning the excavator paused and stood to attention. Even a cleaner, bent over her mop, wiped her wrinkled brow and turned to face the prime minister. Ian Coates cast an uneasy eye over all these observers.

"Bring me a palmtop," he muttered to Miss Bennett, "and patch through a live feed of our satellite imagery on the farm."

"Yes," she replied and snapped her fingers at a nearby agent.

"And also," Ian Coates added, "get the French ambassador down here." Miss Bennett nodded efficiently as Ian Coates turned toward the cell. Even before he was completely through the security barrier, a voice caught him by surprise.

"Congratulations on your promotion, Ian," said Helen softly. Her expression was unforgiving.

Ian held himself opposite her, on the other side of the bars, searching the face of his wife as if he hadn't seen it for decades.

Viggo staggered to the front of the cell. "Prime Minister," he began, "on behalf of the people of Britain, I beg you: call for an election. Let people stand against you and let the population vote for who they want to run the country."

Ian Coates raised an eyebrow, but didn't take his eyes off his wife, who stared back. Viggo carried on. "Then open up our borders again. Let British businesses import foreign goods and let foreign businesses trade in this country." Viggo reeled off his speech as if he had rehearsed it a thousand times. Despite the ordeal of imprisonment and interrogation, he spoke more lucidly now than he ever had.

At last, Ian Coates spat out a response. "Any more demands, Viggo?"

Before Viggo could say anything, Helen's anger bubbled over. "Let us go, Ian!" she shouted. "What do you want from us?"

"I want Jimmy," Ian replied instantly. "He is a threat to the security of Great Britain. He will either work for me or he will be neutralized."

"You mean killed," whispered Helen, tears gathering in her eyes.

"I will do anything to protect this country."

"I thought Hollingdale was bad, but you're a monster."

Helen pulled away from the bars and put her hand over her mouth.

Ian Coates's eyes flickered almost imperceptibly before he continued. "Paduk tells me that despite his persuasion, you still haven't revealed the location of your safe house."

"There is no safe house," Viggo hissed, but he couldn't help shuddering at the memory of everything he had been through under Paduk's supervision.

Ian Coates snorted a brief laugh. "Don't mess me about," he said. "Where is it?" He cast his eyes across the faces of each of the prisoners. They stared back, hateful. None of them moved.

"Fine," Coates scoffed. "Viggo, you can choose which of these three Paduk interviews next." Viggo seemed to bristle for a moment. "And then," Coates continued, "you can choose who is executed first."

Viggo didn't flinch. He looked first at his fellow prisoners, who stared back, each one looking just as determined, standing strong. Viggo answered the prime minister with disdain. "Do your worst. None of us will ever tell you."

Ian Coates nodded briskly. "That's what I thought you'd say." He held out his hand to Miss Bennett, who rushed forward to hand him the palmtop computer. He held it up to the bars so that the prisoners could see. The screen was only just bigger than his hand.

"Have a look at this," he ordered.

The picture wasn't crystal clear, but it was obviously an aerial view of the farmhouse. The image wasn't still though — this was live video footage taken from one of the NJ7 satellites that kept watch on western Europe. There was no sound to go with the images—only an ominous silence.

"What are you going to do?" gasped Helen. "That's where our daughter is. You know that, don't you?" Ian flicked his eyes across to Miss Bennett. They both remained silent.

"Stop whatever this is," Helen implored again. "What are you doing?"

Stovorsky was standing now, and so was Saffron. They both moved toward the screen, drawn in by the flickering image. "Sir," Stovorsky declared, "if you are about to attack French soil, you make a grave mistake."

"There'll be nothing to worry about if you tell me where Jimmy Coates is hiding."

Viggo couldn't disguise his shock. "You knew where we were in France?" he huffed.

"Of course," Ian replied. "We could have wiped you out in an instant."

"Why didn't you?" Viggo protested.

"You're only alive because Hollingdale was a paranoid old man. He was too scared of the French to bomb your little farmhouse." His mouth twisted into a half smile. "But Hollingdale is dead," he whispered. "And I'm not a paranoid old man."

Silence gripped the prisoners, until Helen Coates forced out her horror. "There are four people in that farmhouse, Ian," she rasped. "Two of them are children. One of them is our daughter."

The prime minister's eyes were blank. "It's your choice," he declared.

"Wilson Street." It was Viggo.

"Chris, stop!" cried Jimmy's mother. "Let's think about this."

"There's nothing to think about," he replied. "Fifty-four Wilson Street. Top floor."

Ian Coates immediately gave a strong nod to Miss Bennett. She in turn cast her eye across the room and nodded at an agent who was clearly waiting for her signal. Now he muttered something into a cell phone.

"What are you doing?" panted Jimmy's mother. There was no response.

"You've betrayed me again, Viggo," sneered Stovorsky.

"No he hasn't, Uno," Saffron insisted. "He's saved lives — and saved France from an attack."

Stovorsky countered immediately. "What about the lives of every French field agent who needs that safe house?" he asked. "You never think about the long term, do you? Maybe that's why you chose the wrong man." Saffron said nothing, but moved across the cell and took Viggo's hand.

Meanwhile, Jimmy's father half turned toward Miss Bennett. Behind her, the dapper figure of the ambassador was hopping from foot to foot.

"Ambassador," Ian called out, "I'm afraid I must apologize. What I am about to do is not an attack on your country, but a defense of my own."

The ambassador looked about him. He was surrounded by hordes of NJ7 agents, who all towered over him. He was visibly shaking. "N-no," he stuttered. "Do not worry — I give you my blessing in whatever you are about to do." Ian Coates held up the palmtop once more.

"What are you doing?" shouted Jimmy's mother. "Are you mad? You have the information you want! *Stop!*" Before the word was out of her mouth, a shadow fell across the image of the farmhouse. Less than a second later the screen flashed white. *"No!"*

The picture crystallized again. Where the farmhouse had been, there was a raging fire. Flames poured out of the rubble in a tumult of black smoke.

"What have you done?" shrieked Helen, falling to her knees in tears. Everyone else was silent. Ian Coates didn't look at his wife, who was crumpled on the floor.

At last, Viggo spoke, his voice so thin it was barely audible. "But I told you the truth."

Ian Coates stepped forward until they were face-to-face. "We'll see about that," he snarled through his teeth. "As soon as a team of agents has located Jimmy, we'll know for sure. If they don't find him, Miss Bennett will come back in fifteen minutes to execute one of you. She will return every fifteen minutes after that until you are all dead." With that, he marched across the floor back to the elevator.

"Get him out of here," he snapped, shoving a finger toward the French ambassador.

Miss Bennett led a procession of NJ7 agents. They followed the prime minister back to the lobby. The prisoners were left in shock with only their guards.

Stovorsky was clutching the bars, quivering. "He has gone too far," he murmured.

"There's nothing we can do," snapped Viggo, rushing to Helen. Saffron was already comforting her, but both were crying.

Stovorsky remained staring out of the cell across the basement. Viggo looked over his shoulder, curious as to what Stovorsky was doing. Then, on the other side of the hall, he noticed the cleaner, that shriveled old lady, shuffling toward them.

"What are you doing?" Viggo asked.

"Coates has attacked France," Stovorsky replied. "I don't care what the ambassador says—such an assault on French soil is an act of war."

The cleaner reached the cell's security barrier, sweeping the floor as she went. The guards inspected her pass and waved her through the glass doors as they slid open. She approached the cell. Stovorsky dropped to his knees. He reached out between the bars and with his finger he wrote something in the dust. Viggo strained his neck to see what it was. The letters were clear, but he had no idea what it meant: ZAF-1.

Even before he had finished forming the last letter, the cleaner brushed the floor clean. Then she gave an almost indiscernible nod.

"What's—," started Viggo, but Stovorsky spun around and cut him off with a finger to his lips. The sound of Helen's sobbing hadn't abated. Viggo watched a sly smile creep onto Stovorsky's face.

21
REUNION

"I don't understand," Felix called out to Georgie, who was sitting up on her bed. "I'm sure I'm doing just what Jimmy did, but when I do it, I don't get disguised at all. I just get mucky."

Georgie stifled a laugh. She didn't want to encourage him anymore. But then Felix popped his head around the door and she saw what a mess he'd made. She burst out laughing. He had fragments of soap drooping off all corners of his head; some was even sticking out of his ears. His hair was knotted with some weird sticky substance he'd obviously concocted himself, and his chin dribbled rivulets of black water.

"Great disguise, Felix." She grinned. Felix laughed too and wiped his face on his sleeve.

"Do you think it worked?" Felix asked. "His disguise, I mean. And do you think he's okay?"

"Yeah." Georgie shrugged. "Of course he's okay. He's Jimmy." She wished she could say it with more confidence.

"He'll be back any minute."

"Then we'll know what's going on."

"Yeah," Georgie agreed. Then she added, "I wish there was at least a TV here or something, for while we're waiting." They sighed, both with the same anxiety. There was nothing to distract them from their concerns for Jimmy. Just then, there was a tap on the door. They looked at each other, startled.

Silently, Felix mouthed, "Jimmy?" Georgie shook her head. Then a voice followed the tapping.

"Quick, let me in." It was a man's voice, deep and commanding, but not one they knew. "My name's Roebuck. I'm a friend of Christopher Viggo's. He sent me for you. It isn't safe here anymore."

Felix and Georgie kept their eyes firmly on each other, searching for what they should do.

"It's okay," the voice outside continued. "I know you're in there. And you're right to pretend you're not, but you have to believe me. NJ7 are on their way right now. Can you hear the helicopters?"

They strained their ears. Georgie gently pushed herself off the bed. She couldn't believe it. The noise was faint, but it was there. A bass whir, as if the sea were rumbling toward them.

"Okay," Georgie replied at last. "If you know Chris, what's my name?"

"That's Georgie, isn't it?" came the response from outside. "Is Felix in there with you?" Felix snatched in a breath and stepped toward the door.

"You're running out of time," the man outside insisted.

Felix and Georgie were studying each other's expressions,

neither one of them knowing what to do. "It's a trick," whispered Felix.

"But what if it isn't?" Georgie replied. There was another long silence. Only the drone of the helicopter in the distance filled the room. In their imaginations it was magnified a thousand times. At last, Georgie marched right up to the door and unlocked it.

She was greeted by a tall man, with close-cropped blond hair. His jeans were muddy but looked expensive, and the same was true of his overcoat.

"Georgie, Felix, great to meet you," he whispered. "I'm Roebuck. I'm sorry there's no time to meet you properly. We have to get out of here. Where's Jimmy?"

"He's—" Georgie stopped herself. Her natural suspicion still pulsated within her. "He's out."

Roebuck frowned for a second. "That's okay," he said carefully. "He'll work it out for himself when he hears the choppers."

He didn't even wait for a response. He dashed down the stairs. Felix and Georgie followed, mesmerized by his forceful movements. At the bottom of the stairs he held the front door open for them and waved them past.

"But what about . . . ," started Felix, looking quizzically toward Georgie. He didn't have time to finish his question. Roebuck bustled them both toward a traditional London black cab that was parked directly outside the building.

They piled into the back, and Roebuck slammed the door shut. Felix and Georgie slumped into the black leather seats. It was an old-fashioned London taxi with space for three across the back, plus two flip-down seats opposite. A Plexiglas screen separated the passengers from the driver. They were on their own for a matter of seconds while Roebuck walked around to the driver's seat.

"What do you think?" Georgie asked quietly.

"I don't know. What about Jimmy . . ."

By then, Roebuck was back with them. He started up the taxi, and they pulled away with a jolt. Perhaps it was tiredness, but neither Georgie nor Felix noticed the discreet green stripe on the driver's taxi license.

Jimmy raced on. Sweat clogged his T-shirt. His pulse boomed in his ears, mixing with the steps of the agents so close behind him. The embassy was only a block away. I'm nearly there, thought Jimmy. At the next corner there were more agents, then more. Jimmy changed direction again. They closed around him like a net. There were dozens of them. Wherever he looked, Jimmy saw more black suits, more thin ties fluttering in the wind.

Suddenly, with dread in his heart, Jimmy threw himself forward onto the sidewalk. The concrete smacked his hands. As soon as he landed, he rolled off the curb into the line of traffic, just catching a gap between two cars. The sky and the pavement flashed into his eyes one after the other, mixed with the red faces of men in black suits, and their green stripes.

At the center of the road he spluttered exhaust fumes out of his lungs. His eyes focused. There was the French embassy. Then shadows plunged across his face. A ring of black suits converged on Jimmy's body.

"Don't shoot!" Jimmy shouted. He was surprised by how

calm his voice sounded. Inside he was jelly. The agents pounced on him. Jimmy felt huge hands tearing at him. Who knew how many? He didn't resist.

"Take me to Miss Bennett!" Jimmy ordered. "She wants me alive!" he improvised. With ease the agents flipped him onto his front. Then he felt someone grab his wrists and the cold touch of handcuffs. Jimmy kept a deliberate check on his programming, making sure at every moment that it wasn't about to do anything drastic. For the time being, Jimmy's insides remained all too human. He wondered whether the agents had noticed that he was shaking.

His cheek was pressed into the muck of the road. He tasted mud on his tongue as he gasped for breath. Then he realized that he wasn't gasping for breath. His lips were smearing across the surface of the road. It was disgusting. Then through the dust came the cold touch of metal. The key to the elevator. Just as instructed, Eva had stuck it down, bang in the center of the road, precisely in front of the embassy doors.

Jimmy clasped his teeth around it, pulling it into his mouth. Just in time, he closed his lips. One of the agents yanked Jimmy's head up by the hair and forced it into a black cloth bag. Even night vision wasn't going to help him—he couldn't see through the material. The agents patted him down roughly. Then he heard the click of a pistol. He let himself go completely limp, giving himself up to NJ7. One agent had him on each side. One more pressed a pistol against the back of Jimmy's head. Like this, they escorted him into the embassy.

❖   ❖   ❖

"Where are we going?" Georgie called out from the backseat of the taxi. There was no answer.

"Did he hear me?" she asked Felix. Felix shrugged. "Where are we going?" she shouted, louder. Still there was no response.

"I don't like this," muttered Felix, jabbing her in the ribs. "Now we're out of the safe house, we'll be okay on our own."

"Mr. Roebuck," Georgie shouted, "thank you for coming to help us at the safe house, but we've decided we'll be okay on our own now. You can let us out of the cab."

Still the only response was the churning of the engine as London's streets rushed past them outside the window. Georgie was suddenly at the edge of her seat. "Hey!" she cried out to the driver. "Stop the cab!" She hammered on the Plexiglas at the back of the driver's head. "Stop!"

The driver didn't respond. He didn't even look around. Felix rattled at the door. It was locked. "Let us out!" he yelled. He lay on his back and kicked at the window. It was solid.

The taxi gathered speed, heading out of Central London, putting more and more distance between its passengers and Jimmy. Felix and Georgie stared at each other; they were trapped.

Jimmy felt like he was entering the lion's den. Even the smell of the air was hostile—a mix of cleaning fluid and the oil the guards used on their guns. Jimmy held himself still, trying not to show his alarm. He was unarmed, his hands were cuffed behind his back, and now he couldn't see. He was completely helpless.

He walked unsteadily, dragged along by the agents. He

thanked his luck that they had only searched him after placing the bag on his head. He used his tongue to push the key right down between his bottom teeth and his cheek.

As they walked, he paid careful attention to the texture of the floor beneath his feet and the sounds that his footsteps made—first the marble of the lobby, then sometimes carpet, then wooden floorboards. He counted the steps they mounted—if anything went wrong, he would need to know the quickest way out.

After a few minutes he was pulled to a stop, and the bag was whipped off his head. Jimmy squinted at the light that blasted in through the tall windows. He worked out that this was a third-floor office that overlooked the front of the building. It was probably directly above the main entrance. Miss Bennett sat opposite him, behind a grand wooden desk.

"Jimmy," she said, making his name sound like a taunt. "Give me one good reason why these men haven't killed you already."

Jimmy set his jaw and consciously made it look like he was talking normally. "Shouldn't you be in a classroom some- where, setting extra homework?" The words sprang out from the anger that swamped him as soon as he saw the face of his old schoolteacher. He couldn't help himself. Once he had trusted her. She had spent years building a world of deceit around him.

"Don't mess me about, Jimmy Coates," Miss Bennett snarled, her expression deadly serious. "You're going to do as I say."

Jimmy held himself tall and looked her in the eye. The key cut into his gums, but so far he was managing to sound normal.

"Release my friends and my mother," he demanded.

Miss Bennett leaned back in her chair. "You say the cutest things," she purred. "You really think that's possible, don't you?" Jimmy's face fell. "The group of prisoners currently held in the basement represents a major threat to the welfare of this nation." She smiled a full, luscious smile with her scarlet-red lips. "Think about it, Jimmy. We sent you to kill Christopher Viggo and you failed. We now have him locked up. We can kill him at any time without anybody finding out, and without any awkward questions being asked."

Jimmy's mind was swimming with the horror of the situation, as Miss Bennett's soft voice mesmerized him. "But the reason we kept them alive, Jimmy, is—"

"Me," he gasped.

Jimmy couldn't believe he hadn't seen it coming. When Viggo and Saffron had gone after Felix's parents, they had walked right into a trap. The Muzbekes had been bait to lead Jimmy back to NJ7. That should have been a warning. The same thing was happening now that Stovorsky, Viggo, Saffron, and Jimmy's mother had all been captured.

"Will you release them in exchange for me?" Jimmy asked, desperate to find his way back to a position of strength. Miss Bennett let out a peal of laughter.

"You!" she scoffed. "As far as I can see, we already have *you*."

"But I thought—"

"You know, Ares Hollingdale was obsessed with you. He was a paranoid old man. A political visionary, yes, but he was slowly losing his mind."

Everything within Jimmy was suddenly empty. He had nothing left to negotiate with. The only thing NJ7 wanted was him, and here he was, as vulnerable as a newborn baby. They could do with him whatever they wanted. So why hadn't they killed him? As the last bit of energy drained out of his body, he worked it out. It had been Hollingdale who had wanted Jimmy dead. But there was a new man in charge now—his father. Did that mean he was safe?

The glimmer of hope was enough to keep Jimmy standing there, putting up a show of resistance to Miss Bennett. She was examining him silently. Though she had been undercover at the time, she had always been a good teacher. She knew when to let a student work something out for himself and could tell when he had. Now she was smiling at Jimmy in a way that made him want to run screaming from the building.

Before he could do anything, a side door opened, and in walked the only reason that Jimmy was still alive. His heart and head both washed clean of any emotion, Jimmy coughed. "Hi, Dad."

Out in the suburbs, the taxi pulled off the main road into what could almost have been a country lane. It crawled along until it was out of sight of the passing traffic, then stopped completely.

Georgie looked across at Felix, whose eyes twinkled. He gave a discreet thumbs-up, and a second later, bent double, coughing his lungs out.

"Quick!" Georgie cried. "I think he's going to be sick." Felix fell to the floor of the cab, clutching his stomach and running through an astounding series of disgusting noises.

"Stop that!" shouted Roebuck from the driver's seat. "Pull yourself together."

"There's no air in here!" Georgie shouted back. "I think he's having a panic attack. Are you okay, Felix?" She bent down, pretending to check on the boy writhing at her feet. "Urgh! that's gross," Georgie howled. "There's some disgusting yellow stuff dribbling out of his mouth."

"Oh no," the driver exclaimed, hauling himself out of the taxi. "Don't you puke in this cab." He opened the passenger door next to Georgie, but, just in case, he reached into his over-coat and pulled out a gun.

"Oh, so you're a friend of Chris's, are you?" Georgie mocked. Her anger was doubled by her feelings of foolishness for ever trusting this man. She hopped out of the cab. Felix crawled across and leaned his head over the side.

Roebuck stood over him, watching carefully as he dribbled and spat through yet more foul grunts. "You stay right there," the man said to Georgie. "If you run, I'll shoot you and your friend." Then, in the split second that his face was turned to Georgie, Felix pushed himself up from the floor. The back of his head slammed into Roebuck—right between his legs.

The man let out a holler of pain and bent over. He tried to lift his gun, but Georgie spun around and crushed his hand against the taxi with a precise kick. By then, Felix was up on his feet. He pounded the agent's chest with a combination punch and jumped into the front seat. Georgie followed him in while the NJ7 agent lay groaning by the side of the road.

Georgie tweaked the engine into life, and the taxi hopped forward.

"Can you drive?" Felix called out.

"How hard can it be?" Georgie replied.

The agent was staggering to his feet. Felix obviously couldn't punch as hard as he thought. "*Go!*" he shouted. And that second, they were roaring away.

In the rearview mirror, Georgie caught a glimpse of the diminishing figure of the NJ7 agent. "Should we go back and kill him?" she asked.

"We don't need to kill him," Felix replied, trying to disguise a smile. "But no tip."

"You'd better leave us for a moment, Miss Bennett," Jimmy's father said, his voice unnecessarily loud for the intimate surroundings. Miss Bennett nodded and walked past Jimmy to the door.

"If anything . . . happens," she announced just before she left, "dial seven to raise the alarm."

Jimmy heard the door shut behind him. He was alone with his father. A small part of Jimmy wanted to run over and hug him. But that part had been buried too deep for too long. And his hands were still cuffed behind his back. Why didn't his father come and embrace him? Jimmy felt a tear creeping down his cheek and hated himself for it.

"Stop crying, Jimmy," his father ordered. He sounded harsh, but Jimmy could hear the subtle crease in his voice. His father was finding this hard too. "I gave orders that you were not to be killed."

Jimmy allowed a drop of joy to lighten his feelings. But then his father continued. "I gave those orders because I think you will listen to me." He looked across the room, not at Jimmy, as he spoke. "You have been told some lies by the prisoners downstairs. Some horrible lies."

"No," Jimmy panted. His joy exploded into a thousand drops of despair. "You let me live so that I could try killing again?"

"Listen to me, Jimmy Coates!" his father roared. "Hollingdale was right. Absolute power is the only efficient way to run a nation. It is the only way forward for this country! You should be a part of that!"

Jimmy shut out the words. "You kept me alive so that you could convince me to kill for you?" he gasped. His fury was surging over him now, but he clung to control. "I thought it was because you loved me."

"I love my country," Ian Coates whispered.

"What about your son?"

"You're not my son."

Ian Coates's voice echoed around the room and through Jimmy's head. His tears had stopped as if they had been frozen by shock. He tried to speak. Only a breath came out. "You're not my son." Jimmy repeated it in his head. Had his father stopped seeing him as human, or did he mean something far simpler? Did he mean that somebody else, and not him, had contributed to Jimmy's DNA?

There was so much Jimmy wanted to ask. He felt like he would blurt it all out at once if he could, but because that wasn't possible, he was silent. He kept his eyes fixed on the man he called his father, who looked shocked himself. Perhaps he had never meant to reveal this information to Jimmy.

"Will you do it?" asked Ian Coates, his voice flat. Jimmy didn't respond. He hardly even took in the question. "I told

Miss Bennett that if anybody could convince you, it would be me."

All Jimmy could think about as he looked into the man's face—a face that was suddenly colorless—was that for eleven years they had lived together as a family, basically happy. How could his father claim now that his only reason for keeping Jimmy alive was in order to convince him to kill for NJ7? How could he deny that he loved him?

"Join me, Jimmy," insisted Ian Coates as he lifted the receiver of the phone on his desk. "It's what you were made to do." In that moment, Jimmy loved and hated his father more than he ever had.

"Give me your answer," Ian Coates urged. "Just one word." His finger hovered over the 7 key.

Jimmy felt his programming bubbling now. It knew that the human part of him felt weak. It was as if Jimmy could hear a whisper. Yes, it said, urging him to accept the offer. Refusing would put him in danger. His programming wanted to avoid that, but there was more. His programming was reenergizing Jimmy's insides with a kind of excitement—glee at the chance to rejoin NJ7 and take on the tasks of an assassin.

"The killer in you will only grow stronger, Jimmy," his father declared. "You'll never be anything else. Can't you feel it?"

Jimmy's father was scrutinizing him. Jimmy stayed absolutely still. He didn't want his father to know that everything inside him was desperate for him to say yes. Then, gradually, Jimmy shunted his nerves aside. As he did it, he grasped his programming with his mind and turned its power upside down. He needed it, but he needed it to work for *him*, not NJ7.

"I don't feel like a killer," Jimmy pledged through clenched teeth. "I feel like there are people who love me. And they love me because I'm human."

Ian Coates's expression changed. Jimmy had said enough. The man he had always thought was his father now dropped his gaze to the phone. Something vanished from his eyes. Any trace of compassion dissolved. His finger hit the keypad.

22

INVASION

Somewhere over the south coast of England an A400M tactical transport aircraft entered British airspace. The four eight-bladed propellers along its wingspan were unmistakable. In a matter of minutes it was approaching London. The pilot checked each of his nine display screens, then gave a thumbs-up.

Behind him, a team of four moved toward the paratroop doors. All five people were dressed head to toe in black leather. Black helmets with tinted visors covered their faces.

Then, at the push of a button, the roof of the cockpit burst open. The pilot exploded out of the plane, ejected at a speed of over thirty meters per second. His team followed out of the loading doors. The plane zoomed on, steered by the FMS400 flight management system, turning in an arc to return to France by the most direct route.

The parachute on the pilot's back opened automatically, as

it was designed to do. The small, slim figure plummeted to earth under a blanket of black silk. After twenty-five seconds, he assumed the "flat and stable" position—back arched, arms and legs spread, hands flat and facing the earth. From here it was less than six hundred meters to the ground. But this parachutist wasn't aiming for the ground.

By shifting his body weight, he steered himself through the air as easily as if he were flying. The roof of the French embassy lurched up to meet his feet as he broke into a run. After barely a step, he had unclipped the parachute harness. His team copied his actions precisely.

Suddenly, the roof of the embassy was awash with people. An NJ7 team had monitored the drop and now they burst into the open. The pilot dropped down in a forward roll and came up with a knife in each hand, plucked from his belt. He moved too fast for the agents to even cry out as one by one their weapons were cut away by the curved blades of the two daggers.

The team plunged through the fire escape. The French embassy had once again been breached.

As soon as Ian Coates touched the number 7 on his phone, Jimmy exploded into action.

He harnessed the full force of his programming, fueling it with his rage. With his hands still trapped behind him, he jumped onto the desk. Ian Coates was stunned for just an instant. He must have feared for his life. No, Jimmy thought. Have the strength to ignore him. Their eyes met, and before Ian Coates could do anything, Jimmy bent his knees and sprang into the air once more. He flew straight over Ian

Coates's head, slamming into the window.

He led with his shoulder and closed his eyes. The glass shattered. He soared through it into the open air, but kept his eyes shut, protected from the splinters of glass. Unable to see where he was falling, he had to trust his calculation about the location of the office.

Jimmy stretched his legs directly out in front of him and reached down behind him with his hands. They hit metal — the flagpole where the French flag had once hung so proudly. It dipped slightly as he caught it, and when it sprang back, he pushed himself up. As he twisted in the air, he saw the two guards below him brush the glass off their uniforms and ready their weapons.

Jimmy landed on his feet. He tottered from side to side. It was hard to balance himself with his hands still behind his back, but he did it — he was standing upright on the flagpole. With the precision of a gymnast, he spun around on the spot. Ian Coates stared at him out of the broken window. He was holding the receiver of the telephone to his ear. Jimmy heard the guard below shouting into his walkie-talkie.

"I have a shot," he cried above the noise of the traffic. "Do I take it?"

Now a team of NJ7 agents flooded out of the embassy onto the street. From the safety of his office, Ian Coates kept his eyes on Jimmy. His face was twisted, but empty. Jimmy couldn't hear the words, though he read the man's lips perfectly: "Shoot to kill."

Jimmy felt like his heart had stopped as the first shots ripped toward him. But his programming wouldn't let him die. He flipped over, performing a complete somersault above the flag-pole. The bullets sprayed past him. Then there were more.

Jimmy looked down through the haze of a tear, focusing on the barrel of a single gun. He concentrated all his energies on the one bullet that erupted from the chamber. His ears picked out that one shot above all the others. His eyes processed what he was watching with such clarity and speed that the bullet seemed to be flying upward no faster than a feather would fall. Jimmy contorted his body and jumped toward the bullet, stretching his hands out behind him.

Perfect aim—the bullet pinged into the metal of his cuffs, snapping them with ease. Jimmy's hands were free. He instantly caught the flagpole and threw himself toward the building. The agents continued to shoot, but their target was moving like the swirls of a hurricane.

Jimmy's legs hit the wall of the embassy. He pushed himself off so fast that one of the agents couldn't turn in time. Jimmy landed right on the man's back, gripping him around the neck. Now he had a shield against the rest of the NJ7 fire. The agent flailed about, trying to throw Jimmy off and trying to twist his gun around to shoot over his shoulder. Jimmy was in control though. He grabbed the agent's right hand and forced him to spray bullets all around them at knee level.

The whole NJ7 team crumpled to the pavement, some of them wailing in pain. Jimmy pushed down on the agent's shoulders and flipped over his head, knocking out the agent on the way with a jab to the temples.

Why weren't there more agents closing in on him? Jimmy thought. Why weren't there snipers in all the windows? It was as if half of them had been called to some other emergency.

224

For a split second, Jimmy peered down the street. He could run. But he knew that wasn't an option. In the basement there were four people relying on him to get them out. He prayed that he wasn't too late. He dived back into the building.

Forty meters above the street, a window opened and a head poked out. Mitchell needed only a glance. He saw the agents lying helpless on the ground and a boy disappearing into the embassy. Mitchell had no sympathy for the wounded NJ7 team. He allowed himself a tiny smile, pleased at what Jimmy was capable of. Of course they couldn't kill you, he thought— that's my job.

Where was everybody? Now that Jimmy was in the lobby of the embassy, there should have been dozens more men to stop him from dashing to the elevator. Even the guard who was usually posted by the elevator was gone.

With relief, Jimmy spat the key from his mouth. He tried to lick away the disgusting taste as he wiped the blade of the key clean on his trousers. Then, without pressing the button to call the elevator up, he slotted the key into the panel on the wall. He hurriedly twisted it, and the doors slid apart. Were those gunshots coming from somewhere up the stairs? he thought. Who else could NJ7 possibly be shooting at? There was no time to find out. He slipped between the doors. There was no elevator there to step into of course, so Jimmy jumped.

The elevator shaft was deeper than he had expected. Dust blasted his face as he fell. He reached out and caught one of the pylons that ran down the center of the shaft, then wrapped his legs around it. His hands scraped down the thick wire. He winced as the wire bit into him and the friction burned his skin. He had no choice but to trust in the construction of his remarkable body.

He landed with a thump on top of the elevator cabin. He squeezed his hands together, wishing away the pain, and realized he was sweating. Come on, he urged himself. His programming responded, softening the scorching wound.

With a sharp stamp, Jimmy pounded on the roof of the elevator. It was tougher than he had expected—reinforced with concrete. He poured all his effort into a second stamp. The reverberations jarred up his leg. Come on, he urged, suddenly doubting whether he had done enough to rebuild the strength in his legs.

He stamped again. There was no pain from the impact, but Jimmy cursed his body. If only he had been strong enough to keep his leg out of that shredder. Mustering all his concentration, he banged his foot down again and again.

At last a crack shot through the concrete like a vein. With that encouragement, Jimmy doubled his efforts. In no time, he busted through. He coughed and blinked in the cloud of dust that he'd created, then dropped himself through the hole.

He landed on his feet, still coughing, and pushed the lowest button next to the doors of the elevator. They slid open. The dust slowly cleared, like curtains being drawn apart to reveal a scene. There, filling the cavernous hall, was a whole army of NJ7 agents. They stood in small groups, positioned to cover every corner of the basement. There were others, too, who had been digging through the wall, expanding the NJ7 complex. They carried tools and wore hard hats, but their black suits were unmistakably NJ7. Even the industrial excavator bore a

226

green stripe. Jimmy gulped.

Then, looking past the agents, Jimmy saw something that terrified him even more. At the bars of the cell, a pistol in her fist, was Miss Bennett. She was taking careful aim through the bars—straight at Christopher Viggo.

"No!" cried Jimmy. Every face in the room snapped around to look at him. The scores of agents stared through the fog. At the same moment, they all realized it was Jimmy. As one, they took aim. Jimmy stiffened, ready for action. Then, suddenly, the lights went out.

23

DEATH BY SHADOW

"Sir, we're under attack," Paduk repeated. "We think it's the French."

The prime minister seemed reluctant to move. At last, he nodded and crossed the office to the door.

"It is a matter of national security that the prisoners do not leave this building alive," he ordered.

Paduk was well schooled in detecting the secrets behind the tremble in a man's voice or the shiver in his eyes. For him, it wasn't hard to see that Ian Coates's decision had wrenched his heart in two.

"Yes, sir," Paduk replied. "But my job is to make sure you *do* leave the building alive."

Ian Coates nodded and patted Paduk on the shoulder in a gesture of thanks. Paduk was surprised to feel a surge of compassion threaten his calm disposition. As a soldier, he had very little room for emotion. But Paduk knew, of course, that one of the prisoners was Ian Coates's wife. He respected a man who could place the safety of his country above the woman he loved. It was a wretched choice to have to make. He knew that from experience.

In the corridor, Paduk's elite team was waiting to escort the prime minister off the premises. They hurried to the end of the corridor, where Paduk unhitched a clasp hidden in a ventilation grate at the level of his shin. A section of the wall slid a few centimeters to the side, revealing a sliver of the darkness behind. Paduk efficiently replaced the grate and guided his team into the secret passageway.

"Sir," Paduk whispered as they scurried down a dim staircase, "if I may suggest—we still have one card to play."

The prime minister didn't answer immediately. He knew what Paduk was about to suggest. "I know," he muttered, "but they are not to be hurt, understand?"

"Yes, sir," Paduk replied.

"Okay," the prime minister began quietly. "Have someone radio the agent. Tell him to bring Georgie and Felix to me at Westminster." All the power in his voice seemed to evaporate for a moment as he added, "We can use them as hostages."

In less than a minute the prime minister was stepping into an unmarked car in the side street next to the embassy. A limousine pulled away in front of them—an obvious decoy, but it worked in a surprising number of situations.

"How is this possible?" Ian Coates seethed when his car was safely a few streets away. Paduk shifted uncomfortably next to him.

"It's unfortunate, Prime Minister," he muttered, cracking his jaw. "Two security issues at the same time."

"I could have foreseen that the French would respond with

a guerrilla offensive," Coates whispered, "but how have they responded so quickly?"

"RAF shot down an unmanned French transport over the North Sea a few minutes ago."

"Good. We'll need that evidence if we want international support."

"International support?" Paduk gasped.

"Of course—we can't go to war without the U.S. on our side."

War—the word shot deep into Paduk's brain. He tried to ignore it, but it sat there, enormous and horrible.

"I'm sorry, Prime Minister"—Paduk sighed—"but as head of Special Security I have to ask you this: do you think your son is part of French plans, or is he working alone?"

Ian Coates drew in a sharp breath and averted his gaze. "He's not my son," he fumed, his breath fogging up the window. "You know that very well. I won't have him referred to as my son anymore." Coates turned back to Paduk, his nerves once again steady. Then the prime minister spat his final condemnation. "He's nothing but a traitor."

It took no more than a second for Jimmy's night vision to kick in. Nobody else in the basement was so lucky. In the eerie blue haze, Jimmy made out their expressions of shock and, in some cases, fear. But they still knew which direction the elevator was in and exactly where Jimmy had been standing. There was only the slightest hesitation before the agents opened fire.

That hesitation was enough. Jimmy lunged to the floor and rolled out of the elevator. Staying low, and moving as quietly as possible, he pelted through the crowd. Around the room blazed dozens of flashes as the agents fired at where Jimmy had been standing. Then some of them pulled out flashlights, which streamed through the darkness in an ever-shifting web. Jimmy ducked and twisted to avoid being spotted.

Why are the lights out? he wondered. It was nothing to do with him, and it didn't look like NJ7 had done it on purpose because the agents hadn't been ready for it either. Jimmy fixed his eyes on Miss Bennett, but suddenly he was aware of a dark figure charging through the basement alongside him. At first, he thought it was his own shadow, but when he glanced across, it was gone. He knew there was something there—it swept between the flashlights just as he did, but it did more. All around him, NJ7 agents were inexplicably crying out and falling to the floor, hacked down like grain at harvesttime.

Jimmy was drawn to find out what could possibly be causing it, but he had to focus on the immediate threat. Miss Bennett felt for one of the security guards and snatched his flashlight. She raised her gun, holding the flashlight on top of the barrel to illuminate her target. The beam pinned the four prisoners to the back wall of the cell. Miss Bennett was about to shoot. . . .

Jimmy threw himself through the door in the screen that Miss Bennett had left open. He battered into her back, knocking the wind out of her. The gun went off. It fired straight into the ceiling. Jimmy had her pinned to the floor, but he couldn't stay there—the other NJ7 agents heard the shot and found her with their flashlights.

As she brushed the dust off her skirt, she was suddenly washed in an intense light. Someone had flicked on the headlights of the excavator. Jimmy skipped to the side, just out of their range. Miss Bennett shielded her eyes and scrabbled for the gun. The excavator rumbled doggedly toward her. Despite their artillery and their numbers, NJ7 couldn't stop it. Who is in there? wondered Jimmy.

Miss Bennett snatched her flashlight from the floor. She panned the beam across the shadows. It hit Jimmy. The heat of the beam was nothing, but on his face it felt like a laser.

"There!" shouted Miss Bennett. Nobody could hear her, but a couple of agents saw her pointing. They plunged toward Jimmy. He ducked into the shadows. Still they came for him, aiming their flashlights as well as their guns.

"Can't you drive?" Felix shouted, his fingertips white from hanging on to his seat.

"Of course not!" Georgie shrieked back as the taxi swerved all over the road. "Can you?"

"No," Felix shouted. "But I know you're supposed to go in a straight line."

Georgie was struggling with the gears, let alone the direction of the car.

"Okay," Felix announced, "you do the gears, but let me steer." He reached across the cab and planted his hands firmly on the wheel. Immediately, the car steadied. Georgie reluctantly let go and looked down at her feet.

"I think I've got the hang of it now," she said.

Suddenly, a voice came crackling over the radio. "Location Tricolore under attack," it said. Georgie and Felix looked at each other.

"Watch the road!" Georgie cried.

The radio continued: "Bring the two children to

Westminster as hostages. Do you copy?"

There was a moment's pause. Felix and Georgie glanced at each other. The only noise was the roar of the engine and the crackle of static on the radio. Then Felix plucked up the mouthpiece. "Copy," he huffed, putting on his deepest voice. "On my way." With that, he clicked the radio off.

"Location Tricolore," Georgie gasped. "That has to be the French embassy."

"Yeah," cried Felix, bouncing with excitement. "And it's under attack—that has to be Jimmy!"

"Well, let's get there. He's going to need a getaway car." Georgie forced her foot down on the accelerator, but instead of roaring forward, the taxi hopped and lurched.

"Hey!" protested Felix. "Warn me before you do that!"

"Sorry."

"And where are we going?"

"It's Central London, isn't it?" Georgie muttered. "Just keep going this way and there'll be signs."

"Turn on the SatNav," Felix chirped, reaching for the gadget on the dashboard.

"Yeah? And what address are you going to put in?"

"Oh. Let's stop and ask someone." Felix cast his eyes around for a pedestrian.

"No way. Look at a map."

"Er, I'm no good with maps. What's wrong with asking for directions?"

"And we won't look at all suspicious?" Georgie shouted sarcastically.

"Fair point," Felix grumbled. "But this is ridiculous. Let's get a cab."

"We're *in* a cab."

"I mean one where the driver knows how to drive."

Georgie thought for a second, examining the dashboard in bewilderment. "You're right," she announced. "I thought it would be easier than this."

She managed to bring the car to a stop, with Felix aiming it gently toward the side of the road. They both jumped out and ran along the sidewalk.

"Do you have any cash on you?" Georgie asked.

"Of course. I'm always prepared for action." Felix flicked a piece of soap out of his hair.

Then, reaching her arm up to the sky, Georgie spun around and yelled with all the air in her lungs, "Taxi!"

Jimmy ran toward the agents, zigzagging to escape the light. The agents caught glimpses of him too quick to shoot. When he was close enough, Jimmy dropped to the floor and snapped one of the agents' knees with a vicious chop. By the time the other agent had swiveled to fire in the right direction, Jimmy was on him. He leaped into the air, rotating as fast as he could, and landed, feet first, in the man's face, like a giant drill. Jimmy rolled forward, then jumped to his feet.

At last, the excavator crunched through the security barrier, flattening the sliding doors and a metal detector. That didn't even slow it down. It kept coming. Miss Bennett rolled out of its way just in time. Then the excavator's teeth crunched into the iron, twisting the bars with a screech. It echoed the question screaming in Jimmy's head: Who is driving that excavator?

The four prisoners ran from the rubble—Stovorsky, Viggo, Saffron, and, finally, Helen Coates. Jimmy wanted to embrace her, but this wasn't the time. They couldn't stop moving. Jimmy led them straight to the elevator, blasting through any agents who stood in his way. All the time he felt an extra presence—someone was helping him. It wasn't any of the prisoners he had just freed. It was somebody else, or more than one person—a team of dark figures he could only glimpse, even with his night vision.

Helen and Stovorsky reached the elevator with Jimmy. They hauled themselves up through the hole in the ceiling. Jimmy waited on the ground, watching in desperation as Viggo and Saffron ducked and dodged, seeing only by the reflected light of the flashlights. At last Saffron was close enough. Jimmy snatched her into the elevator.

"You're in the elevator," Jimmy whispered. "You can climb the wires to the lobby." He bent down to give her a leg up, but she didn't move.

"Where's Chris?" she asked.

Jimmy looked out into the basement. Viggo was only a few meters away. An NJ7 team was running toward them, coming to block off the only escape route. Jimmy closed his eyes and searched internally for his programming. He knew exactly how to draw attention away from the elevator. His programming responded to the call. Jimmy felt a grating in his chest, an itch in his throat. Then he barked at the top of his voice, "Head for the cells!"

But it wasn't his voice, it was his father's, and it sounded like it was coming from a distant corner of the hall. The very noise turned his stomach, but it worked. Like a school of fish, the agents changed direction.

Viggo dived to the floor and rolled into the elevator. He

jumped up straightaway to reach the hole in the ceiling. But behind him was a woman as glamorous and as terrifying as any Jimmy knew: Miss Bennett. The lone beam of her flashlight pierced straight through to the elevator. She drew up her gun.

Jimmy mashed the panel of buttons with the palm of his hand. The elevator doors started sliding closed.

"Go!" Saffron shouted to Jimmy. "I'll be right behind you."

Jimmy stretched up his arm and thrust himself off the ground. He easily caught the crumbling concrete ridge.

The elevator doors were only open a crack now. Miss Bennett stopped running. She took aim. Marksmanship was not her specialty, but her bitter determination more than compensated. She pulled the trigger, releasing a single bullet. It whistled through the air as the elevator doors slid closer together. They were almost completely shut now, allowing only the tiniest sliver of light through. The bullet shaved off the edge of the rubber that would seal the doors tight. That didn't deflect its course. It was heading straight for the base of Jimmy's spine.

That split second Jimmy's ears picked out the tiniest noise, hidden deep amid the chaos. Into his brain came a high-pitched hiss—the sound of the miniature torpedo spinning through the air from the barrel of Miss Bennett's gun. He didn't even have time to think about it. It was instinct. The noise connected directly with the muscles in his arm. They contracted instantly, throwing him up through the hole in the elevator ceiling. But, just as she had promised, Saffron was right behind him.

Jimmy found himself standing on top of the elevator,

face-to-face with Viggo. Beneath them, Saffron let out an anguished gasp. Jimmy saw the terror crack Viggo's face. Viggo dropped to his knees. His arm plunged down. He caught Saffron by the wrist.

Her grip was weak. He heaved her up to join them on top of the elevator, where she slumped into his arms.

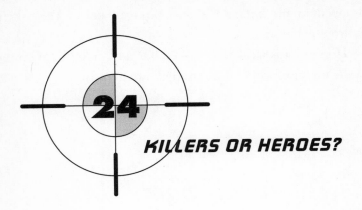

KILLERS OR HEROES?

Jimmy watched the steady drip of blood falling past him, pattering onto the floor. He looked up. Viggo was dragging himself up the wire with one hand. Over his other shoulder was Saffron.

Jimmy pulled himself up toward the light of the lobby. NJ7's constant efforts to breach the elevator hammered in his ears. In no time, they would pry the doors apart.

At last, Viggo passed Saffron gently into the lobby, where Jimmy's mother and Stovorsky took her. But there were other figures silhouetted there. Surely it couldn't be more NJ7 agents.

"Faster!" came a shout from above. Jimmy could hear the rattle of the elevator doors beneath him. The agents had broken through. He didn't look above or below, just concentrating on moving himself up the elevator shaft as fast as possible.

Then there was a crackle. A spark lit up the darkness. As it rushed past Jimmy's face, he picked out the unmistakable whiff of dynamite.

"Move!" came another shout. Whose voice was that? It had a strange accent.

Jimmy blistered his way up the wire. The stick of dynamite tumbled through the air, end over end. Jimmy was nearly at the lobby. He wasn't going to make it before—

Boom!

Jimmy felt as if his head had burst at the sound. He pushed his legs off the wire with all the strength he could muster. A scorching heat rose to hit him. The force of the dynamite carried Jimmy upward, stretching his leap. He caught the floor of the lobby and pulled himself out of the elevator shaft. A tower of flames coursed past him. Jimmy crawled frantically away from the intense heat.

"Jimmy!" called a familiar voice.

Was that Eva? Jimmy's hearing was still muffled from the explosion. He pushed himself up. There she was: Eva Doren, peeking out of her hiding place behind the reception desk.

"Eva, are you okay?" Jimmy asked, dazed.

"The whole place is under attack," Eva panted.

"That's why we're leaving."

"Oh, Jimmy!" Helen shouted, running to embrace him at last. "Have you heard from Georgie and Felix?"

Jimmy looked at his mother's face. It was twisted with worry. "They should be at the safe house."

"So they're in *England*?"

"Yes. Why?" Jimmy asked. "What happened?"

His mother didn't answer. Then Jimmy was distracted by Stovorsky, who strode forward to shake hands with three figures who were covered in black combat armor.

"Thank God you made it," he muttered in French.

Images sped through Jimmy's mind: the basement of the embassy in utter devastation; a carpet of NJ7 agents groaning and quivering. This team had done that.

"You sent for an assault team?" screamed Viggo, jabbing a finger toward Stovorsky.

"There's no time to argue," he replied. "Let's get out of here." He strode off toward the exit.

"All this could have been avoided!" Viggo screamed after him. "What if . . . ?" He dropped his voice, and glanced down at where Saffron lay groaning, blood seeping out from under her. He bent down and gently lifted her up.

"Come on," Helen cut in. "We have to move." She guided him forward, but Stovorsky stopped dead and turned to face Viggo.

"What did you expect me to do?" he bellowed. "Call on my country to attack the British just to save my own skin?" Viggo didn't have an answer, but he was seething with rage.

Stovorsky continued, "I called for help only when Coates committed an act of war against France."

"You put us all in danger," Viggo whispered, venom in his voice. "You told us the DGSE had no idea where you were."

"You were a fool to believe me."

Stovorsky waved a hand in Viggo's direction, then marched away. The three soldiers escorted him out. By the sound of it, there were more in the building, somewhere up the stairs, holding off the rest of NJ7. They moved with an efficient swagger. It was strange—they were all the same height except for one, who seemed much too small to be assigned to a French military assault team. Yet there was a power about them all Jimmy couldn't explain. He couldn't take his eyes off them, but he knew that above all things, they were killers.

Jimmy felt a sickness swirling in his chest. Then Stovorsky and his soldiers were gone.

Jimmy's mother grabbed him by the shoulder. "Come on," she insisted.

They all sprinted out of the embassy. Jimmy could hear sirens somewhere in the distance. Viggo was fuming with aggression when they hit the street. He was still carrying Saffron in his arms, dripping a trail of blood behind him.

"You did this!" he screamed. Stovorsky was nowhere to be seen.

"No" came a cry from above them. Jimmy looked up. There were the DGSE attackers, surging elegantly up a rope ladder, almost at the top of the building already. A few meters below them was Stovorsky.

"Britain did this!" he shouted. "And the next time we come to Britain, it will be at the head of an army!" With that, he clawed his way up to the roof.

Jimmy had no idea how they would escape from there. He listened for the roar of a helicopter or even a plane. He heard nothing but the approaching sirens. Perhaps there was transport waiting for them in Hyde Park on the other side of the building. Whatever it was, Jimmy trusted completely that this devastating team would find a safe means to take themselves and Stovorsky back to France.

At that moment, Jimmy was snatched from his thoughts by the revving of an engine. He looked up and down the street. From out of a side road roared a black cab, gliding toward them. It pulled up outside the embassy. In the backseat was a sight that flooded Jimmy's heart with joy: Felix. He stuck his head out the window and chirped, "Taxi, anyone?"

"Felix!" exclaimed Jimmy's mother. Then she saw Georgie was in there too. "Georgie!" she cried, running around to give her daughter a huge hug.

"Hi, Mum," Georgie answered, as calmly as if nothing was happening. "How's it going?"

"I thought you'd . . . ," Helen gasped, tears in her eyes. She held Georgie's face in her hands.

"What are you crying for?" Georgie asked. Her mother just smiled, and they hugged again. "All right, Mum," Georgie said uncertainly. "I'm glad to see you too."

Meanwhile, Viggo and Jimmy had climbed into the back of the cab. Together they lay Saffron across the floor.

"Come on," Jimmy urged. "Let's get out of here." Jimmy's mother let go of Georgie and heaved open the driver's door.

"Oi!" shouted the driver. He was an old man with a face so worn it looked like a map of London.

"Out!" Helen ordered.

"What?" The driver's voice had more gravel in it than the Thames River. "No way."

At that, Helen grabbed him by the collar, undid his seat belt, and heaved him out of the taxi.

"Sorry about this," she said as she planted the poor man in the road. "We've got your details on your license. We'll make it up to you."

The driver's face went a color Jimmy had never seen before on a human—such dark purple that he was sure some bits were black. Helen ignored his ranting and took her place at the

242

steering wheel. Felix scurried into the front passenger seat with a gleeful smile.

"Let's go," he shouted. The sirens were growing louder.

"Wait." It was Eva, still standing in the doorway of the embassy. Jimmy jumped out of the taxi to drag her away with them. But she didn't move. What was so important that it delayed their escape?

"They'll keep coming for you, Jimmy," Eva said softly. "They'll never stop."

Jimmy looked at her hard. What was she thinking? The sirens howled more intensely. Any second, they might be overrun from every direction by security services.

"They trust me," Eva continued. Jimmy had never seen her so unsure of herself. "If I stay here, I can help you. If I go, they'll come after us both."

Jimmy didn't know what to say. He was astounded at what she was suggesting. She had already done so much to help him, putting herself at enormous risk. Standing in front of him now, she was a completely different person from the girl he used to find so annoying before any of this started. He had never realized how smart she was or how brave. And he knew she was right.

If Eva escaped with them now, Miss Bennett would hunt them both down. If she stayed, she could be Jimmy's informant. It was a huge risk. Here was Eva Doren, volunteering herself as a double agent.

They stared at each other, each one trying to understand the other. Without another word, Eva turned around and disappeared into the embassy. Jimmy almost wanted to stop her. Such a big decision needed time for consideration. But they had no time.

He forced himself to dash back to the taxi. "Okay," he announced, his voice slightly croaky. "Now let's get out of here."

At last they moved away, roaring down the street and passing a cavalcade of police cars that were rushing back the other way. As they passed, Felix slid back the Plexiglas screen and leaned over his seat.

"I knew you'd do it, Jimmy," he beamed, throwing him a playful punch. "I declare Operation Thumbjam a complete success."

"What's that stuff in your hair?" Jimmy asked.

Felix picked out some dried gunk. "Er, disguise?"

"Where am I going?" Helen asked as she powered the taxi through the traffic of Central London. She snatched an old atlas from the floor and threw it back to Jimmy. He leafed through and in a couple of minutes found the page he wanted.

"There," he announced, his finger firmly planted on the map, in the middle of an expanse of green.

"What's there?" Felix scoffed. "It's the middle of nowhere."

Jimmy looked at him and allowed himself a sly smile. "Your parents."

Felix went into a full celebration. He bounced in his seat, punching the air. But Jimmy was looking at Saffron. More color drained from her face every second.

"She'll be fine," insisted Viggo, seeing Jimmy's concern. "So long as there are no more jolts to her system and we get her somewhere I can operate."

Thud!

"What was that?" shrieked Felix.

"Did we hit something?" Viggo yelled.

Bang!

A meaty hand slammed through the window. Glass spattered the floor of the cab. Then a face appeared upside down outside the window. Somehow, Mitchell had landed on top of the taxi.

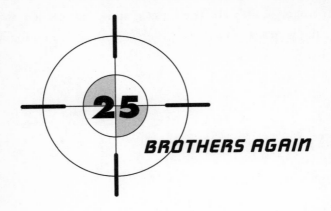

BROTHERS AGAIN

Before anyone could react, Mitchell snatched Jimmy by the collar and dragged him until his head was sticking out the window.

"Stop!" shouted Georgie. "He's got Jimmy!"

"Keep driving," ordered Viggo.

Jimmy could hardly hear the voices inside the vehicle. Mitchell's eyes ripped into him as powerfully as the wind that rushed past. Mitchell took him by the throat. Jimmy strained every muscle in his neck. Then he felt hands on his legs. Viggo was trying to pull him back in from inside the cab.

Jimmy darted his eyes to one side. A truck was charging straight for his head. Jimmy kicked Viggo off, drew his hands out of the broken window and grabbed Mitchell's shirt. Then, at the instant the truck lurched past, Jimmy pulled himself completely out of the taxi. He flipped over and landed with a thud on top of Mitchell.

Inside the cab, Felix ducked instinctively as a dent appeared in the roof. "How did he find us?" he cried.

"Chris," Helen hissed under her breath, "we still have tracking chips in our heels."

"They put tracking chips in your heels?" Georgie said in astonishment. "And you *forgot* about them?"

Viggo grunted in frustration. Then he twisted to peer out of the back window up at the sky. "How did they get a chopper up there so fast?" he snarled.

Georgie bent to see for herself. Sure enough, a helicopter hovered above, haunting them like a spider crawling across lead.

On top of the cab Jimmy and Mitchell exchanged blows with the speed of machine-gun fire. Jimmy spun and ducked on his knees, sliding on the smooth surface of the roof. They moved like break-dancers, yet lashed out with devastating force.

"You don't have to do this," Jimmy yelled. Mitchell responded only with his fists. Jimmy parried the blows and tried again, shouting, "You don't have to be a killer. This is your programming. You can control it."

"I *am* my programming," Mitchell snarled back. "There is nothing else."

The taxi whisked around a corner, flinging them both out to one side. Jimmy's arm snapped out to catch the radio antenna. He curled his fingers around it so tight they were hooks of white muscle. He hung off the side of the vehicle. Then, just as the taxi straightened out from the turn, Jimmy kicked himself off the door. Keeping hold of the antenna, he swung around the front of the cab in almost a complete circle. He half twisted in midair, aiming his knee at Mitchell's jaw. They collided with a perfect crunch.

"Pass me that pen," ordered Viggo inside the cab. Felix plucked a ballpoint from the dashboard and handed it to Viggo. In an instant, Viggo had his shoe and sock off.

"They're following the signal from the tracking chips," he went on. "They'll have a visual on the vehicle any second. Every truck you see, drive alongside it. Head for every tunnel you can."

He dug the nib of the pen into his foot without making a sound. Only the grimace on his face betrayed the pain. Blood spurted out, mixing with the pool that grew slowly beneath Saffron. After less than a minute, Viggo twisted his pen and out flicked a tiny metal ball. Georgie picked it up and wiped off the blood.

"Don't throw it out yet," Viggo ordered, in obvious pain. "Wait until we have all of them then throw them out together. That way NJ7 will keep following them and lose us." Georgie nodded.

"Your turn," Viggo said, leaning over to Helen. She swung her legs around until she could barely see over the top of the steering wheel. Still she kept the taxi snaking between obstacles. Viggo stabbed the ballpoint into her heel and almost immediately plucked out another small metal ball. Georgie collected that one too and examined it, amazed at her mother's resilience. Despite the ribbons of blood and the pain, Helen Coates plunged her foot back on the accelerator. Their speed hardly dropped.

Jimmy was operating at the very limits of his ability. He could feel his programming blossoming within him with every second, adapting to the new situation, learning at every turn. Still there was the human locked inside. Why is nobody helping me? he thought. He realized that his mother had to keep the taxi moving. It was vital that they get out of the city before NJ7 could catch up with them. But surely Viggo could reach out of the window and drag Mitchell off the roof? Before the thought was finished, Mitchell was at him again.

"Do it quickly," gasped Saffron, lying on the floor of the cab. "Then help Jimmy." Her face was like death and her eyes had lost their color.

"You won't survive," Viggo croaked, the words catching in his throat. Saffron forced a smile. To Georgie she looked like an oasis of beauty amid the blood and chaos.

"You have a simple choice," Saffron whispered. "You either throw out the tracking chip or you throw out . . . me."

Viggo had tears overflowing in his eyes now. "You're not going to die," he sobbed.

Saffron nodded serenely.

On the roof of the taxi, Jimmy pressed Mitchell's face against the metal. His programming roared inside him, forcing the human part back. Suddenly, Mitchell's body jerked. In a flash, he flipped over, throwing Jimmy off him. Jimmy was startled at the force with which Mitchell escaped his hold. Then he felt the full weight of the older boy crash on top of him. The air to his lungs stopped. Mitchell's forearm clamped down on his neck with the power of a hydraulic press.

"You should have stayed in the shredder," Mitchell barked. He knelt over Jimmy, squeezing the life out of him. Jimmy's face flashed red then blue. As the oxygen ran out, his mind threw up tricks. He saw images of his bedroom at home. He knew he would never go back there, but he could see it now as if it were all around him. He could hear Georgie's voice playfully mocking him.

Jimmy's vision blurred as the world flew by. He tasted blood. Where did that come from? he wondered. He tried to throw Mitchell off by sweeping his arm up underneath the other boy's body. Mitchell saw it coming and grabbed Jimmy's wrist with his other hand.

Inside Jimmy's head, his programming swirled, utterly confused. Then, beneath it, Jimmy made out a small voice. It was a human voice—his own. It was his only chance. Slowly, Jimmy's lips began to move.

"What's that?" bellowed Mitchell. "Your last words?"

"Mi . . . Mi . . . Mitchell," panted Jimmy, straining to shape the words. His tongue felt cold in his mouth.

"How about I kill you first," crowed Mitchell, "and then you tell me your last words?" He forced out a laugh. It took all his strength to hold Jimmy in position. Then, at last, Jimmy heaved out his message.

"Your brother's still alive." Jimmy felt the shock jar through Mitchell's body. His grip relaxed.

"What?" Mitchell gasped.

In that instant of hesitation, Jimmy pulled his wrist free from Mitchell's clutch. He slipped his hand into his pocket and pulled out the only weapon he had. His programming had been so strong that he'd forgotten about it until now—the key to the elevator doors.

Jimmy jabbed it into Mitchell's side. Immediately, he felt

the life surge back into him as Mitchell jumped back, letting go of Jimmy's throat. Not stopping even to breathe, Jimmy kicked out with both feet, slamming them into Mitchell's face.

Mitchell reeled backward. Jimmy turned and watched Mitchell's despairing grasp as he slid off the taxi into the road. "Jimmy!" he screamed, rolling onto the pavement.

Jimmy rested for a moment on the roof of the taxi. He looked back and saw Mitchell lumbering to his feet, clutching the key that was embedded deep in his side. Their eyes met.

Jimmy saw Mitchell shouting something. He strained to hear it above the noise of the traffic. Then the words echoed into his ears: "Where's my brother?"

For the first time in a long while, Jimmy felt no anger. The fighting instinct inside him ebbed away. All that was left was the deep sadness, mirrored in Mitchell's expression. The two boys stared at each other until the taxi whipped around a corner.

As soon as Mitchell was out of sight, Jimmy eased himself back into the belly of the taxi with a sigh. Inside, he saw at once why Viggo had been unable to help him.

The man was bent over Saffron, who was lying on her front. Viggo clasped a pen in his hand and his shirt was spattered with blood. His face was scrunched, totally focused, as he teased at Saffron's wound, searching for the bullet.

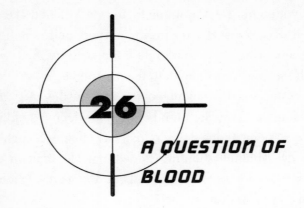

26
A QUESTION OF BLOOD

The taxi sped along the banks of the Thames. No longer in Central London, the river was far more peaceful here. As they charged across Kingston Bridge, Georgie turned to the cracked hole in the window beside her. With all her might, she flung out the three tracking devices, aiming for a boat that was about to pass beneath them.

Three small metal balls soared through the air for several seconds, then came to land, bouncing along the deck. Above them, the drone of a helicopter grew more and more faint. But the danger hadn't passed. Jimmy saw the tears in the eyes of every one of his companions. None of them met his gaze directly.

Saffron was lying face down in blood. Jimmy knelt above her, holding her head so that she could breathe while Viggo tended to the wound. He looked hard at Viggo and saw a reflection of his own anguish. The man's eyes were shot with red. Every few seconds he had to wipe the tears away with the back of his sleeve. Wait, thought Jimmy, do I do that when I'm wiping my eyes? It was a gesture that anybody might make, but Jimmy couldn't help peering closer at Viggo. Do we look the same? The strength in his arms vanished, and he nearly dropped Saffron's head.

"Steady, Jimmy," Viggo muttered. He was unaware of Jimmy's scrutiny. He lowered his head until his mouth was right next to Saffron's ear. "Don't worry," he mumbled. "You're going to be fine."

The man's voice trembled, and Jimmy could only just make out his words.

"I will always love you," he hissed, almost silent. "And I'll get revenge for this."

Revenge. The word chimed in Jimmy's head.

The rest of the journey was silent. Jimmy's mind ached with questions, but every time he thought to speak, the words seemed to evaporate on his lips. Nobody wanted to distract Viggo. He spent every second ministering to Saffron's injury. They would have been arrested immediately had they tried to take her to a hospital.

At last they reached the village. The Muzbekes had been right to choose this place, thought Jimmy. It was small and perfectly innocuous. The houses were a dull, gray brick and each one looked identical to its neighbor. This was no tourist spot. It was the sort of place even the residents forgot about.

Jimmy's mother slowed down so that they could search for the right building. Then Jimmy saw it—up ahead, a dilapidated sign hung above a front door. It bore only one *B*—the other had rotted away.

"Looks like this place is on its last legs," Jimmy said quietly.

Next to the building was a driveway. Helen turned down it, pulling into a small, closed courtyard.

Felix was the first to jump out of the taxi. He ran to the door of the old guesthouse. "Mum!" he shouted, "Dad!"

Before he even reached the door, it burst open. Neil and Olivia Muzbeke smothered Felix in their arms. His cries of joy were stifled in the enormous hug. The family was reunited. Georgie was next to be inside with them, and the sounds of delight didn't stop.

Jimmy stepped out of the cab slowly and lingered in the courtyard. He could hear Felix gabbling inside at a thousand miles an hour. Jimmy knew he would be recounting the tale of flying to France, then how he had come to be in England and everything else that had happened. Jimmy wasn't in the mood for it. He certainly wasn't in the mood to be thanked again.

"Helen, wait." It was Viggo, stepping out of the cab and wiping blood from his hands. Jimmy's mother turned.

"How's Saffron?" she asked.

"It's touch and go. But I think she'll be okay—as long as I find her a doctor."

Helen hesitated, so Jimmy asked the question she must have been thinking. "Where are you going to find a doctor who won't . . . you know, ask about us?"

Viggo sighed. "I'm going to try to track down some old friends of mine. There are still some people in this country who remember what a real democracy is. Any day now, more and more of them will want that back."

"Do you need help?" Jimmy asked immediately. "Do you want us to come?"

Viggo grunted the closest thing to a laugh he could

manage. "No, Jimmy. But thanks for your help. You stay here. You'll be fine. You're in good hands." He looked up at Jimmy's mother. "The best."

Helen handed Viggo the key to the taxi without a word. They stared at each other for what Jimmy thought was an awfully long time, and embraced. Then Viggo ruffled Jimmy's hair and jumped into the taxi. In a few seconds, he was backing out of the courtyard. Through the glass, Jimmy caught sight of his face as it flashed past. He looked like a man whose work was just beginning. By the time Jimmy raised his hand to wave, Viggo was already gone.

"Are you coming in, Jimmy?" his mother asked gently.

Jimmy snapped out of his daze but hesitated. He suddenly felt as if a huge weight was pushing him down. He wanted to crumple into the ground. He couldn't look at his mother.

"Who is my father?" he whispered. He spoke so quietly that he could barely hear himself.

"What did you say, Jimmy?"

Jimmy looked up at his mother. What secrets does she have? This time, he asked more boldly: "Who is my father?"

Helen Coates was absolutely still, stunned by the question. "Your father . . . ," she started, but trailed off.

Jimmy fixed her with a stare. "He told me. He said he wasn't my father." Jimmy spoke slowly and clearly. His mother put a hand to her mouth. After a few seconds she took Jimmy under her arm. They walked together to the far corner of the courtyard and perched on a couple of upturned flowerpots.

"That was a terrible thing for him to say," she began, trembling. There was a long pause. Jimmy waited, impatient for her explanation. "Scientifically, it's true," she continued at last.

"There is another man whose genes you carry. But that's not all it means to be a father. Your father is also the man who raised you and loved you—and I'm certain that he still loves you."

Jimmy gazed straight ahead, not focusing on anything. "Who is the other man?" The words rushed out of his mouth. He felt his mother tense up and turned to look at her. He saw again the toughness that had been in her face when they had been in their most dire situations.

"Jimmy," she said, "you are your own person." She studied his expression. "You have a chance that I never thought you'd have. You can live a life away from NJ7. Maybe not here because they will come after you again. But you'll be ready."

Jimmy looked away, frustration rising inside him. Why won't you tell me?

"Who is my biological father?" he insisted, closing his eyes for a moment as if to shut out his mother's long explanation. Just a name, he thought, that's all I want.

His mother drew in a deep breath. "One day I think you'll understand why I can't tell you," she announced.

Jimmy's eyes shot up to meet hers. He wanted to plead with his mother to tell him, but something in her face froze the words in his throat.

"I know you're going to think about it a lot, and that's okay," his mother continued, "but all you need to know is that the man is dead."

Jimmy felt something inside him crumple. His question still hadn't been answered. Then she said it again, louder this time, and with a categorical wave of her hand: "The man is dead."

With that, she squeezed Jimmy close to her and ruffled his hair. "You come in when you're ready," she whispered. Then she pushed herself up, glanced at Jimmy with a smile, and limped back to the house. Her steps left bloody footprints on the gravel.

Jimmy couldn't move. He was only just able to keep himself from crying. He used to have a normal life. He used to go to school, watch TV, play computer games. He thought he used to have a father. How can he be my father? he asked himself. My real father is dead. He was suddenly flooded with anger. It was more intense than he had ever felt. His hands were shaking and his face was hot. A million thoughts blasted through his mind.

His mother had lied to him all his life. And still she kept the truth from him. What had he done to deserve this life of secrets and violence? It was no longer just the programming inside him that pounded with the urge to kill. The lies of his parents had forced him into brutal fights.

He walked toward the guesthouse and greeted his friends with a fake smile. He knew very well how to act automatically. More than ever before, he felt like someone had stolen away his humanity, and the man he blamed was the prime minister.

Ian Coates fingered his glass of brandy nervously. The flight was rock steady and the private plane was the quintessence of understated luxury. Nevertheless, Coates's troubles were etched into his brow. The hand that wasn't fiddling with his drink clasped a phone to his ear.

"I don't want your excuses, Miss Bennett," he growled. "I want a nation ready for war." Around him, his entourage busied themselves with piles of papers.

"Forget Dr. Higgins," the PM continued. "He's gone. We

need the very best man to replace him, and that's Ark Stanton."
The earpiece of the phone almost exploded with a tirade from
Miss Bennett.

"I don't care how many times he's been sacked, Miss
Bennett, or how many terrorist organizations he's associated
with. The man's a genius and he's the only person who can possibly replace Dr. Higgins." Coates paused again, but this time
he cut off Miss Bennett's protestations.

"Listen," the prime minister snarled, "if we have to go to war
with France, we need two things: the U.S. on our side, and the
most advanced technology. I'll make sure of the first one, and
you do the second by getting me Ark Stanton."

He was about to slam the phone down, but something Miss
Bennett said stopped him. He listened intently. Over the next
few seconds, his face faded to an almost pristine white. When
Miss Bennett's voice stopped, he said nothing. Then, very
slowly, he dropped the receiver of the telephone into its slot at
his side.

"Paduk," he whispered. His voice refused to come out. He
cleared his throat and repeated, "Paduk." The huge agent
bounded up the aisle of the plane and slid into the seat opposite the prime minister.

"What is it, sir?"

"Miss Bennett . . . ," Ian Coates began.

"Yes, sir, what about her?"

"She assigned a couple of agents to clear Dr. Higgins's
files."

"I know," Paduk interjected, sounding far more confident
than Coates. "She wanted them to go through the files and find
whatever information they could that might be useful to his

successor." There was a pause that betrayed the prime minister's horror.

"What did they find out?" Paduk gasped.

Ian Coates spoke slowly, dropping his voice in the hope that only Paduk would hear him. "Thirteen years ago Dr. Higgins worked with Memnon Sauvage on the NJ7 team, before Sauvage fled."

Paduk nodded. "I know," he said. "They were friends."

"But . . . when Sauvage defected . . . ," Coates rasped, "some kind of secret project . . ."

"Project? What project?"

"They were working on their own project. A third chip." Paduk looked confused. "A third assassin chip," Coates repeated, raising his hand to his mouth in fear of the very words he spoke. "Each assassin is programmed using a unique computer chip. A third chip means . . ." He trailed off. His eyes wandered the cabin. "When Sauvage went to France, he took with him the means to build . . ."

His voice seemed to disintegrate. He finished his sentence with only air escaping his mouth. Paduk leaned in closer.

". . . a third assassin."

Ian Coates downed his brandy with a jerk of his head, then began fixing his tie. In a few minutes, the plane would start its descent into Washington, D.C.

That night Jimmy, Felix, and Georgie shared a room again. It turned out that the bed-and-breakfast hadn't had guests for years, but the elderly couple were more than happy to accommodate everybody.

Jimmy lay in the dark, his mind growing more tired every

moment. Every time he closed his eyes, he saw the pool of blood surrounding the agent on the floor of Neil Muzbeke's cell. In his imagination he could feel the warm liquid lapping at his feet. He didn't have the energy to stop himself from reliving those horrible moments. Then, hardly realizing it, his concentration was invaded by thoughts of his father. Where had the man been when NJ7 had sent Mitchell after him? What about years before, when Viggo escaped NJ7 for the first time? Had Jimmy's father been there? Or had Ian Coates been out in the field, at work to support his wife and baby daughter—killing?

Jimmy opened his eyes. If those were the thoughts sleep had in store for him, he'd rather stay awake. He sat up in bed and glanced over at Georgie. He couldn't tell whether she was asleep or not. Should he tell her everything he had found out about their father? Not now, he decided. Probably not ever.

"Hey, what's up?" It was Felix, whispering through the darkness.

"Hey," Jimmy replied, a little taken aback.

"Are you awake?"

Before Jimmy could reply, Felix asked, "Are we going to stay here, do you think?"

"I don't know," Jimmy whispered back. "I doubt it."

"You're right. We have to keep moving." Then Felix's eyes sparked. "I know, we should get ourselves a boat, and load it with all these computers, and live like techno-pirates—"

"What are you two on about?" Georgie was sitting up in bed now. She didn't look like she'd been asleep at all.

"Well, we could, like, live off squid . . . ," Felix started, and off he went on one of the finest rants Jimmy had ever heard. It sounded like being back with his parents had inspired Felix to greater madness. Jimmy soaked it all in. Georgie couldn't help but laugh, and after a minute or so it infected Jimmy as well. Gradually, with every chuckle and every smile that his sister threw across the room, the distress in Jimmy's heart deflated from the size of the whole globe to a soccer ball then a Ping-Pong ball.

They sat up half the night like that, until none of them had any energy left. Then, much later, when they were all lying down, just as they were dropping off to sleep, Jimmy heard a tiny whisper.

"Do you think Saffron's going to be okay?" Felix asked.

"I don't know," replied Jimmy.

In his head, he remembered Viggo's expression as he'd driven off in the taxi. There's no chance that man is going to let Saffron die, he thought. He knew Viggo would do anything before that happened. But what if it does happen?

Now there were only the sounds of soft breathing in the room. Not enough to stop Jimmy's spiraling thoughts. Viggo's words still echoed in his mind: "I'll get revenge for this," he had said. Jimmy couldn't forget that.

As he fell asleep, his mind tormented him with the image of one face: the man he had thought was his father. At first, he tried to push it away, but then he focused on it until he could see nothing else. Inside, the killer stirred.